THE SYRIAN STONE

The "Stone Collection" Book 6

NICK HAWKES

Hawkesflight Media

Titles in The Stone Collection:

The Syrian Stone

Published 2021 (*v.1.3*)
by
Hawkesflight Media

The characters in this novel are purely fictional.
Any resemblance to people who have existed, or are existing, is coincidental.

ISBN 978-0-6487041-6-4

www.author-nick.com

Cover Design by Karri Klawiter

To my dear friends Allan and Merilyn,
who have encouraged me in my writing…
and helped bring it to the world.

The Syrian Stone

A novel

by

Nick Hawkes

Chapter 1

Syria, 2019

Abbas was naked to the waist. He couldn't see much of himself in the traveling mirror hooked onto the tent post. It was a pity, for he liked to see his reflection. He used the time he shaved, which was once every three or four days, to critique his appearance. It was his ritual when at home in Damascus. But he'd been away from domestic luxuries now for six weeks. He did, however, see enough to notice a few gray threads beginning to appear in his hair. None, mercifully, were yet visible amongst the black curls on his chest. He still looked young and strong. That, at least, was a blessing. *Allah be praised.*

Outside, he could hear the camp begin to come to life. Pots and pans were being banged down onto the metal cooking range outside the kitchen tent, and workers were beginning to chat and argue as they stirred themselves for a new day.

For Abbas, and many others in the camp, the day had begun early. He got up before sunrise for *Salat al-fajr*, the first of the five prayer rituals for the day. It was something he rarely failed to do. The great advantage of doing so in the flat, semi-arid, lands

1

surrounding Ebla, was that you were up to see the sun rise. It was the best part of the day. The sun had not yet generated any spite, and the air was cool and ethereal—clear of the dust that would pollute the day, along with the frustrations and worries that inevitably attended the supervision of an archaeological dig.

If the challenges of bringing order to an archaeological dig were not enough, doing so in a time of war made it doubly hard. The 9mm Makarov semi-automatic pistol hanging from his belt was a constant reminder of the conflict. He'd worn it nearly every day for the last nine years.

Abbas sighed. The civil war that had ruined him and his nation for so long had paused long enough to allow some peace, but it was an uneasy peace. No one yet trusted it. The issues causing the conflict had not been addressed. The simmering resentments, particularly of the poor of Syria, remained. But at least there was enough of a respite to begin addressing the ravages and ruin at Ebla, the archaeological site that was the cradle of Syrian civilization.

Many civilizations had marched through history's page in these lands: the Sumerians; the Akkadians with their fearsome leader, Sargon; the Amorites; followed by the Hittites; and then the savagely cruel empire of Assyria. It was extraordinary to think that all of them had existed before 2,000 BCE.

Abbas pondered briefly on the Amorites—the people from the West—and thought grimly that he would inevitably, at some stage in the day, be locking horns with the woman from the British Museum. She, sadly, was not extinct.

He grunted.

Outside, he could hear the distinctive sound of an Otokar Cobra growling its way around the ring road that circled the site. The vehicle was the Turkish equivalent to the American Humvee. It's pungent diesel fumes penetrated the ablution tent where he stood. Soldiers were doing their rounds seeking to minimize looting of the site by locals.

He leaned on the trestle table, closed his eyes, and allowed the personal grief brought by the conflict to pass through his heart. The ache never seemed to go away, but he was familiar enough with it to at least function.

A tent flap moved.

It was only the slightest of sounds.

Abbas opened his eyes.

No one had entered the tent.

He waited for more noise, but all was quiet.

Abbas frowned, and dismissed the sound. It was nothing, and he was glad to still be alone.

He reached for his shaving brush and freshened up the soap on his face. With the practice born of many years, he began to scrape away with a cutthroat razor. He found it easier to use a cutthroat, as access to modern luxuries such as disposable razors was not something that could be relied on in times of war. War only supplied grief, waste, and ruin. He shook his head. So much history and cultural heritage had been destroyed.

He felt, rather than heard, the noise again.

The noise was too discrete to be innocent. Abbas stiffened, and the hairs on the back of his neck stood up.

He looked around.

Nothing.

The razor was losing its edge. Abbas looked at it critically, wiped the soap away, and walked over to where he'd hung the razor strop.

It was as he was scything his razor up and down that he saw a movement. An overlapping piece of canvas near the end of the trestle on which the washbasin stood, twitched.

He paused.

The canvas had pulled aside enough for him to see a pair of eyes. Even though a dirty scarf obscured the lower part of the face, Abbas could see that the eyes were those of a young boy.

The boy's eyes looked at him without blinking—as if time had frozen. There was a curious intensity to them that Abbas found disturbing.

A moment later, a hand snaked around the edge of the canvas flap and reached out for the leather bag that normally held Abbas' shaving kit.

Abbas dropped his razor, snatched the Makarov from his holster, and cocked it in one movement. He pointed the gun at the boy.

"*Ibn al Kalb* (son of a dog). Leave the bag alone."

Rather disturbingly, the boy did not retract his arm. For a moment, no one moved. Then the boy spoke. It was only a single syllable.

"Ab...."

Abbas knew that he should shoot the boy. He'd every right to. The boy was a thief. But how did the boy know his name?

The boy continued to stare at him.

Abbas found he could not bring himself to press the trigger.

Then, as quick as a flash, the boy grabbed the leather case and disappeared.

Abbas, still brandishing his pistol, roared with anger and ran out of the ablutions tent. He spun around on his feet looking left and right, but could see no one.

"*Allah Yakhthek*" (may God take your soul) he growled and spat on the ground.

Chelsea Thompson felt neither refreshed nor restored in optimism by her sleep. She stood on the perimeter track of the excavation site of Ebla and wanted to weep. Evidence of ruin and desecration was everywhere. She was part of a small group of international archaeologists who were helping the Syrian government restore order to one of their most significant archaeological sites, and it was a daunting task.

A puff of wind stirred the head-scarf she wore. At least the air was still warm and had not yet surrendered to the chill of autumn. It had been a hot, dry summer. Many of the trees in the orchards that existed nearby were dead through lack of water and attentive husbandry. Only a few now struggled to keep hold of their green leaves.

She glanced across the site with its sunken pits and low walls. The entire area had been pegged out by string-lines into six by six meter squares. Her job was to photograph and record what lay in each square whenever any archaeological 'finds' were discovered.

No excavation work had been done at Ebla since 2011. This had left the site ripe for looting when the area came under the control of the Fattah opposition army that had occupied the area for many years. They were fighting troops loyal to the Ba'athist Syrian Arab Republic led by President Bashar al-Assad. The locals had used this time to dig tunnels into the site with the aim of finding and looting artifacts. There was not much evidence of mounds of dirt from the tunnels because the villagers had even removed the soil after discovering it was suitable for making ceramic liners for their bread-baking ovens.

In the process of digging, the locals had, rather remarkably, discovered a crypt full of human remains. These had been discarded by the robbers and left carelessly over the surface of the site. There was also evidence that they had unearthed a room that held collapsed shelves carrying clay tablets. Shattered pieces of tablets with cuneiform writing had been found in many of the grids marking out the site.

Chelsea heard footsteps behind her. She turned and was not surprised to see Major General Abbas Shamon, the Syrian officer in charge of reopening the excavation. He was in a crisp army shirt and trousers. As usual, he was looking disdainful.

She swallowed, summoned all the optimism she could find and said, "*As-salam alaykom*" (peace be upon you).

Abbas gave an elaborate sniff and replied, "*As-salam alaykom*" (peace be upon you, as well).

It was as close to rudeness as Muslim etiquette allowed. She looked at him sharply. Abbas' mouth was set in a straight line. As disturbing as his grim visage was, it was his eyes that particularly disturbed her. She wondered briefly how eyes that were so dark and intriguing could simultaneously seem so bleak.

She found herself saying, "I thought you could use as much peace as you could get."

Abbas ran his hand across his forehead. It was a movement that betrayed the infinite tiredness of his soul. She elected to steer the conversation to something safer.

"Are you having much success reclaiming the looted tablets from the locals?"

"Hassan is doing well. He has a budget he can use to buy them...and has shown himself to be..." Abbas paused, "very persuasive."

Chelsea was careful not to show any emotion. She did, however, permit herself to draw in a deep breath. Hassan was Abbas' right-hand man, and he was huge. Intimidating as his physique was, it was his face that bothered her. It never showed any emotion. She did not doubt for a moment his capacity to be 'persuasive.'

"How many tablets have you recovered?"

Abbas looked down his nose. "That is no business of yours."

Chelsea gave Abbas an irritated glare, and wished she were six inches taller so that she could match his height. "Am I not allowed to love your country and be intrigued by its history? It is after all, the reason I am here."

Abbas said nothing.

Chelsea turned away and gazed over the site to the town of Tell Mardikh that lay one mile to the northwest. Remarkably, the thin tower of a mosque still soared above it. It was unusual. Most of the mosques had been destroyed by the Fattah rebels.

She forced her heart rate to slow down and said, "You and your family must be pleased that peace has finally come to your country."

Abbas coughed a bitter laugh. "There is no peace." His mouth settled again in a straight line before he continued brutally. "And my family are dead."

"Dead?"

He shrugged. "My wife and two daughters—they were killed in Damascus six years ago in a bomb attack."

Chelsea was appalled. Instinctively, she began to reach out a hand to him...but withdrew it when she reminded herself of Muslim sensibilities.

"I am so sorry. That must be..." she swallowed, "hard to bear."

The morning sun began to warm the back of her shawl. She

lifted it from her head and shook her hair free. There was a lot of it to shake. Although slight in frame, her hair was thick, black, and very long. It was a very feminine movement—almost instinctive, and she was not quite sure why she did it.

She forced herself to look across the excavation site. Archaeologists from the World Archaeological Congress were busy scraping away with trowels, whilst teams of locals were carrying baskets of soil to be sieved before being dumped on the discard piles. She should be amongst them sitting at her trestle table photographing and documenting the 'finds' that were being unearthed.

Abbas interrupted her thoughts. "We have managed to locate and collect 465 clay tablets."

Chelsea was shocked. "Wow! So many. Do you have any idea about their content or purpose?"

"Nothing certain at this stage. Most of them are written in Eblaite cuneiform. From the few I've examined, I suspect that the room the locals discovered and plundered was some kind of school. I don't think it was another library. None of them contained administrative records." He shrugged. "But as we know so little of the language, it is difficult to tell."

Chelsea tried to disguise the surge of excitement that coursed through her. Having 465 new clay tablets to add to the 2,000 found in 1964 could help unlock the secrets of what was recorded on them. As the tablets represented the earliest record of human writing using an alphabet, the value of being able to understand them was incalculable.

"Why won't you let me see the tablets?" She'd blurted out the question before she realized it.

Abbas lifted up a hand in warning. "It is forbidden...as you know very well." His eyes glittered with passion as he spoke. "You Westerners cannot be trusted with our heritage. You have imputed meaning to the tablets which is false and damaging to Islam."

Chelsea threw back her head in frustration. She was all too familiar with the ongoing archaeological fight over the Ebla tablets. Paolo Matthiae from the University of Rome had unearthed them in 1964, when he discovered the collapsed remains of a library in

Ebla. The library had contained over 2,000 clay tablets written in two languages. One was Sumerian, and the other was a previously unknown Eblaite language that also used Sumerian cuneiform when written. The trouble was, no one was very sure how to translate it. The only person with some expertise in the field was a colleague of Matthiae, Giovanni Pettinato.

Pettinato had become very excited about the discovery of what appeared to be an Eblaite geographical atlas containing over two-hundred place names. At a meeting of the Society of Biblical Literature in St. Louis in 1976, he claimed to have identified the names of Sodom, Gomorrah, and Zoar—locations known from Genesis 14 of the Hebrew Bible. This, of course, gave credence to the Jewish claim that they were the original and rightful owners of Palestine.

The Syrian government reacted by withdrawing research privileges and making counter-claims in support of an Islamic heritage. The fight thereafter became ugly.

Chelsea sighed and turned her gaze to the heavens. A falcon was circling on the first of the day's thermals looking for prey. She plucked the shawl from her shoulders and shook it to free herself of her frustrations. After looping it over an arm, she turned back to Abbas and gave him a speculative look.

He saw her and reacted. "Why are you looking at me that way?"

"Your surname—Shamon: it is an Arabic form of Simon, a name mainly used by Christian Arabs."

Abbas scowled. "Muslims had the name first."

The ridiculous claim broke what little self-control she still struggled to exercise. She threw back her head and laughed. "Who discovered America? A Muslim. Who first flew an airplane? A Muslim. Who did anything first and fastest, indeed anything distinguished? A Muslim." She jabbed a finger at him. "Truth is not a foundational concept for you Muslims. You re-invent history. Your overarching value is the honor of Islam…but in the mad pursuit of it, you actually dishonor it with lies."

She became aware that a deathly hush now hung between them.

Chelsea was appalled at what she'd said. She immediately lowered her head. "I…I am sorry for my outburst. It was disrespectful to you and to Islam. Although what I said was unforgivable, I ask your forgiveness." She paused. "I seek to honor Islam with truth…and I have the passion of a frustrated archaeologist."

She was all too well aware that her future as a researcher at Ebla was now in peril. What Abbas said next would determine her fate, and it was a fate that could see her imprisoned or at the very least, deported.

She kept her head bowed.

Abbas said stiffly, "You are a guest of my nation, and permission for you to stay here is entirely contingent on your behavior. I can have you thrown out of my country like that." He snapped his fingers.

Chelsea raised her head and looked into his eyes. Abbas' face was stony and grim. He glared at her for a long while. Then, she was shocked to see his countenance change. For a moment it softened, and he looked almost wistful.

She lowered her head quickly.

Abbas turned on his heel and marched back toward the tents.

Mahdi could remember very little of the day his mother was killed. It was almost four years ago to the day by his reckoning, and he'd been eight years of age at the time. He rubbed at the scar that deformed his left forearm. The old wound had healed, but it never ceased to itch.

The old men of the town later told him that his house had been hit by a US-made rocket, a BGM-71 TOW, captured by the al-Nusra Front from the Western-backed militia. The hell that rained down that day did not end when night came. Next day, the town of Tell Mardikh—his town, and the town of Saraqib four miles to the north, were both counter-attacked by forces loyal to Bashar al-Assad. But it didn't really matter. His mother was dead by then. She'd worked as a teacher in the local school. He never knew his father.

Mahdi glanced up at the woman who now called herself his

mother. She was mad of course, but at least she cared for him. The downside of her affection was that she called him 'Jamal,' the name of her dead son.

He rubbed again at his forearm and looked to see if it was safe to uncover his secret hiding space.

The old woman was cooking *falafil*, fried balls of spiced mashed chickpeas, which she would serve on Arabic bread—sometimes with hummus, if she could buy or barter for it. Her *falafils* were actually very good, and she managed to feed both herself and Mahdi by selling them to the locals. The trouble was, it was almost the only thing she cooked.

She was currently standing at her charcoal-burning stove, spooning boiling oil over a new batch of them.

Good: that meant she would be busy for the next twenty minutes.

He ducked back into his room. Calling it 'a room' was perhaps being generous. He actually slept on a mat in the washroom where the toilet was. But he didn't always sleep there. Sometimes he would awaken at night screaming, and the woman would take him into her own bed, wrap her arms around him, and croon away in her crazed way until he fell asleep. Over the years, Mahdi had become used to her smell and her strange ways, and was grateful for her affection.

The corner of the washroom was badly damaged, and it had been necessary to block a hole in the wall with a blue, plastic sheet. At least it kept some of the elements at bay.

Mahdi took a length of steel reinforcing rod and prized up the corner of a flagstone that lay under his mat. He heaved up the flat stone until it rested against the wall. A cavity had been excavated under where the stone had once rested. The cavity was large, extending under two of the neighboring flagstones. He smiled. This was his space. Everything in the world that belonged to him was in this place. It held one photograph…and twelve clay tablets inscribed with strange writing—writing that looked as if a child had pressed the head of a nail thousands of times into wet clay.

These were his tablets, and he'd found them.

In the years that followed the time when his town had been

driven mad with rockets and bombs—the time when the Fattah 'Army of Conquest' controlled the region—he'd joined with some of the locals in looting the excavation site at Ebla. The men raiding the site were grateful to have him with them, because he was small enough to squeeze into the tunnels they'd dug and the cavities that were unearthed.

The looting, however, proved to be only mildly productive. All they found were piles of clay tablets. No gold or jewelry was found at all. Mahdi would dig out the tablets and pass them back to the men, who would reward him with sweets, or sometimes with nothing at all. The men would then take their booty to Mr. Khaled. He was a slug of a man. Regardless of the time of year, he only wore a singlet over his expansive belly, and his hairy shoulders always seemed to be covered in a sheen of sweat. Mr. Khaled had 'contacts' and was able to sell on the tablets found at Ebla. People in the West were hungry for them, evidently.

One night as he was digging, a cavity broke open at the side of his tunnel, and there, covered in dirt, were two piles of tablets. As he brushed away the dirt, he discovered there were six tablets in each pile. He resolved then and there that these would be *his* tablets. He would come back in the early hours of the morning and retrieve them one by one until he had them all. And then he would visit Mr. Khaled.

The fruits of his labors now nestled in the cavity he'd dug under the flagstones—three piles of four tablets.

Mahdi reached behind him for some pages he'd torn out from an old exercise book. He laid a page on top of the nearest clay tablet and began to rub its surface with a piece of charcoal. It wasn't long before a smudged impression of the tablet was left imprinted on the paper. Then he turned the tablet over, and repeated the process on the other side.

Satisfied with his work, Mahdi lowered the flagstone back into place and covered it with his sleeping mat.

Then, taking his pieces of paper, he went to visit Mr. Khaled.

Mr. Khaled's shop ostensibly sold tobacco, together with all the accoutrements that went with it. This chiefly meant hookahs, or 'hubbly bubblys,' as he was told Westerners liked to call them. He liked the term 'hubbly bubbly.' It described the hookah well. He was fascinated by their shape, particularly that of the older traditional hookahs. They were ornate and richly decorated. On top of the hookah was a ceramic head in which the *shisha* was burned. Beneath that was a brass tray, and below that was the port to which the smoking hose was attached. All of this sat on a central shank that rose up from the bulbous vase containing the water through which the smoke bubbled.

Yes, he liked the term 'hubbly bubbly.'

But he had no interest in hookahs today.

Mr. Khaled was seated, as usual, behind his battered wooden counter. When he saw Mahdi enter his shop, he snapped shut a ledger he was inspecting and leaned on his elbows.

"And who do we have here, *abu Reiha* (the father of stinky smells)?" He gave a derisive smile that showed off his bad teeth.

Notwithstanding the forced smile, Mahdi noticed that the man's pallor was unusually bad. He also noticed that the little finger on his left hand was heavily bandaged. Two lollipop sticks had been used as splints.

Mahdi swallowed and said without preamble, "I have old clay tablets from Ebla to sell."

Mr. Khaled's response surprised Mahdi. The man lifted his hands up as if defending himself, and shook his head vigorously. "I'm having nothing to do with any more tablets from Ebla. A government official came last week…" he paused as a shudder caused his flesh to quiver…"and they took all my stock before I could sell it." He waved Mahdi away. "So go away. It is not safe to have these tablets anymore."

Mahdi was both appalled and amazed. Mr. Khaled never passed up an opportunity to make money from the labors of others. Taking a deep breath, he began to appeal to the only thing he could think of that would motivate him—greed.

"These tablets are particularly good, and I will let you have them at half the price you normally pay. Here, take a look." Mahdi placed the pieces of paper with the charcoal rubbings on them onto the counter.

Mr. Khaled turned his head away, but a moment later, his eyes darted back to the piece of paper. After a few seconds, he bent over and peered at it.

"How many of these do you have?"

"Twelve."

"Are all of them as good as this?"

"Yes. They are all the same."

Mr. Khaled grunted and took out his Smartphone. After taking some pictures of the pieces of paper, he slid them back across the counter to Mahdi.

"I'll pass the word around and see if anyone is interested. But I won't carry any stock here unless I have a buyer. I can't afford to be found with any more tablets." The man mopped his forehead. "I will pay a third of the normal price. Come back next week."

Mahdi was very tempted to say *Telhas Teeze* (kiss my ass), but managed to say instead, "Thank you."

Outside the shop, Mahdi glanced at the sun. It was well down toward the western horizon. He would have to hurry if he was going to get to the excavation site at Ebla in time. He worked there in the mornings and evenings for Miss Chelsea. She would be looking for hot water to wash her hair. Miss Chelsea was always washing. Every evening he fetched hot water for her from the kitchen in a large black-bottomed kettle.

She was the cleanest person he knew—and the most beautiful.

Chapter 2

Kent (England), 2019

The last strains of Claude Debussy's 'Clair de Lune' faded away into silence. The finish of the piece was exquisite. Tony Patterson settled deeper into his car seat and allowed the peace of the music to soothe his soul. Music was his safe haven. It was something timeless and beautiful in a world that was too often ugly, unjust and violent—particularly his world.

He waited patiently for the next track to play. It would be the Meditation from Thaïs by Jules Massenet. Tony Patterson knew the playlist well.

He guided his Hyundi i30 through the country lanes of Kent. The car was gray, demure, and unremarkable...and he liked it that way.

Unsure of what he would be facing in the next hour, he did a mental inventory of his readiness to meet any surprises. He adjusted the rear-view mirror to give himself a quick inspection. The action had nothing to do with vanity, and everything to do with presenting a face that betrayed nothing.

A tanned face looked back at him. It was clean-shaven and showed the strong features of his chin and aquiline nose. Pale blue eyes that had spent too long in the sun inspected him briefly. Crinkle lines had appeared at the corner of his eyes. He noticed too that his blond hair had been given lighter streaks by the sun. It was now considerably longer than a regulation military cut—not that short hair was always a requirement in his particular branch of the military. It didn't matter now anyway, because he was no longer an enlisted man.

He returned the mirror to its driving position and reflected on the fact that, sadly, his was not an easy face to hide.

Outside the car, the morning sun was trying to make an impact on a gray, watery sky. It was early autumn, and the countryside was beginning to surrender to the starkness of winter. The hedgerows were becoming a tangle of wickerwork. Tony thought he could still identify hawthorn, beech, and the occasional willow.

The road was single track, and he was forced to slow down to make way for a tractor. Tony drove patiently behind it. Eventually, the tractor pulled into a farmyard. The driver waved an apologetic hand—which was perhaps a wave of thanks.

He drove his car through the village of High Halstow and on into the bleak flatlands of north Kent. Arable land eventually gave way to pasture, which in turn gave way to marshland. Its tussocky grass was bisected both by tidy drainage channels and very untidy natural rivulets of water. He knew that somewhere in the distance, a sea wall would be hiding the mighty Thames, but he could see no sign of it from the car.

A few minutes later, he saw a silver Mercedes station wagon pulled off from the side of the road—just where he'd been told to expect it. It was parked a hundred yards down a muddy track. The car's tailgate was open.

Tony elected to park his car at the entrance of the track where it was slightly drier. Leaning back in his seat, he removed the pistol from his shoulder holster and checked again that the magazine was full and the safety switch was on. The gun was a 9mm Glock L137. Being quite large, it was not an easy gun to keep inconspicuous. It was, however, a very reliable weapon—and reliability was everything.

Tony splashed along the muddy track toward the car. He could see a man standing in gumboots thirty yards beyond it. He was wearing a shooting jacket and was holding a shotgun. A Golden Retriever was sniffing around at the grass, pausing occasionally to lift a leg against a tussock of sedge.

Tony called out, "Mr. Carlisle."

It may or may not have been his real name; it didn't really matter.

The man lifted a hand in acknowledgment. "So you're Tony Patterson?"

"Yes, sir."

A hundred yards away, two geese launched themselves into the air and flew almost directly overhead.

The man swung the shotgun up to his shoulder and blasted into the sky.

High above, the two geese continued on in their flight unscathed.

"Damn and blast it. Missed again," he said.

Tony ventured a comment. "You know it's not open season for shooting birds for another six months, don't you."

The man broke open the shotgun, ejecting the spent cartridges. "The blasted Canadian geese here are overpopulating the area." He loaded two more cartridges into the gun.

For a moment, the only sound was the sighing of the wind.

Three more geese took to the air.

The man suddenly tossed the shotgun at Tony.

"Here, you try."

Tony caught the gun. He saw briefly that it looked expensive and had been beautifully made. Calmly, he broke the gun open, ejected the cartridges, and handed it back to Carlisle.

The man raised an eyebrow.

Tony shrugged. "I don't kill unless I have to."

"That's a surprise. I've read your file."

"Files can still have their secrets."

"I don't like secrets—not in my line of work. My job is to uncover them." Carlisle turned and trudged back to his car. He placed the gun in the back of the car and sat down under the tailgate. Reaching for his hip flask, he said, "You were offered the job, then?"

"Yes."

"But you will now also report to us. You doing so was contingent on you winning the job, so well done."

Tony nodded.

For a moment, nothing was said.

Carlisle broke the silence. "You give us eyes on the inside. But most of the time, I expect you will see nothing."

"That doesn't bother me. My official job will be interesting enough in itself."

Carlisle grunted. "London is probably the most international, multi-cultural city in the world, but not all of the international interests domiciled here are benign. This is particularly the case in the place where you will be working. It is the focus for a lot of foreign interest. The people there have to field a lot of claims and cope with the political hubris of many international agencies." He paused. "We're not always sure where this pressure comes from, or who the people are that are being leaned on."

The Golden Retriever finished inspecting Tony and slumped down beside the front tire of the Mercedes. The man continued. "Your job, as it pertains to us, is poorly defined and messy, but never doubt, it is important." He paused. "It might sometimes be dangerous."

The grass beside the car leaned over in the rising wind.

Carlisle took another swig from his hip flask. "You say you don't like killing. You've not become gun shy have you?"

Tony said nothing. After a few seconds, he stepped forward and took the hip flask from Carlisle, then reached into the wicker basket behind the man and removed a plastic bottle of water.

He placed both the hip flask and the bottle of water on the roof of the Mercedes.

"Please step away from the car," he said as he began to walk away.

Carlisle's mouth dropped open. "Hey," he said, raising a hand in protest. "That's a very expensive car."

Tony ignored him but was gratified to see him scuttle to the side.

Twenty yards away, Tony unsheathed the Glock and cocked it. Then in one fluid movement, he turned and loosed off two shots.

The plastic bottle of water exploded, and the shattered hip flask spun through the air.

"Dammit man," said Carlisle. "That was a Macallan single malt."

Tony put the Glock back in its holster, covered it with his jacket flap, and walked behind the vehicle to pick up the exploded plastic bottle and the ruined hip flask. If there was one thing he couldn't stand, it was litter.

"Open sights at twenty yards," he said handing the hip flask to Carlisle. "No. I am not gun shy."

Chapter 3

Ebla, Syria

A bbas looked at the medical officer darkly.

The man shrugged. "I'm sorry sir, but I am certain."

"We have an outbreak of MERS?"

"Middle East Respiratory Syndrome; yes, sir."

"How serious is it?"

"It's a coronavirus; so it's serious."

"How many people?"

"Two of the team from Switzerland and, I suspect, some of the locals."

Abbas was sitting behind his trestle table in the administration tent. It was the nearest thing he had to an office. He leaned his elbows on the table and put his head in his hands.

"How does this wretched disease spread?"

"It spreads from an infected person's respiratory secretions—through coughing and the spray of people speaking."

Abbas groaned. This was the last thing he needed. He had an international team of scientists and scores of workers from the local town—a town where people's health was already degraded by years of war.

"What does it mean?"

"The medical officer bobbed his head up and down obsequiously. "It means isolation, sir. Self-imposed quarantine for two weeks." He paused, but couldn't bring himself to continue. "Err…""

Abbas lifted his head from his hands and barked at the man. "Spit it out, man. What else?"

The medical officer took his glasses off his nose and rubbed them with a handkerchief. "Umm…because this archaeological dig involves foreigners, it will also be necessary to spray everything using a disinfectant registered by the Environment Protection Authority."

"Everything?"

"Everything."

Abbas sat back in his chair, leaned his head back, and closed his eyes. He desperately tried to think. "Does this include the artifacts salvaged from this site?"

"Yes, sir. Everything that has been handled."

Abbas swore.

For a long time, nothing was said. Outside, the noise from the camp could be heard clearly through the walls of the tent. Everything seemed so ridiculously normal. But it wasn't. He now had a catastrophe on his hands.

The medical officer broke the silence. "What do you want me to do, sir?"

Abbas drew a deep breath. "Send the workers home and call the international team together. Tell them to meet me outside this tent in one hour." He heaved himself up from his chair. "Cooping them up in here might not be a good idea." He pointed to the medical officer. "Both you and I will address them."

"Yes sir."

"And one thing more."

"Yes?"

"Warn the doctor in the local town, Tell Mardikh. Make sure he knows what's happened here. He has to understand the quarantine measures he'll need to put in place. We can't have the camp and the townsfolk continually cross infecting each other." He paused. "If he prevaricates, tell him he will be shot."

"Yes sir. Err…and what if there is no doctor?"

"Then tell the local clerics." He pinched the top of his nose. *Think. Think.* "In fact, tell them anyway…and take Hassan with you."

"Yes sir."

The international team of archaeologists chatted away to each other without any appearance of concern, as they milled around in front of the admin tent. Abbas looked at them sourly. *So privileged, entitled…and boring.*

His eyes searched out and found Chelsea Thompson. She, however, was definitely not boring. Dr. Thompson stood out like a candle. *No*, he corrected himself, like a roaring fire—a dangerous fire. Her petite figure was shapely, and she was conspicuously beautiful. The only other woman on the international team, was a painfully thin, middle-aged lady from Belgium. He couldn't remember her name.

It wasn't long before the mood of the gathering changed. The medical officer had delivered the news about the MERS outbreak and was outlining some of the consequences.

"Your food will be delivered to the front of your tents. You will collect it and eat it alone inside your tents."

The medical officer turned to Abbas and invited him to take over.

Abbas stepped forward.

"I've organized for two hand-held temperature guns to be shipped here from Damascus. They will help us monitor the situation. In the meantime, and until I say otherwise, no workers from the town will be allowed on site. They will do no more digging."

Groans and complaints immediately erupted from the group in front of him.

Abbas held up a hand. "This is not negotiable. You will be

allowed to work on site provided that you feel well and can stay four meters from each other." He glared at his audience. "Any breaches of this protocol, and you will be confined to quarters."

One of the archaeologists called out, "What will we do with the 'finds' we collect?"

You will take them to the central collecting table and leave them there to be disinfected." He paused. "We will take charge of them from there."

This comment was greeted by another wave of murmurings.

"And what about the clay tablets you've collected? You said you were planning to ship them out this week. You can't disinfect those. They could be ruined. Even slight dissolving of the features could represent an incalculable loss."

The voice, of course, belonged to Chelsea Thompson. He watched her as she pushed her way to the front of the crowd and stood in front of him. Although Abbas was taller than most Syrians, somehow he didn't feel tall in front of Chelsea. She had an aura that demanded respect—and he didn't like it.

Chelsea was carrying her camera in one hand. She held it out to him. "It is now more important than ever that the tablets be photographed." She paused. "You have to allow it."

Irritated by her demands and audacity, he lashed out with one hand, smashing the camera from her hands. The sound it made as it hit the stony ground did not bode well for the camera's continued functionality.

Everyone gasped, and for a moment there was silence.

Abbas was surprised by his own actions, but elected to plow on. "There will be no photographs. It is forbidden." He lifted his chin in what he hoped was a haughty gesture. "You may go. The quarantine regulations are in force as of now."

As the research team began to disperse, Abbas looked at the woman in front of him, now bending down to pick up the camera. "You stay," he ordered.

Chelsea stood up and looked at him defiantly.

In an instant, he was transported back in time to when a woman, just as feisty, had looked at him in a similar way. And somehow, it had transmuted to love—a forbidden love. He shook his head. Whatever it was, it was not a love to be underestimated. It was strong. Young love made up in fervency what it lacked in wisdom.

He ran his eyes over Chelsea's dark hair and fantasized about touching it...scrunching it, feeling it. For a moment his hand moved forward, but he let it fall to his side. Abbas risked glancing at her eyes. They were brown and flecked with gold, like those of a falcon.

He swallowed. "Why is it always you?"

"What do you mean?"

For a long while, Abbas said nothing. Then he lifted his gaze to the scene beyond her, and seeing nothing of it, said, "I am expelling you from this archaeological investigation. As soon as the quarantine period is over, you will be driven to Khmeimim Air Base, put on a plane, and deported."

Chelsea stormed back to her tent and tossed the camera on her bunk. It's lens or its housing was probably broken, but she doubted that the pictures stored in the camera had been corrupted. She'd plug it into her computer and check later.

She stood in the middle of her tent and drove the palm of her hand into the central tent pole.

It shuddered pleasingly, so she hit it again, and again, and again. Finally she stopped, leaned her forehead against the pole and wept. *So stupid. The man's so wretchedly pig-headed and foolish.*

Then she wept some more.

"Miss Chelsea. Miss Chelsea."

The small quavering voice interrupting her grief was full of concern. Chelsea sniffed, released one hand from the post and forced a smile.

"Hello Mahdi." She wiped her nose with a handkerchief. "Don't worry. I'm just a bit upset."

Mahdi was standing in the entrance of her tent. As usual, he wore a dirty tee-shirt and shorts, and stood in bare feet. His face was puckered with worry. "Do you want some hot water?" he asked.

Chelsea smiled. Hot water seemed to be the remedy for every-thing. She couldn't help but think Mahdi could do with a bit more of it himself. His long, tousled hair was gray with grit and sand. She reached out and put a hand on the boy's cheek.

The boy's reaction to this intimate gesture surprised her. Suddenly, he threw his arms around her, buried his face into her thigh, and wept.

Chelsea was shocked.

After a few moments, she knelt down, folded her arms around him, and began to whisper endearments into his ear. It was the instinct of a mother, instincts that she rarely allowed herself to feel.

After a while, Mahdi had himself under control enough to step away. He stood with his head bowed, looking forlorn.

Chelsea felt obliged to at least give Mahdi some sort of explanation.

"Don't worry Mahdi. I'm just a little disappointed. I…I will have to return to England in a few weeks, and I had hoped to be taking some things found here with me to show to the world."

Mahdi nodded solemnly and began to rub his disfigured forearm.

"What things did you want to take?"

Chelsea sighed and forced another smile. "Don't you worry about it."

"What things?" the boy insisted.

"Some of the clay tablets…collected by the townsfolk." She ruffled his hair. "They speak about a great kingdom that existed long ago…that is part of your history."

Chelsea lay on her bunk, tossing and turning uncomfortably for the next hour. She was emotionally exhausted, and struggling to think. So it was a shock to her when the idea came. One moment she was in deep despair, lying on her back with her forearm pressed against her forehead, the next, her hands were at her side gripping the blanket with excitement.

The idea was audacious, insane…and probably unworkable. But the more she thought about it, the more convinced she became that it was worth a try. Anything was worth a go in the circumstances. She chewed over the idea for the next twenty minutes, until she could bear it no longer. Her watch told her that it was nearly midday. That would mean it was almost 10am in London.

Taking a deep breath, she took out her mobile phone and put a call through to a colleague she had great affection for in the British Museum—'Beanie,' known formally, and rarely, as Dr. Jamie McKenzie. Most people at the museum had a soft spot for Beanie. He was a character. His dress rarely varied. He typically wore shapeless cord trousers that hadn't been in vogue since the 70s, and disreputable pullovers that looked as if they'd been salvaged from a charity shop. His nickname came from the fact that he always wore a beanie jammed on top of his bushy red hair. They were always knitted with bright bands of colored wool, making him look as if he was parading a succession of tea cozies.

Those who worked with him knew that he was an easy man to underestimate. His personal scruffiness was in stark contrast to his technical work, which was meticulous. In his own way, Beanie was a genius.

His cheerful voice came through on the phone. "Hiya Chelse. How's it going in Syria?"

Chelsea couldn't help but smile. "It's pretty wretched, to be honest. But listen; I've got a crazy idea, and I want you to tell me if it's technically possible. I need to know before I call Megan and ask permission to give it a go."

There was a chuckle at the other end of the phone. "Well, you've got my attention, girl. What nefarious scheme are you hatching?"

"You remember those rotating laser beams we've used to map the underground water caverns in Rome?"

"Yep."

"Didn't you build a miniature table-top version that was used to scan the bas-relief on Babylonian wall tiles a few years ago."

"Yeah. I've still got it. Why?"

Chelsea took a deep breath. "Could you build a radiation unit into it…the sort of thing that might be used to sterilize medical instruments?"

"Wow!"

"Beanie, is it possible? What sort of rays do people use to sterilize things?"

"There are a number: gamma radiation, X rays, or high-energy electrons. Why?"

"I'd need one that would explain the sort of light produced by your scanning laser."

Beanie gave a low whistle. "Now you've really got my attention. What are you wanting to scan?"

"This is strictly confidential, Beanie…as in 'losing your job' confidential." She rubbed her forehead. This was the crunch. "I want to scan clay tablets containing cuneiform writing without anyone knowing—under the pretense we are sterilizing them to get rid of MERS virus which has broken out here."

"You're kidding!"

For a long while there was silence at the other end of the phone.

Finally, Beanie continued. "How big are the tablets?"

"About thirty by thirty-six inches."

After the briefest of pauses, Beanie continued. "Yeah. That should be pretty easy. I can fit a radiation unit into the machine I've got here."

Chelsea expelled the breath of air and pressed on.

"But that's not all. We'd need some pretty hefty external hard drives to hold the information. We'll be scanning about five-hundred clay tablets. And it would have to be done in secret."

"Are you wanting to scan both sides of the tablets?"

"I'm told they are just inscribed on the top, but we'll have to irradiate both top and bottom to kill any viruses."

"Leave it with me. I'll think of something." He chuckled. "Finally, I've got something worthy of my singular talents."

"Are you happy for me to talk to Megan Caplan to get her permission? This is high risk, and it can't happen unless she pulls some strings. We haven't got much time."

"Sure, go ahead. I'll fix things from the technical side." He paused. "Trouble is, the table-top unit will need a lead apron around it to contain the radiation, so it'll end up being quite heavy. If I'm bringing it out, it will be nice to have someone to give me a hand."

"Thanks Beanie, you're a darling. Needless to say, this is dynamite if the wrong people get to hear about it."

"So you're telling me to keep it under my hat."

She pictured him with a beanie pressed down on his red hair. "Yes."

"Don't sweat it. You've made my day."

Chelsea rang off.

Her heart was racing.

Not daring to wait until common sense urged her to call off the whole harebrained scheme, she rang another number—that of her boss Megan Caplan.

After a brief pause, she spoke. "Hello Megan. I have a problem; Syria has a problem; and the archaeological world has a problem…" She paused, trying to work out what to say next.

"Tell me more." Megan's no-nonsense voice helped settle her.

"I've an idea that is as desperate as it is irresponsible…and I need your permission to make it happen."

She went on to outline her plan.

After ten minutes, she heard Megan say, "I'll get back to you in three days. Meanwhile, keep clear of MERS. It's nasty."

Chelsea's phone rang three days later. She nearly dropped it in here excitement as she snatched it to her ear. "Hi Megan."

"How are you going?"

"I'm going stir crazy being cooped up in my tent. I can only get down to the site on my own for a few hours each day."

"Is everyone well?"

"There are no new confirmed cases here. But I understand

things are not so good in the local town. There have been some deaths."

"Well…take care."

Without any more ceremony, Megan continued. "Beanie is ready and willing to join you, with his, er…radiation equipment." She paused. "I'm putting the feelers out for someone to go with him. Quite frankly, the idea of Beanie being abroad in another culture without a chaperone, is scary."

Chelsea quite understood. Beanie was unorthodox enough in social settings at home, let alone abroad. She put a hand on her forehead, unable to believe that anyone was taking her plan seriously. Should she be delighted or terrified?

Megan's voice carried on calmly. "If the Syrian authorities want the radiation equipment, we'll fly Beanie, and whoever goes with him, in via Akrotiri in Cyprus. They can then transit to a small plane for the hop over to Khmeimim Air Base."

Megan went on to give Chelsea further details. "Funnel everything through me. I'll liaise with the RAF at Akrotiri if the Syrians give permission for this to go ahead."

Her boss's matter-of-fact voice helped Chelsea believe that what they were planning might actually be possible. She reflected briefly on her boss. Megan seemed able to do things that few other people could do. In her time at the British Museum, she had earned a reputation for being a no-nonsense manager. Although only a few years older than Chelsea, she had already risen to become the curator responsible for the museum's display of Ancient Levant and pre 1500 BCE Mesopotamian artifacts. She'd brought a brutal efficiency to the role that had swept away sleepy inefficiencies and under-performing staff. As a result, the museum's displays had improved, and research funds had doubled.

Meagan eventually ended the call, leaving Chelsea standing in the uncomfortable heat of her tent trying to come to terms with what she had heard. One thing she was very sure of: the success of the next step in the plan was entirely up to her.

She pulled a hairbrush through her hair in a perfunctory fashion, squared her shoulders, and ducked through the door-flap of the tent.

A few seconds later, she was standing outside the entrance to the camp administration tent.

Abbas was sitting behind a table entering information from a ledger into a computer. She didn't dare go in. Instead, Chelsea cleared her throat and called out. "Mr. Shamon, may I have a word with you. I…I have an idea that might ensure your tablets are made free of contamination by the MERS virus."

For a while, Abbas refused to answer her. Eventually, he said, "Go away. You should not be here. You are in quarantine."

Chelsea rolled her eyes in frustration. "You are safe from me if I remain standing here." She paused and said again. "I have an idea that may be of benefit to you."

Abbas leaned back and inspected her. "What?" he demanded.

"The British Museum has a machine which can irradiate artifacts to sterilize them and make them safe. I can give you the details so you can have it flown out here, together with the people who operate it. The whole operation need only take a few days."

Abbas frowned and then banged his fist on the table in frustration. "It's all a damnable waste of time. There is almost zero chance of the MERS virus being present on the tablets—and you know it."

"But you can't take the chance."

Abbas said nothing.

Chelsea pressed on. "I'm offering an opportunity for you to be certain…so you can get the tablets out of your hair and safely stored away." She arranged her face into what she hoped was a winning smile. "You'll be able to prove to the international community that you are both responsible and thorough—someone worthy of respect."

Abbas picked up a pen and jabbed it at her. "And if we do this, do you promise you will have nothing to do with this… this…radiation?"

Chelsea held up her hands. "I'll have nothing to do with it. I only want the tablets preserved, so scholars can examine them in the future." She sighed. "So much has been destroyed in recent years.

We can't afford to lose anything more. Syria's history is part of the world's history, which we all share."

It was a pretty speech, and she spoke it with a degree of sincerity because she believed most of it.

Abbas frowned.

She allowed her proposition time to marinate.

When she judged it was time to press on, she continued. "If you want help, it's probably best that we act quickly—while there is a window of opportunity with this machine."

"How will it get here?"

"My boss, Dr. Megan Caplan, says we can fly the radiation machine in via Cyprus. You can pick it up from Khmeimim Air Base...provided your government can give suitable assurances and landing rights." She paused. "You could have it here within two hours once it arrives there." Chelsea laid a piece of paper on a folding chair that sat to one side of the entrance. "I've written the details down for you."

Abbas leaned back, put his hands behind his head, and laced his fingers. He ran his eyes over her, then said, "You should have been a Syrian."

Chelsea's eyes opened wide. "Why?"

"You care for our culture." He sniffed in a way that wasn't quite derisive. "But you are rude in a way that Syrian women are not."

She couldn't think of anything to say. Finally, she blurted out, "Will you ask Dr. Caplan to send the radiation machine?"

He gave her a dismissive wave. "I shall think about it. Go away. You should not be in anyone's company. You are in quarantine."

Two days later, Chelsea received a text message from Megan. *Your parcel is being sent. Expected arrival: afternoon of Thursday, October 24.*

Chapter 4

Syria

T ony sat in the front seat of the little jeep. He recognized it as a Russian manufactured UAZ Hunter...and it was none too comfortable. The driver sitting next to him was a taciturn Syrian soldier who spoke poor English. Tony therefore had plenty of time to nurse his own thoughts.

Beanie was slumped sideways in the back seat, fast asleep. His initial excited chatter had long since surrendered to the weariness of travel. They'd taken off from the RAF base at Brize Norton and landed in Cyprus six hours later. From there they had flown in a Britten-Norman Defender, a demure light transport aircraft, to Khmeimim.

Tony had found Khmeimim Air Base a disturbing place. It was an active military airfield operated by the Russians. When they landed, he could see some modern Mig-29s parked next to some older Su-24 *Fencer* jet fighters. Bizarrely, the airfield facilities were shared with Bassel Al-Assad International Airport, an airfield that serviced the city of Latakia twelve miles to the northwest. This was despite the fact that Khmeimim housed one of Russia's most important international surveillance sites.

An hour's driving in the little jeep eventually delivered them to the excavation site at Ebla. The driver steered through a gate in a wire fence and pulled up in front of a collection of tents. Signs warning people that this was a quarantine area were everywhere.

Beanie spluttered to life, stretched, and cautiously opened the door of the vehicle. From his expression, he looked as if he'd just discovered the end of the earth. Tony could sympathize. He gazed across to the excavation site. There was not much to see—just some low walls, some pits, a few stone steps, and what appeared to be a couple of stone troughs. It wasn't much to excite the imagination.

"Is this it?" he asked.

"Yeah. Welcome to Ebla. Believe it or not, it was a flourishing city of 30,000, four-and-a-half millennia ago."

"The night life must have been stupendous."

Some curious faces appeared at the entrances of a few tents. However, before he had time to check whether one of them was Dr. Chelsea Thompson, an imperious voice called out to them. "Do not go near any of the tents. The occupants are in quarantine."

The owner of the voice stood at the entrance of one of the larger tents. He was tall, fit-looking, and obviously in command. Standing not far from him was a large, bullish man who regarded the new arrivals with a poorly concealed expression of hostility. Both men were dressed in military uniform and were wearing side arms.

Tony acknowledged him with a wave and helped Beanie lift the metal case containing the radiation scanner from the back of the Hunter. He and Beanie then reached in to collect their rucksacks.

"I've got the case, Beanie. You just carry your rucksack."

The metal case had tiny wheels that, whilst good on hard surfaces, were of limited use on a surface of sand and stones. He tugged it across to the two men, stood himself upright, and introduced himself.

"My name is Tony Patterson. I'm here to assist Dr. Jamie McKenzie." He waved a hand at Beanie."

Beanie was looking more than usually disreputable after his long journey. He sketched a wave and said, "Hiya. I'd kill for a good coffee. Any chance?"

The larger of the two men gave him a stony look. "You don't look much like an academic doctor."

Beanie pulled his multi-colored hat further down onto his red curls and grinned. "We come in all sorts of surprising packages these days."

The man turned his attention to Tony. "I am Lt. Col. Abbas Shamon, commander of this camp. You both will answer to me and to no one else. Is that clear?"

Beanie stood with his mouth open.

Tony nodded.

Shamon indicated the man standing next to him. "This is Hassan, my adjutant. He will be assisting you. At no time will you be working without him being present."

Tony felt himself being inspected by Hassan. He could sense the cold insolence of the man as he did so. Tony had elected to wear a military style uniform, but one that was colored blue rather than khaki green. Sewn onto the chest of his jacket were two patches. One simply read, 'Patterson.' The other read, 'World Archaeological Congress,' and in larger letters underneath, 'Security.'

Tony cleared his throat and said, "We'll be very grateful for any help we can get. Thank you."

Shamon glared at him, making it clear that he hadn't expected his orders to be mistaken for magnanimity.

"Hello Beanie." It was a soft, feminine voice—one that was totally out of place in a world of war, men, and competing egos.

Tony turned to see a woman dressed in a simple local caftan. A blue shawl hung over her shoulders. She was small, shapely, and beautiful. Her skin had been turned honey-colored by the sun, and black hair cascaded down her back. The woman was standing behind them, five yards away.

Beanie threw up his hands in delight and before anyone could stop him, bounded across to her and gave her a hug. "Hi Chelse. How'ya doin'? It's good to see you, girl."

Shamon roared. "Step away from her. She is in quarantine."

The woman disentangled herself from Beanie and regarded the camp commander with a look of defiance. Tony could see the fire in her eyes as she spoke. "Mr. Shamon, it is highly unlikely that I am infected. I've been in quarantine for over a week, and these men have just arrived from the UK, which is free of MERS."

The camp commander lifted his chin. Tony had the impression that he was about to argue, so he elected to diffuse what he felt would be an inevitable fight.

"Sir, we very much want to co-operate with you and adhere to whatever rules you have put in place. However, it will be necessary for both Dr. McKenzie and myself to work alongside yourself and your adjutant for the next few days. Perhaps, in the circumstances, you'd also allow us to be in each other's company during the evening." He paused. "And we'll be gone from here in a couple of days."

The camp commander looked at him stonily. "Dr. Thompson is to have nothing to do with the irradiation of the artifacts. Is that clear?"

Tony nodded.

The commander continued. "As Dr. Thompson will be leaving with you when you go, I suppose there is minimal risk to the rest of the camp." He shrugged. "If you choose to fraternize, be it on your own heads. Just make sure you keep well away from other people." He stepped to one side. "Bring your machine in here and set it up on that table over there. I want to inspect it. If I am satisfied, you can start work tomorrow morning."

Tony nodded. "Will any others be assisting us?"

"I have arranged for two men to be brought in from a military camp outside the quarantine area. They will help carry the artifacts to and from the truck." He pointed to what looked like a furniture removal van parked beside the tent.

Tony helped Beanie unpack the irradiation unit and set it up on a trestle table. Beanie gave a running commentary as he assembled it.

"The unit is essentially very simple. It's just a series of lights that emit the radiation we want, and a fan to keep them cool." He stepped away from the machine and invited Shamon to inspect it."

The camp commander did so.

When Shamon finished examining it, Beanie hefted a lead-lined apron onto the table and began to clip it into position around the machine's top hood. "I didn't have time to build in a conveyance roller to move the artifacts under the radiation light, so we have to poke them under the lead curtain with a stick." He turned to Shamon. "Have you got a wooden stick?"

The commander looked at him as if he'd stepped in something unpleasant. "A stick?"

"Yes."

Shamon sneered. "Very primitive." He declined to answer and pointed to the black rectangular objects Beanie was plugging into the radiation unit. They were about the size of a large bar of soap. "What are those?" he demanded.

"They are Kobalt 40-Volt, 2.5 amp, rechargeable batteries, my man. We need to plug them into the unit. If there is a generator failure, they'll keep the unit powered up so the fans can cool it down slowly, and we can avoid expensive damage."

Shamon nodded. "How long will all this sterilizing take?"

Beanie pushed his hat back and scratched his head. "What sorts of things are we sterilizing?"

"Clay tablets—465 of them."

"If we get a production line going, it will take a bit less than a minute per tile."

"They're tablets," Shamon corrected.

"Tablet, tile—whatever."

"How long will it take?" said Shamon again.

"We could probably get them done in seven to eight hours." Beanie interlaced his fingers, bent them back and cracked his knuckles. The action caused the camp commander to wince.

Shamon turned on his heels to leave, but on seeing Dr. Thompson, he paused and pointed to her. "You are not allowed to come near this tent tomorrow."

Chelsea lifted her chin, extending her neck so that she looked regal, and spoke words of compliance that her body language denied. "Of course."

Shamon stalked out of the tent.

As soon as he had left, his adjutant, Hassan stepped forward. The man took his pistol from its holster, grabbed Beanie in a head-lock and ground the gun into the side of his head.

Tony kept his eyes lowered and did not move.

Hassan snarled at Beanie. "No funny business from you, silly man, or I will kill you. Do you understand?"

The sudden violence took Beanie so much by surprise that he was unable to do anything other than to splutter, "I say: steady on."

Hassan let Beanie go and inspected the pistol in his hand. "This is a 9mm Browning. It holds thirteen shots in the magazine." He looked speculatively at the bulge under Tony's jacket. "Do you carry a gun?"

"Yes."

"What gun do you have?"

"A 9mm Glock."

"The Glock 26?"

"No, the L137."

Hassan nodded slowly. "That holds seventeen rounds."

Tony kept his eyes lowered. "Yes, it does."

Chelsea stole a covert look at the man called Tony. He had wide shoulders, and the late afternoon sun was causing his blond hair to shine like gold. The man had noticed that Beanie was still badly rattled by Hassan's violence, because he had picked up both his and Beanie's rucksacks and slung both over his shoulder.

He turned to her. "Where are we sleeping?"

Chelsea pointed to the end of the row of tents. "You're both in the end tent. It got erected yesterday ready for your arrival."

Tony nodded and set off across the compound.

She fell in step with Beanie.

"Are you alright?"

Beanie managed to conjure a smile. "I'm not feeling very much love in this place. Just a lot of negativity." He rubbed his neck. "It's generating bad karma, man; bad karma."

For a while, they walked across the compound in silence. However, a question kept disturbing her. In the end, she gave way to it.

She whispered, "Beanie, where are the hard drives?"

Beanie's smile broadened. "Did you see the little black batteries with the blue tops?"

Her mouth dropped open. "You're kidding."

He grinned. "Some of my best work."

"Seriously?"

He nodded.

She pointed to Tony who was striding on ahead of them and whispered, "How much do you know about him?"

"What? Tony?" Beanie shrugged. "Nothing. He's fairly quiet. You get the impression he's...sort of...watching."

"Watching?"

"Yeah, but not in a creepy way. He's basically a nice guy who keeps to himself." He paused. "And he's pretty fit. Don't take him on in an arm wrestle."

Chelsea nodded and quickened her step in order to come alongside Tony. However, once she was beside him, she wasn't sure what to say. A storm of emotions was wreaking havoc with her sensibilities.

In the end, she needn't have bothered because Tony began the conversation. "Dr. Thompson, how bad is the MERS outbreak. What's the risk?"

"You're not scared are you?"

"What's the risk?" he repeated.

She sighed. "MERS has only killed about 800 people since 2012, so there's never been a massive pandemic. The risk of MERS is probably fairly minimal here in the camp." She pointed across to Tell Mardikh, "But the disease is pretty significant in that town over there. Four have died already. Lt. Col. Shamon has lent them a backhoe tractor to dig some graves. They've dug a number of them as they are expecting more deaths soon. Muslim law requires the dead to be buried within 24 hours."

Tony nodded.

She paused. "What do I call you?"

"Tony."

"Then, I suppose you'd better call me Chelsea." She was appalled to hear the lack of enthusiasm for him doing so, so clearly in her voice. Chelsea hoped he didn't notice. She rushed on.

"I didn't know the World Archaeological Congress had a security department."

He looked at her levelly with disturbing gray-blue eyes.

"They don't."

"Then who exactly are you? How come you are here with Beanie?"

"Someone recommended me to your boss, Dr. Caplan."

"Why would they do that?"

"I've had a little bit of experience in the Middle East."

"But what is it that you actually do?"

"It's probably best to think of me as a civilian contractor."

"In some parts of the world, that's a euphemism for being a mercenary."

Tony shrugged.

"So you're a mercenary?"

"Not really."

"Well, if you're meant to be 'security,' I think you're pretty useless. That man Hassan is a brute." She shuddered. "You didn't move a muscle to defend Beanie."

He regarded her again with his unsettling pale eyes.

"No, I didn't."

Chapter 5

Chelsea wasn't at all sure that she had come off very well in her conversation with Tony. The wretched man had refused to take on board her censure and had remained infuriatingly self-possessed. But she knew that wasn't the full reason for her feeling so out of sorts. The truth was, she'd been rude to him, and she was a person who was very rarely rude. She realized that she should apologize, and it was not something she looked forward to.

She stood in the middle of her tent in a lather of indecision, clenching and unclenching her fists. Finally, she could bear it no longer. She threw back the entrance flap of the tent and set out across the compound.

The last of a dusky red sunset had given way to a lingering twilight. It was her favorite time of day—a time when the day gave a quiet sigh, rested on its elbow, and lay down to dream.

Her thoughts were interrupted by a shadow that darted out from behind a tent. A second later, a little hand tugged on her caftan.

It was Mahdi.

"What are you doing here?" she hissed. You'll get yourself into big trouble." She frowned. "And how did you get into the compound? There's a wire fence and a gate guarded by soldiers."

"Pah!" Mahdi waved a hand dismissively. "They said that dirt carriers can no longer come here." He pushed out his chest. "But I am not *khadim* (a lackey), I am *wasif*" (personal valet)." He reached for her hand.

Chelsea came to Tony and Beanie's tent, grateful that it was the least conspicuous tent in the compound and flipped back the entrance flap.

"Quick, get in here before you're seen," she ordered.

As she ducked into the tent, she heard Beanie say, "Hello, hello, hello. Who have we here?" Beanie lay sprawled out on his camp stretcher. Tony, she noticed, was sitting in a plastic chair, reading something on a Kindle.

"Sorry to barge in," she said. Chelsea reached out and ruffled Mahdi's hair. "This rascal shouldn't be here and will get into big trouble if he's discovered. He's called Mahdi. He's my best friend and my indispensable helper at the camp."

"What's a rascal?" demanded Mahdi.

"Someone who is very important, but who occasionally breaks the rules," she said.

"How do you do," said Beanie, shaking Mahdi formally by the hand. "I'm Beanie."

Tony simply nodded a welcome.

It only took a few seconds for Mahdi to overcome any sense of nervousness. "Do you guys want anything? If so, I can get it for you."

Beanie cocked his head and smiled. "You speak very good English."

"My mother taught me. She…" he paused, "was a school teacher."

"Was?" inquired Tony.

"She's dead now." The boy lifted his chin. "I also speak Hebrew and Arabic."

Beanie nodded. "That's very impressive, young man. And what sorts of things could you get for us?"

The boy grinned and rushed on enthusiastically. "You want hashish, or maybe cigarettes, or a hookah?"

Beanie sat himself up on his camp bed. "What, you mean one of those hubbly bubbly things?"

"Yes."

Tony pointed to the unoccupied plastic chair and invited Chelsea to sit down.

She nodded her thanks and did so. Chelsea tried to formulate the words of her apology but was forestalled by the banter going on between Beanie and Mahdi.

"Wow!" said Beanie. "I've always wanted to try one of those hookah things." He cracked his knuckles. "Can you really get me one?"

Mahdi put his hands on his hips. "Of course. You pay me American dollars, and I will buy for you."

Chelsea felt obliged to intervene at this point. "Beanie, the water in a hookah cools the smoke and removes some of the toxins in the nicotine, but it is still addictive. Are you sure you want to go down that path?"

"Absolutely," enthused Beanie.

"It will be difficult to transport," added Tony.

"I'll find a way," said Beanie. He turned back to Mahdi. "I don't have American dollars."

"What do you have?"

"Syrian pounds."

Mahdi sniffed. "Not as good. But okay. What sort of hookah do you want?"

Beanie shrugged. "I dunno. What makes a good hookah?"

"You can have an old fashioned one—very beautiful, or a modern one."

Tony put down his Kindle. "Connoisseurs say that solid brass is best. They are the heaviest and don't corrode. The trouble is; you have to polish them regularly. The important thing to check is that the gaskets are sound and that they seal properly."

Chelsea looked at Tony with raised eyebrows and said nothing.

Mahdi rushed on. "You want a small hookah or a big one?"

"What's the best?"

Mahdi held out a hand so it hovered about thirty inches from the floor. "About this size." He paused. "How much do you want to pay?"

Beanie shrugged.

"You pay 100,000 Syrian pounds, and it will get you the best."

Tony again interjected. "If you pay 30,000 Syrian pounds, you should get a very good one. That's about 45 British pounds."

Beanie reached for his wallet.

Mahdi stared at the wallet with a barely concealed look of triumph and continued on enthusiastically, "What *shisha* do you want to smoke?"

"*Shisha?*"

Chelsea laid a hand on Mahdi's shoulder to try and restrain his enthusiasm. "*Shisha* is what you smoke. It's made of tobacco and molasses, and has any one of a number of flavorings."

"Which one do you want?" insisted Mahdi.

Beanie raised an eyebrow. "No idea. What flavors are there?"

Mahdi ticked them off on his fingers. "Apple, ambrosia, peach, or mint."

Moments later, the transaction was complete.

Mahdi hopped from foot to foot in his excitement. "I will buy it for you tonight and give it to you tomorrow."

Beanie looked surprised. "Are the shops open this late?"

Tony answered. "Shops and restaurants stay open late at night in Syria, although very few will be open now because of the MERS virus."

"I get it for you anyway," said Mahdi.

As the boy made his way to the entrance of the tent, Tony called after him. "Mahdi, you'd better also bring everything he needs to smoke it, including some charcoal."

Mahdi waved a hand. "No worries," and disappeared into the night.

Chelsea turned back to Beanie. "Beanie, I'm going to give you some disinfectant, and you have to promise me that you will disinfect everything Mahdi will bring to you. Do you promise?"

Beanie laid himself back down on his camp stretcher with every expression of happiness and put his hands behind his head. "No problem."

Conversation turned inevitably to the task that lay ahead of them next day. Somehow, Tony's demeanor had made it clear that Chelsea's apology was not necessary. He appeared quite at ease with her. She was aware that whilst Beanie knew that they were about to engage in clandestine work, Tony would have no idea what they were actually doing. She couldn't help but feel that he must be mystified by the hostile reception he and Beanie had received. She wondered how much she should tell him.

Chelsea cleared her throat. "I'm really sorry for the reception you received today. The Syrians are pretty touchy about these clay tablets."

"Geesh, you're not wrong," said Beanie. "What's the story?"

"It's a long story. It begins way back in 3,000 BCE when humans first started to write. The Sumerians of southern Iraq invented a form of writing called cuneiform, which literally means 'wedge-shaped.'"

"Why?" asked Beanie.

"Because they wrote it using a reed stylus to press wedge-shaped marks onto a clay tablet."

"And how does that relate to Ebla?"

"Because the kingdom of Ebla was pretty much contemporary with the Sumerian civilization. Both wrote their languages down using cuneiform."

Chelsea noticed that Tony was paying her close attention. His eyes were fixed on her. She felt emboldened to continue.

"From what we can gather from the few clay tablets people have managed to decipher, the kingdom thrived on trade." She smiled. "Some of the things they recorded were their recipes for beer. They also had pretty enlightened views about women. Women had high status, and the queen had a major influence on both state and religious affairs."

Beanie grinned. "Wow! Now you've got my interest. I knew this place must have had something going for it for people to bother living here. Beer and emancipated women—wonderful."

"How many of the tablets have been translated?" asked Tony.

"About fifty—from a total of 2,000."

"That all?"

"Yes. But already we've discovered the earliest known references to the words, 'Ugarit,' 'Canaanite,' and 'Lebanon.'" Chelsea chewed her lip wondering how much more she should say. She continued carefully.

"It was also thought they made reference to the existence of the Old Testament figures of Abraham and David, as well as the towns of Sodom and Gomorrah," She shrugged. "But this has since been disputed—and things have become pretty political."

"Why?" demanded Beanie.

"Because if the Old Testament names really did exist on the Ebla tablets, it would verify the Jewish claim to sovereignty over the land of modern Israel."

Beanie gave a low whistle. "So understanding what's on the tablets could be political dynamite."

"Yes. That's why Shamon and the Syrian government want to get this new batch of tablets secreted away where only they can see what's on them."

Tony nodded and looked at his watch. "Well that may be his concern. My concern is to get you both back safely to the UK." He turned to Chelsea. "I understand you'll be leaving with us."

Chelsea dropped her head. "Yes. I'm being deported."

She felt his eyes bore into her.

"That must be hard to bear."

Chelsea blanched. She didn't expect sympathy and under-standing from someone like Tony. His kind words flooded through her like warm syrup…and that, in itself, was deeply disturbing.

Tony watched the truck back up to the front entrance of the tent. A soldier unlocked the back doors of the vehicle, climbed in and levered open the first of five crates strapped onto the truck-bed. He removed some packing and handed the first clay tablet to his colleague, who came into the tent with it and laid it on the table in front of the radiation unit.

Shamon was present watching proceedings. Occasionally he barked an order in Arabic, presumably to urge caution.

Beanie instructed Tony on how to irradiate the first tablet.

"You need to feed it through the radiation unit about ten seconds per meter. That will ensure a good kill of any microbes." He demonstrated what the speed looked like.

Tony had to concede that the process didn't look all that technical. Beanie was pushing the tablet through the lead curtain of the radiation machine with a piece of wood from an olive tree.

After the tablet was irradiated, it was turned upside down and put through again. It was a mind-bogglingly tedious business, but it soon settled down to an efficient routine.

Shamon didn't stay long, but returned from time to time during the day. He'd come into the tent, exchange the briefest of nods with Hassan, and then leave without saying a word.

Every half-hour, Tony and Beanie would swap the jobs they were doing at either end of the machine. It didn't bring much variation, but it helped relieve the boredom a bit.

As the heat of the day built up, the tent got warmer, and Tony's hands became sweaty inside the latex gloves he was wearing.

The two of them pressed on through the day, pausing only thirty minutes for lunch.

Every few hours, Beanie would swap the battery of the back-up unit. When Tony saw him do this the first time, he asked, "If the batteries are not working, why do you have to change them?"

Beanie stood up from plugging in a new battery. "Ah, but it is losing power, my ignorant friend. It bleeds power all the time, as it evens out variations in current flow."

As Tony picked up the tablets and fed them through the machine, it was hard for him to imagine that he was handling something that was 4,500 years old. So much had happened in human history since a scribe had pressed a reed stylus into the clay he was now holding. *Was it all for good or not?* He wasn't sure he wanted to know the answer.

His mind turned to the challenges he might have to face the next day. He felt edgy, and he'd lived long enough to respect feelings of disquiet. The trouble was, he had no idea why. On the face of it, everything was straightforward. They'd be driven to the Khmeimim Air Base where a Britten-Norman Defender would be waiting to fly them back to Cyprus.

To take his mind off his gnawing anxiety, he reflected on the meetings he'd had the previous day with Chelsea Thompson. He still wasn't sure what to make of her. She could be forthright and reactive, but also showed compassion and understanding. He sighed, and wondered how much trouble he could expect from her. Women, he reflected, usually represented some sort of complication.

He acknowledged ruefully that the lifestyle he'd chosen to live made it difficult, if not impossible, to sustain long-term relationships. As a result, a gnawing loneliness had settled on his soul, but he'd grown familiar enough with it for him to accept it as normal.

It was dark when the last tablet was carried to the truck and packed away in a crate. Shamon was there watching as the lid was nailed shut, and the crate was strapped to the floor. He personally shut the rear doors of the truck, locked them, and handed the key to the driver.

Without further ado, the truck lumbered off into the night.

Tony and Beanie returned to their tent, exhausted.

To Beanie's great delight, his hookah was waiting for him inside the tent. Tony suspected that Mahdi had delivered it under the cover of darkness not many minutes earlier.

Beanie, of course, wanted to get it going straight away, but Tony forestalled him.

"I'll get it going for you after we eat. But right now, I'm ravenous."

They'd missed the usual evening mealtime, but Shamon had organized for the kitchen to stay open and for panniers of food to be left outside their tent. On exploring their contents, he discovered Arabic flat bread, a *meze*, and a pannier of minced beef mixed with a herbal *za'atar*. Tony wolfed it down. It was good food, and he was grateful for it.

Once the demands of hunger were met, Tony turned his attention to Beanie's hookah. He recognized straight away that the hookah was of good quality. Beanie could probably thank Mahdi's relationship with Chelsea for that.

He assembled the parts, making sure that the gaskets were all tight. In truth, he was glad to do something that took his mind off worrying about tomorrow.

Tony undid the plastic bag of tobacco and put a ball of it into the ceramic cup at the top of the hookah, taking care not to compact it too much. Then he covered the tobacco with silver foil.

After filling the bowl with water, he pricked holes in the silver foil, lit a tablet of charcoal, and placed it on the top.

He handed the hose to Beanie. "Give it about twenty seconds, then have a puff."

Beanie took the hose enthusiastically, took a puff, and coughed. However, it wasn't long before he was puffing voluminous clouds of smoke, and the water in the bowl was gurgling merrily.

Tony slapped him on the shoulder. "If you add a bit of red wine to the water, you'll find it gives a bit of extra spice."

Beanie's reply was inaudible. His eyes were half closed in lazy contentment.

Tony envied him. It was not a contentment he shared. This was their final night, and he wondered what would be waiting for them when the sun rose.

Chapter 6

M ahdi did not want to wake up. He had no desire to face the day ahead. He'd talked with Miss Chelsea the night before, and she'd told him that she was being sent home to England. A fresh wave of grief swept over him. What would life be like without Miss Chelsea? She represented hope, another world—a beautiful world...one where there was kindness.

He turned his head into his grimy pillow and wept.

It was not a good way to start a day.

The fact that Miss Chelsea was leaving also represented a financial catastrophe. She had paid him well above the normal rates for working for her in the mornings, and again for working an hour in the evenings. It had taken a few weeks for him to realize that Miss Chelsea had arranged the day so Mahdi could eat lunch and dinner in the camp, and so have some reliable, nutritious food.

He hung his head. With Miss Chelsea gone, he needed to look to his finances. Mahdi grimaced. That meant visiting the mean-minded Mr. Khaled in order to find out if he had secured a buyer for his clay tablets.

He rolled off his mat and quietly left the house, making sure he was unobserved by the mad woman.

Mahdi picked his way through the broken rubble on the streets until he came to the back of Mr. Khaled's shop. The steel shutter door hadn't quite been pulled to the bottom. It was locked in a position that allowed six inches for Mr. Khaled's cat to get out. That was good. It meant that the man was up and would be in his shop.

Mahdi lay on the ground and squeezed though the gap. He got to his feet, dusted himself down, and crept between boxes and crates toward the front of the shop.

Before he got near to the front counter where Mr. Khaled would be seated, he heard voices. It wasn't good to be seen visiting a shop during a viral epidemic, so he hid behind two crates and watched what was happening at the front counter.

Two men were talking with the shopkeeper. He heard one of them say, "Mr. Khaled, as you can see from this warrant, we represent the Syrian Government. We are very keen to buy any ancient clay tablets unearthed from Ebla that may have come your way." The man held up his hands. "No questions asked." He paused. "We are particularly interested in obtaining the tablets you advertised by your charcoal rubbings."

Mr. Khaled's response startled Mahdi. The man seemed to take leave of his senses and started to rave.

"You come from the government," he shouted. "Pah! Rubbish! You lie. The government representative has already been here." Mr. Khaled waved a hand in the air showing off his heavily bandaged little finger. "And I should know because he gave me this little gift."

The two men frowned.

He continued to yell as he tugged a mobile phone from his pocket. "I'm going to take a photo of you two and report you both to the authorities. You are obviously deceivers—and very probably thieves." He raised his phone and took a photograph.

The two men did not look overly put out. They did, however, look grim. One of them gave the tiniest of nods to the other.

The other man calmly took out a pistol—a strange looking pistol with a fat barrel on the end of its spout—and shot Mr. Khaled once in the chest and again in his head.

The shopkeeper fell backward onto the floor where he lay outstretched and unmoving.

Everything was so quick, that Mahdi couldn't quite comprehend what had happened.

The man who had shot Mr. Khaled calmly picked up the dead man's phone and put it in his pocket.

Then, without a word, the two of them left the shop.

The strictures of the quarantine meant that there were no farewell hugs from colleagues and no leaving party. Chelsea was actually grateful. She wasn't sure she could have survived much socializing in her current state of heightened anxiety.

She and Beanie were standing alongside Abbas Shamon's personal jeep. His pennant was flying from an aerial—an eagle with spread wings above two crossed sabers, the same insignia he wore on his epaulettes. It denoted his rank—Major General.

Hassan was going to drive them to an army camp where they would join a convoy driving to Latakia, Syria's largest northern seaport. Khmeimim Air Base was just twelve miles to the south of the city.

Beanie had dumped his rucksack by the jeep, but still hugged his beloved hookah to himself. He'd wrapped it in his sleeping bag.

Tony was walking around the little jeep looking at the condition of the tires. Chelsea glanced at the two tires she could see. They seemed fine to her. The man was obsessive.

She leaned her rucksack against the metal case that contained the radiation unit. Chelsea scowled at it, hating the fact that it was still so wedded to them. Its presence continued to pose a very real threat. She leaned over to Beanie and whispered, "What have you done with the batteries?"

"They're in the pockets of my cargo pants. It seemed safest. They've got zips."

She nodded and glanced around at the camp as if seeing it for the first time. It looked uglier than when she'd first seen it six weeks ago. Perhaps it was just her mood. She sighed.

"I had to say goodbye to Mahdi last night. It wasn't easy."

Beanie nodded his understanding. "He's a great kid."

She smiled sadly as she remembered the conversation. "He told me he has some more clay tablets, and that I could have them if I stayed. He said he was going to sell them today if I didn't take them." Chelsea smiled sadly. "It's such a pity I can't buy them and take them with us."

She'd barely got the words out her mouth when she heard a scuffling sound coming from the front seat of the jeep. With a shock, she saw Hassan lever himself up into a sitting position. He was holding some insulation tape that he'd obviously been using to repair something under the dashboard.

She put her hand to her mouth. Had he heard her? Her heart started to race.

Hassan, however, gave no appearance of having heard anything. He unlaced the canvas back of the jeep and helped load their baggage inside. Chelsea frowned and began to feel uneasy. Hassan's behavior was out of character.

Her worst fears were confirmed as he steered the jeep out of the camp gates. He spoke to her over his shoulder. "You will want to say goodbye to the little boy who has been your servant. I have seen that he is your friend. I will take you to his house. You will direct me."

"No, don't do that," said Chelsea in a panicked voice.

The tone caused Tony to turn round with an expression of concern.

She hurried on. "The town is not safe. There's a virus outbreak."

Tony was sitting in the front seat beside Hassan. He said in a measured voice. "I'm not sure that going to town is wise."

Hassan gave a dismissive wave. "I will go in the house first and check all is safe."

Chelsea continued to protest. "It is dangerous."

Hassan grunted. "Life is dangerous. There is not much danger. You show me where he lives."

She thought briefly that she could deny she knew the way, but that was pointless. The whole camp knew that she had made the occasional trip to Mahdi's home. She'd come to regard her trips to Tell Mardikh as a type of pilgrimage—to fix in her memory the devastation caused by war, so she could rail against it and tell the world when she returned to England.

She was sitting directly behind Tony. The man looked relaxed and unconcerned. She wanted to shake him and scream that Mahdi might be in danger. But all she could do was lean forward and grip the sides of his seat, hoping that he would feel her anxiety and be warned of the danger she felt was imminent.

She railed against herself, hating her foolish, undisciplined mouth.

The little jeep had to continually swerve as it wound its way past piles of rubble, twisted reinforcing metal, and shattered concrete. Almost every wall was pockmarked with bullet scars.

Some of the buildings had their front walls blown off. Ripped wallpaper and shattered furniture bore mute testimony to what had once been a normal life. She shook her head. The public baring of what had once been so private was obscene.

Occasionally, they passed some locals. Their dark eyes flashed both fear and distrust. *What new terror are you bringing?* Those who were most disturbing, however, had empty eyes. They belonged to people still shocked at being alive—many doubtless wishing they weren't. Everything they had come to value and cherish, family, home, and faith…had been ripped from them by the ongoing war.

Chelsea wondered for the umpteenth time how anyone could live in such a place. Anxiety seethed within her. Concern for Mahdi, coupled with the appalling devastation of the town, added to the emotional toll that had pressed heavily upon her for the past ten days—the terror that attended her perpetration of a monstrous subterfuge.

She wanted to scream.

The jeep pulled up in front of Mahdi's house with a squeak.

Hassan turned to his passengers. "You stay here and wait. I will check all is safe." He reached under his seat, retrieved a hammer, and opened the door.

Mahdi sat in the corner of his mat with his legs drawn up. He was rocking himself back and forth rhythmically trying to exorcise the demons that haunted him as a result of what he had seen earlier that morning. Occasionally, pathetic mewing sounds escaped from his lips, but he was barely aware of them.

He did, however, become aware of a man's voice barking an order at the mad woman working in the kitchen next door. His head shot up like a startled animal. Who could it be? A sense of dread flooded over him. Should he escape out the back door and run?

Before he could do anything, the huge bulk of a man Mahdi recognized from the camp entered the toilet area where he slept. It was Hassan, and he was holding a hammer.

Mahdi held his arm up protectively and cowered further back into the corner.

Hassan said without preamble, "I have been told you have some of the stolen clay tablets from Ebla. You will tell me where they are, or I will crush your fingers, one by one with his hammer."

"Please sir," said Mahdi, "I don't have any tablets. You have heard wrong. I didn't steal anything." His feet scrabbled on the floor as he tried uselessly to get away from the man.

"I don't have time to waste," growled the man. "I've got people outside waiting for me. Tell me now, or I'll smash your fingers." Hassan advanced toward him.

"No. I have nothing," screamed Mahdi.

Hassan lunged forward, grabbed Mahdi by an arm, and threw him over onto his back. Then, he put a knee on his chest and pinned Mahdi's left wrist to the floor. The man raised the hammer. "You have three seconds to tell me, or I'll crush your little finger."

Mahdi screamed in terror, knowing that he was defeated, but before he could admit to his hidden stash of tablets, he heard another yell. It came from the mad woman, and she was screaming like a banshee from hell.

She flew at Hassan, pummeling him with her fists and clawing at his eyes with hooked fingers. "You leave my Jamal," she screamed.

Hassan swung the hammer sideways with a vicious backward swipe. It caught the mad woman on the side of her temple, flinging her sideways onto the toilet floor.

She lay ominously still.

Mahdi screamed under the weight of Hassan's knee and banged his feet against the floor, trying to escape.

Hassan raised the hammer again, and then paused.

There was a movement at the door.

Mahdi twisted his head sideways and was shocked to see the man called Tony standing just by the door. Beanie and Miss Chelsea were behind him, pressing in to see what was happening.

Hassan dropped the hammer and reached for his pistol. As he drew it out, Mahdi heard an enraged bellow.

It came from Beanie. He pushed past Tony and launched himself at Hassan.

Hassan jerked up his pistol and fired. The noise was deafening.

Beanie spun sideways and collapsed to the floor.

Almost instantly there were two more shots. Mahdi was amazed to see that Tony had a gun in his hands.

Hassan jerked twice in quick succession and collapsed sideways against the blood splatters on the wall.

A second later, Chelsea pulled Mahdi from under Hassan's legs and hugged him to herself.

He clung to her as he wept.

Through his tears, he was dimly aware of Tony going first to the mad woman, and then to Beanie, who was groaning and clutching his thigh.

The woman was dead.

Beanie, however, was very much alive, but bleeding profusely.

Hassan's bullet had plowed through the side of his thigh. Fortunately, it had missed the bone and the femoral artery.

Tony grabbed a blanket from the mat and pressed it down on the wound. "Chelsea, I need you now. Come and press this down on the wound while I cut away his trousers."

Chelsea was white with shock, but she understood enough to disentangle Mahdi from her and scramble across to him. As she pressed the bunched corner of the blanket onto the wound, Tony unsheathed the knife from his boot and began to cut away the leg of Beanie's cargo pants. He hadn't got far before he discovered that Beanie was wearing Mickey Mouse boxer shorts underneath.

After removing one trouser leg, he searched around for something to use as a bandage. Seeing nothing obvious, he ducked through the door and did a quick search of the house. A moment later, he returned with a sheet from the bed he presumed must have been the dead woman's. He fashioned a pad with some of it and tore the rest into strips.

Before long, Beanie's wound was staunched and wrapped tightly.

Tony ran a critical eye over his handiwork. One thing was very certain; he needed to get Beanie to a doctor as soon as possible. The sheet he'd used to dress the wound was none too clean.

He crouched down in front of Mahdi.

Mahdi held his hands up in fright.

"Mahdi, it's all right. You're safe. We're here to look after you. But I need your help. I need to get Beanie to a doctor. Is there a doctor in the town?"

Mahdi didn't answer him. He looked across at the woman who lay sprawled on the floor beside him. "Is she dead?" he asked.

"Yes."

Mahdi's eyes flicked across to Hassan. "And him?"

"Yes. He can't hurt you anymore."

Mahdi dropped his head and began to cry.

Tony let him cry for a moment then laid a hand on his shoulder. "Mahdi, I need to know: Is there a doctor in town?"

The boy sniffed and nodded. "Next to the mosque. It is a modern building with a green door."

Tony nodded his thanks.

All the time, Tony was thinking furiously, trying to work out what he should do, and what he could do, given different contingencies. Two things were a priority. He had to get rid of Hassan's body. There would be a hue and cry if it were found. And he needed to get Beanie to a doctor. He glanced at the dead woman. It would be a bonus if she too could be taken care of in a way that was at least half respectable.

Whatever he did, he knew that it was imperative to act quickly. They needed to be away from the place as soon as possible.

Tony asked Chelsea to take Mahdi into the kitchen and take care of him. "Try and get him to drink something warm and sweet."

He then set about seeing to the dead.

Tony used the blue plastic sheeting covering the hole in the wall to wrap up Hassan's body, together with his hammer and his gun. He used a bed-sheet to wrap the woman. The sheeting was kept tight in both instances by chord cut from the clothesline in the back courtyard. By the time he had finished, there were footprints of blood everywhere. Everything seemed covered by sticky gore. It was fortunate that almost all of it was contained in the wet area of the house, the room set aside for the toilet and for washing. He cleaned up the blood as best he could.

Beanie was propped up against a sidewall. He looked pale, and was, for some reason, clutching onto the leg of his cargo pants that had been cut off.

"Are you okay?" asked Tony.

Beanie said through gritted teeth. "Whatever happens, don't let me lose my pants."

Tony was bewildered. He shook his head. Shock took people in different ways.

As he busied himself cleaning up the pools of blood and the sticky mess, Tony wondered whether anyone would come to investigate the gunshots. He doubted it. War in the Idlib province had devastated the area. Gunshots were common and had come to be feared and avoided.

When he'd finished doing what he could, he went outside, got into the jeep, and backed it against the front door of the house. Then he emptied the luggage from back of the Hunter into the front room. Chelsea and Mahdi watched him as he went back into the toilet area and fetched the two bodies, one by one. He lifted both into the back of the Hunter, closed the tailgate, and refastened the canvas hood. Then he returned to the house, rummaged in his rucksack, and removed a caftan and a head wrap.

After removing his jacket, he dressed himself in the local garb. Then he squatted down in front of Mahdi. "Mahdi, I need Chelsea to help look after Beanie. Are you okay if I leave you here on your own for a while? Can I give you the job of looking after our luggage?"

The boy looked at him with desperation in his eyes. "You will come back?"

Tony nodded. "I promise. I'll try not to be too long."

Chelsea helped Tony support Beanie as he limped to the jeep. Once he was seated inside, Chelsea climbed beside him to help keep him steady.

Tony got into the front seat, gave what he hoped was a reassuring wave to Mahdi, and drove away.

He found the local doctor without difficulty. The man met them at the door dressed in a disposable haz-chem suit, which looked as if it hadn't been disposed of for a very long while. One glance at Beanie assured the doctor that his visitors were not calling because of MERS. He instantly became co-operative and sprang into action.

As Tony turned to leave, he whispered to Chelsea. "Tell the doctor that Beanie's been in a shooting accident at the camp." He paused. "Can you stay with him while I attend…er, to things?"

"What will you do with the bodies?" she asked softly.

"I've got an idea, but if that doesn't work, I'll bury them in a bomb crater." He drew in a deep breath. "There's no shortage of them."

Chelsea looked at him with wide eyes. He could see that she was struggling to take everything in, but so far, she was holding it together.

He laid a hand on her shoulder and gave it a gentle squeeze. "I'll be back in forty minutes or so."

For the briefest of moments, she laid her hand on top of his, as if seeking his strength. Then she took it away.

Tell Mardikh was not a big town, and it didn't take long for Tony to find the cemetery. To the untrained eye, it didn't look like a cemetery, as the graves had no headstones. He wasn't surprised to find it deserted. No one wanted to be near a cemetery during a disease epidemic.

Tony was relieved to see five freshly dug graves. They lay next to four that looked as if they had recently been filled in. Tony maneuvered the Hunter so that its back wheels straddled the first empty grave. Then, trying to look as much like a local as possible, he opened the tailgate and pulled out the body of Hassan wrapped in blue plastic. It fell into the grave with a thump.

Tony unstrapped the shovel fastened onto the front fender of the Hunter and started to fill in the grave. It took some time, as the grave was quite deep.

When he had finished, he repeated the process with the woman's body.

It took him an hour before he was finished—longer than he'd hoped.

When he finally climbed back into the jeep, he took out his phone and put a call through to RAF Akrotiri in Cyprus.

After being patched through to the control tower, he said, "My name is Tony Patterson. Abort the flight to Khmeimim. I say again: Abort the flight to Khmeimim. There is a complication—possibly hostile. The passengers will make their own way home."

Once he'd rung off, he rang another number.

Chapter 7

M ahdi hated being alone. He looked around the house that had been his home for so long. The mad woman who had looked after him was dead, and Miss Chelsea was leaving. His world had imploded in a nightmare of terror, death, and madness. He was giddy with disbelief, and overcome by a dreadful sense of vulnerability. He didn't understand anything other than the fact that he was now, or would shortly be, completely alone.

Mahdi sat down with his back against the cooking bench where the charcoal stove sat. The room reeked of stale cooking oil—the smell that was always present on the clothes of the mad woman. Chelsea had taken the pan of boiling oil off the heat, but it would take a while before the charcoal fire burned itself out.

Then what?

He hugged his knees, rocked himself backward and forward… and wept. Everything was hopeless.

When he stopped crying, he tried to think what he should do. He couldn't stay in the house. Police or soldiers would inevitably come and question him. A fresh wave of fear flooded over him. What could he say? He couldn't explain anything. The authorities would put him in prison.

Only one solution offered any hope: he had to persuade Miss Chelsea to take him with her.

Even as he thought of her, he could recall the smell of the soap she used. It had a lovely fragrance. To be near her and smell it—to know her comfort and kindness—that would be the only thing worth living for, worth hoping for.

His thoughts returned to the clay tablets nestled in their secret place. The tablets that he'd once so treasured, were now a liability. Men came with hammers. He shivered. Whatever else he had to do, he had to get rid of them.

Mahdi wrinkled his brow and tried to think. Unable to think of anything, he picked himself up off the floor and walked to the room of horrors, the charnel house where the killing had taken place. For a long time, he simply stood in the doorway unable to go further. Then, taking a deep breath, he stepped over to his mat and folded it back to reveal the flagstone that covered his secret place.

It was as he moved the mat that he discovered the keys. They had lodged themselves just under the edge of the mat. He picked them up and stared at them. It took a moment for him to realize that they must have fallen from the pocket of the nice man, Beanie, when he fell onto the floor.

He got up from the floor and returned to the front room. There was only one case that had a lock on it—the big metal case that had reinforced edging. He pushed one of the keys into the lock and turned it. He was rewarded by a satisfying click. Mahdi twisted the hasp away from the metal tang.

He rolled back onto his heels and wondered whether he should open the case.

It was then that he had the idea. Miss Chelsea said she wished she had some of Ebla's clay tablets…and he desperately wanted to get rid of them. The solution, when he thought about it, was obvious. He would give Miss Chelsea the clay tablets.

Mahdi took hold of the case and began to tug it into the toilet area. It was not easy. Something inside the case was incredibly heavy. But desperation gave him strength.

Eventually he had the case open beside his secret hiding place. On investigation, he saw a dismantled electric machine of some kind, and some massively heavy sheeting. Both were wrapped in protective padding.

He lifted the strange machine and sheeting out of the case and laid them on the floor. Then he levered up the flagstone with his piece of reinforcing rod and stared at the clay tablets. A leather case lay on top of them.

It took longer than he expected to pack the tiles into the metal case. He had to pack them carefully using the padding in the case and blankets from the mad woman's bed. Miss Chelsea wouldn't like it if any of them got broken.

Mahdi nearly got them all packed without incident. However, in his haste, he let the last tablet slip from his hands. It banged onto the floor, breaking off one corner. He picked up the broken piece and put it inside the leather case.

Mahdi packed the last tablet into place and locked the case shut.

He then set about packing the strange machine and the heavy sheeting into his secret hiding place. When he finished, he looked at the strange instrument nestled in its new home. The hole was not his anymore. It contained things that did not belong to him—things he didn't understand, or want to understand.

He did not have very long to wait before he heard the sound of the military jeep returning. Mahdi stood up beside the luggage in the front room and waited. He watched in fear as the front door opened.

Mr. Tony stepped inside the room. He was holding one hand inside his jacket. On seeing Mahdi, he asked, "Are you all right?"

Not trusting himself to speak, Mahdi nodded.

Miss Chelsea came in just behind him. He immediately ran to her and clung to her.

She cradled his head. "There, there, my little Mahdi. It's okay. You're safe." She voiced endearments that caused him to break down in tears.

It took a while for him to remember the plan he'd rehearsed in his mind. He drew himself back from her and, in a voice of entreaty, said, "Please take me with you, Miss Chelsea. I have no home, no mother…and the soldiers will come and put me in prison."

"No, no, no. We won't let that happen," Miss Chelsea wiped tears from his cheek with her hand.

"Look," he said, picking up the leather case by his feet. He unzipped it and held out the broken corner of clay tablet. "If you take me with you, I will tell you where there are more of these." He paused. "You want them, don't you?"

Miss Chelsea took the broken corner from the tablet and inspected it. He saw her furrow her brow, as if puzzled, and then hand it back to him. Then she drew Mahdi to herself and held him close. "That's very kind of you Mahdi. But you don't have to bribe me to take you with me."

She glanced at Mr. Tony. Mahdi saw him give her a small nod.

Miss Chelsea gave Mahdi's shoulders a squeeze. "You are right. You can't stay here. You're coming with us." She ruffled his hair. "Somehow, we'll make all this work out."

It was a relief to finally be on the move, putting as much distance as possible between themselves and the horrors of Tell Mardikh.

Chelsea was seated next to Tony in the front of the jeep. He insisted that she sit beside him. "You and I will pass as locals provided people don't look too closely."

Beanie and Mahdi were in the back seat.

Any sense that they were now safer was, of course, illusory. They were in a war zone and quite possibly being hunted. Chelsea gave voice to her fears.

"How long do you think it will be before people start looking for us?"

Tony shrugged. "No idea. I suspect that we could have a fair bit of time. Hassan was due to drive us to Khmeimim, so he won't be missed until late afternoon."

"But we were due to join a convoy."

"This is Syria, people are used to things not going to plan."

Chelsea shot him an interrogating look. She suspected he was deliberately putting a positive spin on their situation.

"So we're going it alone," she said eventually.

"Yes. It's only a forty-five mile journey, but it's a dangerous one. We'll be on a motorway that passes through territory notionally held by Jihadist forces and Syrian rebels. They've killed a number of civilians on the road."

Chelsea now wished that Tony had put a more positive spin on their situation. A wave of anxiety washed over her, its acid dissolving what little hope she'd been trying to nurture. She desperately sought for some reassurance.

"But if we get through, we'll still be able to get to the plane, won't we?"

Tony shook his head. "No. I've canceled the plane. I can't risk the plane and its crew being impounded because they're aiding escaped fugitives."

Her eyes widened. "Please tell me that you have another plan."

"I do. We go to Latakia."

Chelsea lapsed into silence as she tried to digest what she'd just heard.

Tony drove north on the Damascus-Aleppo Highway, then turned left up the western side of the town of Saraquib to join the M4. The motorway headed west to the coast. There wasn't a lot of traffic, but what there was, was disturbing. Refugees, with goods strapped on the back of pickups and cars, were heading in the same direction seeking the relative safety of Latakia.

Chelsea gazed out at the flat, dry landscape. It was being strip-farmed by local farmers. None of the farms looked prosperous. Occasionally, she saw an orchard. She remembered that seventy-five percent of Syria had once been covered by trees. Asiatic lions, cheetahs, and Caspian tigers had roamed the area. She shook her head. Today, native trees covered just three percent of Syria, and the animals had long since become extinct. She wondered idly whether Syria could ever recover from the ravages of war and exploitation.

Why was it that the health of the environment always seemed to reflect a nation's spiritual and moral health?

To counter her doleful thoughts, she stole a covert look at Tony. He was certainly more pleasing to the eye than the barren landscape…and thinking about him helped calm her. The realization of this came as a surprise to her. She frowned and tried to work out why.

There was, she decided, a cool, determined certainty about Tony. He was calm, but also capable of unleashing dreadful violence in order to protect those who were vulnerable. Throughout the ordeal of that morning, Tony had not uttered a curse, dithered, or given any evidence of being overwhelmed. Chelsea couldn't help but reflect that she was very different. She often felt that her world was spinning out of control, and she frequently felt overwhelmed by the demands she put on herself.

She knew she'd badly misjudged Tony at their first meeting. He wasn't a mouse of a man who avoided responsibilities. He was simply biding his time. Tony was a panther, patient, waiting to strike.

She cleared her throat. "I was rude to you when I first met you. What I said back then was untrue and unwarranted." Her little speech sounded forced and formal, but she hoped Tony would hear her sincerity.

Tony nodded. "Don't mention it."

The fact that he responded so quickly made her suspect he remembered her words all too well…and the thought of that made her cringe.

Chelsea lapsed back into silence and forced herself to think about something else. She thought of Mahdi. But Tony again intruded into these thoughts. He hadn't demurred for a moment about taking Mahdi with them, despite the fact that the boy represented a complication they could well do without. She had to admit that there was a lot about Tony Patterson that she hadn't first been aware of.

She forced her thoughts back to Mahdi. He'd shocked her when he'd shown her the Syrian stone—the broken corner of an ancient, petrified, clay tablet. She'd only seen it for a moment, but it was long enough for her to know that what was written on one side of the tablet was Sumerian cuneiform. However, it was what was on the other side that excited her. She was unable to read much of it other than to guess at a couple of words. Chelsea very much suspected that the cuneiform writing on it was Eblaite. The little piece of stone quite possibly had Sumerian text on one side, and the same text written on the other in Eblaite.

She was unable to suppress a shiver when she thought about it. If this were so, the tablets Mahdi claimed he had hidden somewhere could facilitate a massive breakthrough in understanding the language written by the ancient civilization at Ebla. She tried to recall what she'd seen, but she'd only held the stone for a few seconds.

Her thoughts were brought back to earth by the sound of Beanie groaning in pain.

She twisted herself round, knelt on her seat, and faced backward.

"How are you coping?" she asked.

Beanie gave her a wan smile. "I've had better days."

Chelsea nodded. The doctor had only managed to give Beanie rudimentary treatment. His wound had been sterilized and wrapped with a clean bandage. Beyond that, the doctor had been unable to do anything other than to give him some basic analgesics, the sort sold without prescription in most Western supermarkets.

Beanie looked pale. She reached over and laid a hand on his forehead. It was clammy, but there was no sign of a temperature.

Mahdi watched her with wide eyes.

She gave him a reassuring pat on the arm.

Beanie whispered, "I nearly lost two of the batteries."

Chelsea put a finger to her lips, warning him to speak more quietly. "How many do you have?" she asked in a voice that was barely audible.

"Four. They're all in the other pockets of my trousers now."

She nodded.

Beanie continued. "Is my hookah safe?"

"Yes."

"Good." He paused. "I keep thinking that everything that happened was a nightmare, but the pain in my leg tells me otherwise."

"It was a nightmare Beanie." She manufactured a smile. "But Tony's got a plan."

Chapter 8

Tony drove as fast as he dared, both to impersonate the impatience of a senior officer in the Syrian army, and because he didn't want to provide an easy target for a rocket-propelled grenade.

The long sweeping stretches of motorway took them past the towns of Mseibin, Arihah, and Urum al-Joz, bypassing them disdainfully, as if wanting to avoid the maize of shattered, white-topped, buildings where people had bled and died.

His musings were brought to an abrupt end when he saw the tail of a military convoy up ahead. The last vehicle in the convoy was an Otokar Cobra. It had a rotating machine gun turret mounted on top.

He speculated briefly whether this was the convoy Hassan was planning to join.

The machine gun on top of the Cobra swung round until its twin barrels pointed directly at him.

Tony gave what he hoped was a friendly wave and drove demurely behind the convoy.

After a few minutes, the Cobra swung to the left side of the road and braked slightly, allowing Tony to overtake him.

Once he was past, the Cobra swung in behind him.

Tony expelled a breath in relief. The Cobra was being a mother hen gathering in its chicks. Presumably, those inside the Cobra had worked out that a military vehicle driven by suicide bombers would not have four people inside—and would probably not be flying an officer's pennant.

The pace at which they were now forced to drive was a lot slower. For the moment at least, Tony felt there was not much to worry about. This gave him the opportunity to dwell on the woman sitting next to him. Chelsea had shown extraordinary resilience and poise in a grim situation—and that had surprised him.

For some reason, thinking about her began to awaken the sense of loneliness he normally kept suppressed in his heart. Her presence seemed to shine a light on it. Tony struggled to find the words to describe the effect she had. He furrowed his brow. It was as if she'd come into that lonely place, given it a fresh coat of paint...and decorated it with pictures that suggested new possibilities.

He shook his head. He was going soft.

Tony forced himself to re-engage with the reality of what was going on around him. It wasn't hard. Now and again they passed military vehicles going in the opposite direction. Most of these were six or eight wheeled Soviet army personnel carriers. They were low, squat, and wedge-shaped. All of them looked dangerous.

After half an hour's driving, the motorway swept north around the irrigation plain of the Orontes River and started to snake its way through the foothills of the Jabal an Nusayriyah mountain range.

Tony noticed that the red limestone soil of the plains had now turned to a sandy cream color. For whatever reason, the pale of the limestone was now more in evidence.

The mountain range was quite narrow, only twenty miles wide. Even so, he felt the temperature drop as they climbed higher and higher. Trees were now more in evidence and many of the hillsides were terraced. The orchards they passed seemed to be flourishing, doubtless because of the higher rainfall.

Soon, they were dropping down to the coastal plain and the city of Latakia. He could see the blue sheet of the Mediterranean stretching out beyond the city into the horizon.

He forced himself to concentrate. Tony had to leave the convoy in a way that wouldn't arouse suspicion.

In the end, it was very easy. When the convoy reached the elaborate four-leaf-clover flyover in the center of the city where the M4 joined the M1, Tony simply peeled away and headed west past the dormitory towers of Tishreen University.

The city of Latakia looked as if it had woken up with a hangover. It was dog-eared and tired. There were, however, plenty of people about. Refugees had swollen the local population considerably and introduced a new level of pathos to the city.

Chelsea surprised him by saying, "Did you know this city used to be the home of Turkish tobacco?"

Tony found it difficult to believe the city would now allow itself to indulge in anything so frivolous.

She continued. "Not anymore. It's now produced in Cyprus." Chelsea paused before asking, "Where are we going?"

"We're heading to the Southern Corniche Peninsular."

"Any particular reason?"

"Yes."

She glanced at him. "Sometimes you're not the greatest conversationalist, you know."

Tony couldn't think of anything to say.

She continued to probe. "How come you know your way around here?"

"Research." He forced a smile. "Always have a plan B."

"And a C?"

"Yes."

Tony was actually thinking hard, playing out in his mind all sorts of different scenarios. He desperately wanted to do everything possible that would keep them safe. Although this was nothing new, the strength of his resolve on this occasion surprised him. He'd been involved in the 'extraction' of personnel from dangerous situations before, but this time things were personal. He told himself it was because of the boy, Mahdi.

Soon, they were driving down the coastal road of Al Hurriyah past resorts that harbored memories of happier days. Tony turned off onto a bleak, treeless foreshore. A gaggle of recreational boats was moored just offshore.

Tony searched the boats, looking for one in particular. When he saw it, he allowed himself a sigh of relief. He parked on the waste ground that passed as a car park for the Taha Café.

The only other vehicle parked there was a rusted, red, pickup truck. As Tony pulled up, a small, wiry figure got out of the truck and sauntered over to him.

Tony wound down the window. "Pietri, how's it hanging?"

The man smiled. "It's hanging well, my friend." He paused. "Any problems?"

"None."

"Good. Back your wagon down the foreshore as far as you can. I'll get the boat."

Tony noted with approval that another man remained seated in the passenger seat of Pietri's truck.

As Pietri walked away, Chelsea hissed, "Who was that?"

"That's Pietri. He's a friend."

"From where? Where does he come from?"

Tony scratched the stubble on his chin. "He's got a bit of every-thing in him. I think he's mostly Italian, but he's married to a Syrian woman—a very beautiful one, actually."

Chelsea raised an eyebrow. "And he lives here in Latakia?"

"Sometimes."

Tony thought that he had already said too much—enough for her to deduce that he and Pietri had a history.

But Chelsea persisted with her questions. "And who is the other guy in the truck?"

Tony put the jeep into reverse and started backing it down to the rocky foreshore. "He's the guy who will take this jeep to a place where he can wash it with water and bicarbonate to remove all signs of blood and fingerprints. He'll then remove Shamon's pennant, park the jeep in the middle of the city, and walk away."

"Oh," she said, weakly.

Tony backed the jeep as close to the water as he dared. He and Chelsea got out and watched Pietri row out to a speedboat in an inflatable dinghy. Moments later, the engine of the boat growled to life. Pietri cast off the mooring buoy and edged the speedboat toward the shore. He cut the engine some way off, stepped over onto the bow of the boat, and lowered himself into the water. Pietri allowed the boat to drift into the shore until he was able to stand in waist deep water. He then turned to Tony and beckoned.

Tony dropped the tailgate of the jeep, unlaced the canvas hood, and began to unload the luggage.

"Why doesn't he bring it closer to shore?" asked Chelsea.

Tony hefted down the metal case. He grunted, forgetting how heavy it was. "Because that boat is not really a boat."

"What?"

"It's a hydrofoil. It has skis under the hull."

Tony waded into the water ferrying out the luggage, one piece at a time. Carrying the metal case was the biggest challenge. It was so unwieldy that he couldn't avoid putting a couple of scratches on the pristine gunwale of the boat.

"That will cost you," said Pietri.

Back on shore, Tony helped Beanie walk to the café in order to use the toilet and get something to eat and drink. He insisted that Chelsea and Mahdi come with him and also avail themselves of the facilities.

Once everyone had reassembled on the beach, Tony carried each one of them out to the boat. Carrying Mahdi was easy. His tiny malnourished frame barely weighed anything. Beanie was heavier. Carrying Chelsea, however, was disturbing. He felt her warmth and femininity—so much so, he was reluctant to let her go.

She gave him the briefest of glances when he finally did.

Pietri walked himself to the side of the boat and heaved himself on board.

Tony stayed in the water, holding onto the bow. He saw Chelsea look around the boat in wonderment.

"It's a beautiful boat," she said, running her hands along the gunwale.

Pietri slid himself into the driver's seat. "It's a product of the Soviet cold war. She was built by a genius: Rostislav Alexeyev."

"I'm afraid I haven't heard…"

"He started the 'Valga Craft' company. They were the first to build hydrofoils from aluminum-magnesium alloy. The Russians even gave one to Fidel Castro."

"Oh."

Pietri patted the dashboard. "This is their updated 'Classic. It's got an American V6 Mercruiser in it." Pietri grinned. "Let's hear it for *glasnost*, eh."

"Where are we going in it?"

"To Cyprus."

Tony saw Chelsea's mouth drop open. He conceded that her reaction was understandable.

"Cyprus…in this tiny boat? Will it get us there?"

"The weather forecast for the next five days says it's going to be calm, so you're in luck. All I need is for the waves to be less than thirty inches high."

"And we'll have enough petrol?"

"We'll be using eighteen gallons an hour for two-hundred miles. The original tank only held forty gallons, but I've installed one three times the size." Pietri pointed to the back of the boat. "Unfortunately, the extended fuel tank means I've had to remove the rear bench seat. You'll have to squash up in the back on the one that remains and put your feet on the baggage."

Chelsea appeared speechless. "How long will it take?" she spluttered eventually.

"We'll be averaging just over forty miles an hour, so it will be a five hour trip."

Pietri started the engine and gave Tony a 'thumbs up' signal.

Tony heaved himself onboard.

With a deep growl, the stern of the boat kicked down, and the boat began to move.

In almost no time at all, the boat lifted clear of the water, and they were skimming over the top of the sea on hydrofoils.

"Are you all right?" asked Tony. He had to shout to make himself heard above the noise of the engine.

Beanie nodded. He was in the front seat next to Pietri. The single-seat offered him the best support and had more space for his legs.

Tony, Mahdi, and Chelsea sat facing backward just behind them. Their luggage was piled up in front of them, forcing them to rest their feet on top of it.

As Tony turned back round, Chelsea leaned across to him. "It's a weird sensation sitting in a boat that's suspended in the air."

Tony nodded. "Get used to it. This will be a long trip."

Mahdi was sandwiched between Tony and Chelsea. The boy had snuggled himself as close to Chelsea as he could and was clutching his leather case. Chelsea had a protective arm around him.

Tony smiled to himself. Chelsea's maternal instincts had been aroused. She may be an academic, but the 'mother' in her was very much in evidence.

Chelsea had obviously been digesting the ramifications of Tony's last comment because she leaned across and said, "What happens if anyone needs the toilet?"

"You've got two choices. You can use a bucket, or we can stop and…"

Chelsea held up a hand. "Don't say it!"

He smiled. "Yeah, you can drop over the side into the water."

She looked at him grimly. "It's just as well for you that parts of my body have shut down and are in a state of catatonic anxiety."

The engine was noisy, forcing Chelsea and Tony to put their heads close together in order to speak. Tony found himself enjoying the intimacy of it.

"How far away is Cyprus?" Chelsea asked.

"The Eastern end of Cyprus is only sixty miles from Latakia. But it's about twice that to the Dhekelia Sovereign Base Area where we're going."

She looked at him with a puzzled expression. "What's a Sovereign Base Area?"

"Although Cyprus is independent, the British Ministry of Defence retains control over two Sovereign Base Areas: Akrotiri in the southwest, and Dhekelia in the southeast. Akrotiri has an RAF base. We'll be flying out from there. But first we've got to stay for a while in Dhekelia—for quarantine." He paused. "And that reminds me, I'd better make a phone call."

"Who to?"

"The authorities in Dhekelia."

She nodded.

After making the phone call, Tony settled into his seat.

The silence was broken only twice in the next two hours. The first time it was broken by Mahdi when he opened his leather pouch and held out a set of keys to Tony.

"These fell out on the floor…in the house."

Tony nodded his thanks and put the keys in his pocket.

The second time, Pietri interrupted them when he handed some bottles of water and some muesli bars to them. "Keep hydrated," he shouted.

Everyone lapsed into silence, and the tedium of the voyage settled on them again.

Tony looked at his watch. It was now well into the afternoon.

Chelsea glanced at him and shivered. "I'd feel safer if I could see the coast."

Tony gave what he hoped was a reassuring smile. "It's actually only about thirty miles to the north. We're starting to track down the northwestern arm of Cyprus."

An eternity later, a pale smudge appeared on the horizon. Tony pointed it out to Chelsea. "Those are the limestone cliffs of Cape Greco. We've haven't got far to go now."

The coast of Cyprus soon came into view. Pietrie took the boat close enough inshore for them to see the features of the coast clearly.

Pietri pointed ahead and shouted. "That's Dhekelia Bay—where we're headed."

The hydrofoil swept past Dhekelia's ugly power station with its red and white chimneys, and turned round the small peninsular at the eastern end of the bay.

Pietri eased back the throttle. The boat came off the plane and sank drunkenly into the water.

The change in the volume of the motor's sound left Tony's ears singing.

Pietri nosed the boat into the tiny marina tucked in at the base of the peninsular.

Chelsea and Mahdi began to look around excitedly, exclaiming at the things they saw. "Is that a church?" she asked. Chelsea pointed to a round-topped building that overlooked the marina. "It seems a fairly odd place to put one."

Tony nodded. "That's the church of St. Nicholas. The Cypriots put them everywhere."

Slightly more ominous was the presence of a military police wagon in the car park at the head of the marina. Two men dressed in hazchem suits stood beside it. One had 'Medic' emblazoned on the front, and the other, 'Military Police.' Both men wore paper masks.

They left Beanie in the boat as everyone else ferried luggage along the pontoon to the car park. Mahdi carried Beanie's hookah.

When they got to the car park, the military policeman called out and said with wry British humor, "Welcome to the sunny holiday isle of Cyprus. Bring your luggage and climb inside."

The back of the military wagon was open, and Tony could see bare metal benches running down each side. There was no concession for comfort.

After lifting the luggage into the wagon, he and Pietri went back to the boat to collect Beanie.

Once Beanie had been assisted into the wagon, Tony spoke to the medic. "This man has a severe flesh-wound on his thigh. It's been dressed, but it's only received elementary aid."

The medic nodded. "We'll take care of him."

Peitri turned to leave. "I'll send you the bill, Tony. See you later."

The military policeman held up a hand. "Where do you think you're going, matey. Sort your boat out, then get into the wagon."

Pietri looked at Tony. "You're kidding me."

Tony shrugged and made a poor show of looking contrite. "Sorry, Pietri. I forgot to tell you."

"Pietri shook his head. "This is definitely going to cost you. And British Army hospitality had better be sensational."

Tony grinned. "That's what I love about you, Pietri: your optimism."

<hr>

Chelsea reflected that ten days in confinement wasn't the most auspicious start to a new life free of the perils of Syria. The room in which she was confined was sensible, practical, and only just sufficient. It was typical army. But its brutal simplicity was a good deal more luxurious than her tent at Ebla, and it reminded her that she was safe. It was an odd feeling.

All of them had been reunited with their luggage and had been escorted to their rooms. Customs and immigration had taken the luggage, ironically enough, for irradiation.

Everyone was allocated a room. Mahdi, however, steadfastly refused to be parted from Chelsea, so arrangements were made for him to share her room and ensuite.

She soon learned two things about Mahdi. The first was that he screamed in his sleep. Chelsea had to spend a good deal of time each night sitting on his bed, soothing the tiny twelve-year old's anguish. The second was that he had a voracious appetite. He ate everything that was provided—and very often a good deal of the food provided for her.

Beyond eating food, there was very little they could do other than watch films on TV. Whilst Mahdi loved films, it didn't take long for Chelsea to become bored and frustrated.

Her thoughts turned to the broken piece of tablet Mahdi had shown her. She longed to see it again.

"May I see your Syrian stone, again, Mahdi?"

"Yes, Miss Chelsea." He jumped up from his chair, fetched his leather bag, and handed the piece of broken tablet to her.

Just holding it in her hand gave her huge excitement. When she inspected it, she saw streaks of black across the stone. Chelsea suspected that the piece of clay tablet had been baked into stone as a result of an intense fire—quite possibly the fire that had razed the city to the ground 4,500 years ago. She was more convinced than ever that the cuneiform writing on one side of the tablet was Eblaite. Chelsea sighed. If only she could have the whole tablet. But events had conspired to make returning to Syria impossible.

Chelsea shivered. She was having great difficulty processing all that had happened. Deeply disturbing images of their final day in Syria kept tormenting her. When everything became too much, she picked up the telephone and put an internal call through to Tony, and occasionally, to Beanie, or Pietri.

Conversations with Pietri usually centered on him saying uncharitable things about the food, or about the wine that accompanied the evening meal. "I would kill for a decent Italian red," he said darkly. All they give me is the local retsina."

Chelsea sympathized, although she thought the sharp flavor of the local white wine was rather nice.

Tony was measured and calm in his conversations, and she always felt better after talking with him. He was in the room next to her. She could sometimes hear him. From the sound of the occasional squeak, his bed was just the opposite side of the wall from hers. The thought of it being so close gave her a strange feeling.

Mahdi had the television on most of the time, but she never heard the sound of a TV coming from Tony's room. She'd put an ear to the wall to check a number of times. What she did hear, surprised her; it was classical music.

Beanie was uncharacteristically quiet for the first few days. Chelsea suspected that he was suffering from post-traumatic shock. He told her that he was ignoring the 'No Smoking' signs and spending the evenings puffing away on his hookah. However, it didn't take long for him to run out of *shisha*, and he was mortified that the authorities couldn't supply him with any more.

On the plus side, he said his leg was beginning to heal, but that the wound would leave a significant scar. He sounded as if he thought it would be rather 'cool.'

After a week, Chelsea was informed that Mahdi would need to stay on in Cyprus so he could be processed and attempts made to track down his nearest relatives.

When she told Mahdi of this, he stood in front of her with his head bowed, rubbing his forearm. "I won't have to go back to Tell Mardikh, will I?"

"No, no, dear. That won't be happening. But a lady from social services will be visiting us this afternoon. You'll be able to speak to her through a glass window via a speaker system."

When the social security woman came, Chelsea was pleased to see that she had the good sense to bring a Labrador puppy called 'Misty' with her. Chelsea had already spoken to her about the traumatic things Mahdi had experienced, and his nightmares.

Mahdi was initially frightened of the puppy, but its antics soon won him over. The puppy, cradled in the social services officer's arms, reached for him with an oversized front paw. It didn't take long before the puppy was trying to lick Mahdi's face through the glass.

Chelsea was delighted. The puppy's unconditional love was the best therapy Mahdi could have.

After the visit, Chelsea knelt down in front of Mahdi. "I've asked the authorities to keep me informed of everything that happens to you. And I've given them my contact details so you can reach me at any time."

He nodded.

Even though both she and Mahdi had several days to get used to the idea that Mahdi would not be leaving with her, there were floods of tears when it came to the actual departure.

Just before she headed out to the minibus taking her to Akrotiri, Mahdi took out the broken tablet from his leather bag and handed it to Chelsea. "I want to give you this," he said. "Please don't forget me."

Chelsea took the piece of petrified clay and didn't trust herself to say anything. She simply gave him a hug.

She didn't see much as the minibus made its way to the highway. It was a while before she could see through the tears. As time passed, she gradually got herself under control. Chelsea was even able to smile when they passed a winery. A sign outside read: 'Caution: Road slippery with grape juice.' The grape harvest was in full swing.

She remained fairly subdued however, until the sight of a castle piqued her interest again. Chelsea spotted it not long after the minibus had left the main highway and begun to head south to Akrotiri. The castle had the simple characteristics of a fortress built by the Knights Templar. But there was no one to tell her what she was seeing, so she slumped back in her seat.

The minibus took them round a large salt lake, past a check-point, and into an area that was unmistakably military.

They were processed with brusque RAF efficiency in a red brick terminal, and in short order, they were walking out onto the tarmac.

Tony nodded toward a huge aircraft that seemed to be squatting on wheels that were too small for it.

"That's us," he said. "It's a C-130 Hercules. I'm not sure how comfortable it will be."

As it was the only large plane on the airfield, Chelsea risked a joke. "I rather hoped it would be one of those." She pointed to a row of fighter jets parked further away.

Tony smiled. "Yeah, sorry." He glanced at the fighters. "Typhoons. You'd get home pretty quick."

He had a nice smile.

Chelsea glanced at Beanie to check how he was going. He was doing well on his crutches, and something of his ebullient self had returned.

"Hey Chelse," he said. "How about we organize some hookah parties when we get back? England is going to be a bit dull after all this."

She smiled, glanced at Tony…and thought that her heart could do with a bit of 'dull.'

Chapter 9

Abbas stared at the cavity under the floor. Lying on the flagstones beside it was the gray, lead-lined apron and the dismantled pieces of the radiation machine.

He squatted down and examined the pieces trying to work out why Dr. Thompson's team had left it behind. Abbas could only think of three reasons: It was too dangerous to carry; too ruined to bother with; or it had been discarded in favor of carrying something more precious. He straightened himself up and ordered the soldiers who had found the machine to carry it to his wagon.

The hidden cavity had been found as a result of Abbas ordering two searches. The first search had uncovered the fact that the boy who had been Dr. Thompson's servant, together with his mother, had disappeared. He'd ordered a second search, and that's when the cavity under the flagstone was discovered.

Just as sobering as the discovery of the machine, was the discovery of a rust-red color in the cracks of the floor. Abbas very much suspected it was blood. He put a knuckle to his forehead, closed his eyes, and tried to think. *What was going on? Think, man. Think.*

So much had happened in the last two weeks that was both disturbing and suspicious. And they had all happened under his nose, whilst he was in command. Even as he thought about it, he felt himself become clammy. He didn't dare think what might happen to him if his political overlords got wind of it.

A whole string of puzzling events had occurred.

Chelsea Thompson and her party had never arrived at Khmeimim Air Base, and no plane had arrived to pick them up.

Hassan had completely disappeared, and Abbas did not hold out much hope that he was still alive. The jeep he was driving, Abbas' personal jeep, had been found in Latakia, stripped of all identifying marks and thoroughly cleaned.

If the disappearance of Hassan wasn't bewildering enough, the chief cleric in Tell Mardikh reported that the local dealer in stolen artifacts had been killed. Evidently, he'd been shot, execution style— once in the heart and once in the head.

Abbas was not greatly surprised to learn of this. He'd just become aware of some of the merchandise the man had recently advertised. What the local dealer purported to have in his possession could potentially be dynamite—if it got into the wrong hands. Abbas sighed. It was just a pity that others had got to him before he did. The disturbing question was: Did those who shot him have the clay tablets he was advertising, or not?

He stared again at the empty cavity under the floor. Abbas drew no comfort from what he saw. All the strange events had to be linked, and he didn't like what they were suggesting.

What could he do? He couldn't go to his political boss. If his worst suspicions were realized, he'd be shot.

There was only one place Abbas knew he could go.

———

Syria and China enjoyed a degree of co-operation. Abbas was under no illusion about the reasons for it. It was their shared antipathy for the West: Syria, for religious and ideological reasons;

China, because it was in the process of challenging America's position as the dominant world power. Under president Xi Jinping, China was engaging in a vigorous expansion program designed to help it dominate, control, and exploit as many nations of the world as possible. It was a scenario that resulted in some unlikely alliances.

For some years, Abbas had enjoyed one with Huawei, the Chinese tech giant. The alliance between Syria and Huawei was not overt, of course, because of the American led sanctions against Syria and Iran. However, no one was in much doubt it existed. Reuters had even reported on the alleged alliance earlier that year. Their claim was that Hauwei maintained its interests through two independent companies: Skycom Tech Co Ltd, and a shell company, Canicula Holdings Ltd.

Canicula used to have an office in Damascus, but it attracted so much attention that the General Director of the local branch placed an article in a Syrian newspaper to say it had "totally stopped operating" in Syria. No explanation was given as to why, and the name of the General Director was not given.

Abbas was now sitting in their new office. It was also in Damascus.

The office barely had anything in it. Although it was Spartan in terms of décor, it had comfortable chairs and air-conditioning.

Mr. Wang looked at him without expression. He was a middle-sized man with round-rimmed spectacles and a balding head—visually unremarkable. Abbas knew almost nothing about him other than that he came from Shanghai.

Mr. Wang put his fingertips together. Light from the window caused the folds of his expensive Western-style suit to reflect a slight sheen. "What can I do for you, Mr. Shamon?"

Abbas pointed to the suitcase he had wheeled in behind him.

"Can you and your tech team look at the machine inside this case and tell me if there is anything suspicious about it?"

Mr. Wang's expression did not change. "Is there anything you are particularly suspicious of?"

"I want to know whether it has the capacity to photograph anything."

Mr. Wang nodded. "Do you want any findings to remain confidential?"

Abbas was unable to repress a shudder. "Absolutely. It is crucial that you report your findings only to me."

Mr. Wang did not blink.

"I understand."

———

Abbas received a text message from Mr. Wang three days later. It simply read. *We should meet.*

As a result of that message, Abbas was sitting in the same seat he had occupied just days before.

Mr. Wang appeared to be wearing the same suit.

Abbas moved uncomfortably in his chair.

The man opposite put his fingers together. His face betrayed nothing, but his voice betrayed everything.

"Your machine is a very cleverly disguised laser scanner." Mr. Wang paused. "The essential parts were embedded in the alloy and could only be found by cutting up the machine. The laser light had been fed into the radiation globe."

Abbas lowered his head in despair and pinched the top of his nose.

Mr. Wang asked solicitously, "Does this represent a problem for you?"

It took a moment for Abbas to reply. Eventually he leaned back and banged a fist down on the arm of the chair. He would have liked to bang it a lot harder. He desperately tried to think. Nightmare scenarios tumbled and tripped over themselves in his mind. Whichever way he brought the facts together, one conclusion was impossible to avoid: The British Museum now had a record of every tablet unearthed from Ebla in the last four years. Dr. Thompson had outwitted him. It was a disaster.

The thought then occurred to him that the underhand behavior of the British Museum was out of character. It always tried to present itself as the reliable, trustworthy custodian of world history.

The museum appealed for nations of the world to trust it with their artifacts…and needed to do so increasingly in recent years as more and more countries tried to regain ownership of their heritage. Abbas frowned. The British Museum would have to be very careful with their stolen information. If they advertised what they had, they would suffer international censure. This meant that the information would be closely guarded, and few people would have access to it.

Perhaps there was hope.

He cleared his throat.

"Mr. Wang, do you have the capacity to hack into the computers kept by the British Museum to find if they make any reference to cuneiform clay tablets found recently at Ebla?"

Mr. Wang looked at him guardedly. "That's a lot of computers."

"I can narrow it down. I can give you a name."

"Who?"

"Dr. Chelsea Thompson. You can start with her and with those who work closely with her."

Mr. Wang nodded.

Silence again descended on the two of them.

"What will you do now?" said Mr. Wang eventually.

"I will go to London."

"…and recover what was stolen?"

"It's a long shot, but I have to try. The only thing I've got going for me is that the information is unlikely to have been disseminated. I might have a chance." He rose from his seat. "First, however, I need to shut down the archaeological dig at Ebla."

"You feel that is necessary?"

"Yes. I think we were foolhardy to ever open the dig. There is no peace, just an uneasy ceasefire that is becoming more unstable by the day due largely to the Turkish invasion of Idlib Province from the north. It has emboldened the rebels.

Mr. Wang nodded. "The Turks and the Jihadist forces they have armed are seeking to displace the Kurds, now that the Americans are no longer present to protect them. It is only the threat from Russia that is keeping the Turks in check, I understand."

Abbas nodded. "It's a mess."

"Who will win the fighting?"

"Only death."

The Chinese man got up from his seat. "We will, of course, cover your expenses in the UK."

Abbas signaled his thanks.

Chapter 10

England

C helsea discovered that military transport planes did not afford their passengers the luxury of windows. She sat on her bench seat along the side of the cavernous interior, with little to look at other than two large crates that had been strapped down in the cargo bay. She also discovered that the noise of the aircraft discouraged conversation. That was a pity. She would have liked to talk to Tony.

She glanced at him. He seemed to be asleep. Quite how he managed that was beyond her. Beanie had his head pressed back against the side of the fuselage and seemed to be lost in his own thoughts.

The loadmaster on the Hercules was a cheerful cockney called Ben. He invited Chelsea to climb up to the flight deck for half an hour. Chelsea found it an extraordinary experience. She stood beside the co-pilot surrounded by a bewildering array of lights, switches, and dials. What particularly intrigued her were the little windows in the nose of the aircraft. One of them was at floor level near her feet. She could see the English Channel burnished gold by the setting sun as they crossed the coast of France.

It wasn't long before the lumbering behemoth landed at Brize Norton, and she was making her way down the plane's sloping cargo ramp.

There was enough light in the day for her to appreciate how green, ordered, and domesticated England was. An October shower had left puddles on the tarmac. Although Chelsea had only been away for three months, she was hard pressed not to kneel down and kiss the ground. England was like a cozy pair of slippers that you look forward to putting on in the evening by the fire.

The three of them waited for their luggage to pass along a conveyor belt past a monitoring station. A customs and excise woman was at the consul.

Chelsea spoke to her. "I thought our luggage cleared customs at Akrotiri."

The woman smiled cheerfully. "Sometimes we do it again." She glanced at the screen as Beanie's metal case stopped on the belt in front of her. The woman pointed to it. "You'll be pleased to know that there's nothing suspicious in there. No bombs, drugs, or metal objects as far as we can see."

Chelsea frowned. *No metal objects. That can't be right!*

When they were in the front foyer of the terminal building, Chelsea led everyone to some seats. "Beanie, have you got the keys to the metal case?"

Beanie nodded and handed her the keys.

"What's the matter?" asked Tony. "There's a guy outside with a Land Rover waiting to take us to the bus station."

Chelsea waved him into silence, turned the keys,…and twisted the hasps to one side. Carefully, she opened the lid.

Beanie was the first to speak. "That's not right," he said, as everyone stared at a dirty blanket no one recognized.

Tony squatted down and folded back the blanket.

What Chelsea saw next, caused her to hold her breath. There, nestled between rows of foam packing were three clay tablets with cuneiform writing on them. She very much suspected that there were more tablets underneath. One of the tablets on the top had a broken corner.

Chelsea reached into her travel bag and pulled out the broken piece of stone given to her by Mahdi. It fitted perfectly against the corner of the tablet. As she removed it and put it away again, her mind was in turmoil.

"Mahdi," she said under her breath. "What have you done?" She shook her head, trying to come to terms with the discovery.

Tony placed a hand on her shoulder. "Are you all right?"

Beanie said in an aggrieved voice, "Where's my bloomin' radiation machine? Which low-life nicked it?"

Chelsea put a finger to her lips and shushed him until he was quiet. "Beanie, what we have here could be infinitely more important than your scanner." She came to a stop, unable to put into words the enormity of their discovery.

Chelsea closed the lid of the case, locked it, and pocketed the key. She wasn't sure if she was shutting a nightmare back in the cupboard or closing the door to an Aladdin's cave.

Tony's voice cut into her thoughts. "Chelsea, what do you know about this…and what does it mean for us right now?"

Chelsea sat with her head bowed, massaging her temples with her fingertips. "Mahdi told me that he had some tablets, and knew I would very much like to have them." She sat back. "The crazy child must have swapped the machine for the tablets when he was looking after our luggage."

"Is that a problem?" asked Tony.

Chelsea glanced at Beanie. "Yes it could be." She drew a deep breath. "You probably should know, Tony, that the radiation machine was not just a radiation machine."

"What do you mean?"

She shrugged apologetically. "The radiation machine was also a laser scanner. It took covert pictures of the tablets when they were irradiated." Chelsea shrugged. "It was something Beanie and I dreamed up because the Syrian government were refusing to let the world see the tablets…for ideological reasons." She trailed off.

Tony nodded. "So we have stolen information and some stolen

tablets." He paused. "Is there anything else we need to be concerned about?"

Beanie interrupted. "You bet your sweet ass. Someone's got my scanner. We have to assume they will find out what we've been up to."

Chelsea groaned. It was all too much.

Tony continued to speak. "Chelsea: you said that these tablets could be particularly valuable. Why?"

"Because they have Sumerian cuneiform written on one side, and Eblaite cuneiform written on the other." She took a deep breath. "In other words, they could help us translate Eblaite…and unlock the secrets of what has been written on all the tablets found at Ebla."

Tony nodded. "And this information has political connotations because of the names and places that might be revealed?"

Chelsea nodded. She paused. "Tony, this has to be kept top secret. I…I'm not sure what to do with it."

"What needs to happen?" he asked.

She hesitated. "I…I think I should get this home, look at what we've got, and then work out what to do next."

Tony nodded. "Than that's what we'll do." He turned to Beanie. "We'll take the case off your hands, Beanie, and I'll escort Chelsea home."

Beanie nodded. He then opened a side pocket of his rucksack and handed Chelsea four battery packs. "Then you'd better have these as well," he said.

Tony frowned in puzzlement.

Chelsea took them in both hands, saw Tony's confusion, and said, "These are actually the hard drives with the scanning information on them."

Tony raised an eyebrow.

Beanie pointed to them. "If you prize off the blue cap with a screwdriver, you'll find a USB port underneath."

"Right," said Tony. "Let's get everything, and everyone, home. He turned to Chelsea. "Where do you live?"

Chelsea bit her lip. "Well…that's also something that's a bit difficult to explain."

———

It was a long and dreary trip, and Tony was dog tired by the time a taxi dropped him and Chelsea off at a side road that ran beside Rochester cathedral. They had caught a bus from Brize Norton to Frideswide Square in Oxford, and from there, they took a train to Paddington Station in London. Beanie had left them at that point and taken a taxi. Tony and Chelsea went by underground to St. Pancras Station and caught the train to Rochester.

Tony looked around at the soaring spire of the cathedral, now picked out by spotlights. It pointed to the heavens, as if in hope. As he did, the bells began to toll the hour. It was 10pm.

Poking above a tall, ancient wall beside the road, Tony could also see the top of Rochester castle. The stolid Norman keep rose uncompromisingly into the sky. Its features were similarly highlighted by spotlights.

Tony had to acknowledge that if ever there was a location suitable for an archaeologist, this was it.

A light drizzle had begun, making the lamplights along the road glow with a fuzzy ethereal light.

He bent over and took the handle of the metal case. "Right, let's get you inside. Where do you live?"

Chelsea turned round and pointed behind her. "Er, in there."

Tony turned round and saw where she was pointing. "You're joking!"

"Um…actually, no."

"In there…on top of that gate?"

"Yes."

Before him, an ancient medieval gate straddled a laneway. The top of the gate incorporated a building that could not be more than a single room. It had an ornate window overlooking the cathedral and the cathedral lawns.

Chelsea swung her rucksack over her shoulder and walked along the cobbled street toward it.

Tony hauled the metal case behind him and followed her. The drizzle had now turned to rain, and he was glad to reach the shelter of the vaulted archway.

Chelsea busied herself opening a small black door tucked in the corner of the archway. "I'll go up first and put some lights on." She ducked through the door.

Tony peered into the entrance. After the briefest of landings, a steep, spiral staircase wound its way up. The ancient steps had their worn surface overlaid with some sort of dark hardwood to protect them. The same wood had been used to make a curving handrail. He was surprised when blue LED under-lighting built into it suddenly came on. It gave the tower a magical look.

Tony bumped the metal case up the stairs, left it on the top landing, and then went back for his rucksack. Chelsea met him at the top landing and pointed to a narrow door that led off it. "That's the bathroom. It's a bit squeezy—just a toilet, sink, and shower. Come in." She stepped back to let him pass.

Tony dropped his rucksack on the landing and stepped into the room. Whilst it was just one room, it had been ingeniously modified so that it accommodated everything a person could want—whilst preserving its medieval character. It was charming.

In front of them was an ancient drop-leaf table with one leaf folded down. Two wheel-backed chairs were tucked underneath it. Backing up against that was a settee that sat in front of a stone fireplace located on the far wall. A gas, log-effect fire was burning away cheerfully.

Chelsea saw him look at it. "Not the real thing, I'm afraid. But I need instant warmth."

Tony didn't say anything. He was still in awe of what he saw. A marble bench ran along one length of the wall. White paneled doors underneath presumably hid cupboards and kitchen amenities. He couldn't see an oven, but he did see a coffee machine and a modern combination cooking-mixing machine.

The cupboards hanging above the bench had paneled glass

fronts and mirrored backs. Any light coming through the front window would be reflected throughout the room. He saw that light would also come in through a small window located above the sink.

On the other side of the room, a bench seat had been built under the ornate stone window that overlooked the cathedral. White paneled cupboards and a desk sat to one side of it. Chelsea's bed was on the other side, against the wall.

Tony looked at the settee and the recliner sitting next to it. "How on earth did you get all this stuff up the stairs?"

She pointed to a door to the left of the fireplace. "A fire escape leads up to that door. It goes into the back garden of the terraced house next door."

Tony nodded. "It's fantastic."

Half an hour later they were both seated in front of the fire sipping hot Bovril. It was the only hot drink they could make, as there were no perishable goods in the kitchen.

They had snatched a meal at Paddington station, so they didn't need to eat.

Chelsea asked Tony to leave the metal case by the entrance door. It was as if she didn't want to see it—at least for a while.

Tony was very content not to see it. He glanced at the discreet lighting played on the old stonework. It brought the stone to life so that it whispered stories of long ago. "What is this place?" he asked.

"It's known as Prior's Gate. It was one of five gates built in 1344 to encompass the lands owned by the cathedral. There are only two left now, this one and College Gate. That one's just the other side of the cathedral on the high street."

The warmth of the fire, coupled with the exertions and anxieties of the day caused Tony to begin to nod off to sleep.

He snorted himself awake as Chelsea got up from the chair.

She knelt one knee on the arm of the settee he was sitting on. "Where had you planned to spend the night?"

Tony rubbed his eyes. "In a hotel. There's got to be one near here."

For a moment, nothing was said.

Chelsea nibbled her bottom lip and eventually broke the silence.

"I think you've done quite enough running around for one day. If you like, you can sleep here on the settee."

"Are you sure?"

She glanced at him. "Are you safe?"

There was another silence.

"Yes." He paused, and tried to grin. "Not that you aren't very…" but he didn't quite have the courage to finish the sentence.

"What?" she demanded.

He waved her question away. "Nothing." He drew in a deep breath. "Thank you. I'd like to stay…very much."

Chapter 11

Tony woke as Chelsea came in through the door. The blind over the window had been lifted and light was streaming into the room. He sat himself up and rubbed his eyes as Chelsea heaved two shopping bags on top of the marble bench top.

"I've got breakfast," she said. "Coffee?"

Tony nodded. "Sorry I wasn't up to help you."

She waved a deprecating hand. "You needed to sleep."

Over coffee and toast, he learned more about the gatehouse. "How did you come to own it?" he asked.

"I don't. I lease it from the Anglican Church. They were only using it as a store room."

"But how did you find it?"

Chelsea passed a piece of toast over to him. "I discovered it when I was digging some archaeological trenches in the gardens of the place next door, Bishop's Palace."

"What were you digging for?"

Chelsea raised an eyebrow. "Are you interested in archaeology?"

"Hanging round you has got me interested."

"Well, we found an old Roman wall; some foundations of a pre 1150 Norman building; and a silver-plated forgery of a denarius of Julia Domna—the third century Roman empress consort."

Tony raised his eyebrows and looked around him. "So the church owns this building. It's not very churchy."

"They do. The Ecclesiastical Commissioners bought it in 1870, and it was given a grade 1 heritage listing in 1950."

"I thought that meant you couldn't change anything about the building."

"Oh no. The heritage people don't necessarily want their buildings frozen in time, but they do insist that you get building consent before you do anything...and that can be tricky." She looked around her. "I've changed almost nothing—just added gas and plumbing—and as there's already a house on top of College gate, they couldn't really complain about me living on top of this one."

The two of them were sitting at the drop-leaf table. "What needs to happen today?" asked Tony. He didn't really want to break the spell of simply talking to Chelsea about things that weren't critical, but he knew it must eventually happen.

Chelsea looked over to the metal case. "I'm going to have a look at what's inside there. Then I suppose I'll take the tablets up to the British Museum." She began to rock her coffee cup around on its base. "But as for the stuff on the hard drives..." she sighed. "As weird as it is for me to say it, I'm now actually a bit concerned about it."

Tony looked at her sharply. "Why?"

She shrugged. "It's stolen information. I could be bringing a world of pain down on the British Museum."

"A few people have gone through a lot of money and effort to get that information."

Chelsea leaned on her elbows and sighed. "I know. Not least yourself...and poor old Beanie got shot."

Tony leaned back in his chair. "What if the information on the hard drives became 'unfortunately' corrupted or was found to be unreadable?"

"But the loss to archaeology could be incalculable." Chelsea threw her hands up in exasperation. "I just don't know what to do."

"If you made copies of what was on the hard drives, and then corrupted them…" Tony shrugged "It would at least give you some thinking time. Your boss would look at the original hard drives and just say that it was unfortunate—and things would go on as normal. You will then have months, or even years, to decide what to do with the information you do have."

Chelsea threw her head back. "Oh, that is so tempting."

Tony nodded slowly. "If these hard drives are causing you moral problems, let them go. Nothing's worth that."

"I…I'd really like it…if it were possible."

"Then, let's do it."

She laughed. "How on earth do you go about corrupting files on external hard drives?"

"I'm pretty sure Beanie would know." Tony paused. "And if you are planning to do this, you should probably see how Beanie feels about it first. As you say, he's had to pay a pretty big price to get the information you will 'ostensibly' destroy."

She looked at him quizzically. "You know, sometimes you don't sound like a mercenary."

He changed the subject. "So what will you do today?"

"I'll look at the tablets and see what I've got."

"And tomorrow?"

Chelsea pushed herself back from the table. "I'll go up to London and see Beanie."

Tony only had two jobs to do before evening. He had to return to his flat in Dulwich, inform his landlord that he was leaving—effective immediately, and hand him one week's rent in lieu of notice. It was an arrangement he'd negotiated when he initially rented the room. Maintaining flexibility was essential to him.

He then had to find new accommodation that was as close to Chelsea as possible—but not so close as to arouse suspicion.

In the end, he was able to rent an attic bedroom in Chatham at half the rent he was paying in London.

Tony then went shopping. He bought eight external hard-drives and a computer that would never be connected to the Internet.

He connected one of Chelsea's battery hard drives and one of the new hard drives to the computer, and copied the files from one to the other. Tony then replaced the new hard drive with another, and copied the files again. The rest of the day was spent repeating the exercise with each of Chelsea's battery hard drives.

He now had two copies of the data he and Beanie had collected in Syria. Tony had been careful to ensure that none of the information from Chelsea's battery hard drives had ever been stored on the hard drive inside the new computer.

That evening he stood under the archway of Prior's Gate and rang Chelsea.

"Hi. I'm at the front the door."

"Oh. Okay, I'll come down."

Tony could hear Chelsea remove the crossbar she used to secure the front door. He reflected approvingly that she'd organized her security well—but was it enough?

Chelsea opened the door to him and stood with one hand on a hip. She ran her eyes over the conservative drill pants and the Tweed jacket. The jacket was demure, with colors no more outlandish than those of a Yorkshire peat bog. Only his shoes gave a hint of the 'man of action.' His clothes, however, manifestly failed to hide the man's physique. Tony was as disturbingly impressive out of uniform as in it. But it wasn't just his physique or his handsome face, it was something deeper; it was a delicious combination of competence and kindness.

"Don't you have a job to do? You can't nursemaid me forever," she said.

"I'm sort-of freelance."

Chelsea gave him a searching look. "I'm not paying you, you know." Even as she said it, she was conscious that her breathing rate had stepped up a notch. She very much wanted to hear a reason that might give her hope—but didn't dare define what that hope might be. It was enough to know the sweetness of it…and the ache it brought to her soul. Increasingly, she found herself constructing fantasies that all-too-easily developed a momentum of their own. One thing she was very sure of, was that she wanted Tony to be in her life.

Tony rubbed his forehead. "The Board of your museum have asked me to keep an eye on you for a few weeks."

Her heart fell. After a few seconds, she lifted her chin.

"I find that demeaning. I'm not a vapid, helpless female needing a man to rescue me."

Tony smiled. "No Dr. Thompson. You are one of the least vapid, helpless people I know."

She frowned. "You've only known me three weeks."

"Yes."

For a moment, nothing was said.

Tony cleared his throat. "I am…or I should probably now say 'was' a soldier, and I was always grateful to have a buddy to protect my back."

He looked at her with those disturbing eyes, eyes that seemed to interrogate her soul. "Could you…perhaps be grateful for that?"

Silence hung between them like a curtain.

Chelsea nodded. "So the British Museum is paying you to watch my back."

Tony dropped his eyes. "Yes."

Chelsea gave a puzzled frown, but managed to hide it the moment Tony glanced back at her. Her heart began to race. Tony's iron self-control had faltered. He had lied.

"I could," she said, slowly.

"What?"

"Be grateful…and I am."

Tony followed Chelsea up the spiral staircase to the entrance of her room, but stayed on the landing. He pointed to the spiral steps that continued upward. "I presume this continues up to the roof turret."

"Yes. There's a door at the top that leads out onto the roof."

Once inside the apartment, he handed her the shopping bag containing one set of hard drives, and the four original ones that had been disguised as batteries.

She accepted them without saying a word.

He turned to go, but paused, and said, "Chelsea, can I ask you a question?"

"What?" she said.

Tony could hear the defensiveness in her voice.

"Why do you live here?"

"Oh," she said with obvious relief. "Because it surrounds me in history…and has a fabulous view."

Tony nodded slowly. "It is also a fortress."

"Oh." Chelsea lowered her head, and for a while, said nothing. Eventually she said, "I'm not sure I'm ready to tell you yet."

Tony knew that he was being shut out of something deep within her. It was not a feeling he enjoyed.

She must have glanced up and seen the disappointment in his face for she hurried on, "Perhaps I will…later."

Tony had the feeling that both of them had retreated to a bunker, a place from which they could hide whilst testing the strength of the other.

Chelsea suddenly blurted out. "How can you kill a man?"

Tony was not surprised at the question. In some ways, he was relieved that she'd finally asked it. He was acutely aware that what he said next, could make or break the tenuous friendship he had with Chelsea.

"It is not…" he paused, "easy."

Her eyes opened wide with shock. "You mean…" she paused. "You mean…you've done it before?"

For a long while, Tony did not answer. Eventually he gave a tired smile. "I'm not ready to tell you yet. Perhaps I will later."

He saw Chelsea bunch her hands into fists.

Tony reached out and took both of her hands in his.

Chelsea looked at him in surprise.

He moved his thumbs over the back of her hands in what might have been a caress.

"You saw something brutal two weeks ago, and you will probably be having memory flashbacks of what happened." He looked her in the eyes.

Chelsea nodded.

He saw tears welling up. "It gets better, but except in cases of severe trauma, you don't forget…nor should you. Life is sacred."

He let go of her hands.

Then he left.

Chapter 12

Chelsea got off the underground at Tottenham Court Road and walked along Bloomsbury to Great Russell Street. She'd made the journey many times over the years, but never tired of entering through the magnificent, wrought iron gates to the fore-court of the British Museum. As usual, it was filled with tourists. The building was the world's oldest national public museum, and it looked the part. It was, however, relatively modern, having been built in 1852 in the 'Classical' Greek revival style. Imposing columns soared up to a triangular pediment on which the 'eight stages of mankind' had been carved.

She walked up the steps and made her way into the Great Court with its spectacular glass roof funneling down to the central museum shop. As she made her way across the court, she found herself walking beside Sir Anthony Spiers, Director of the British Museum. Chelsea didn't envy him his job. He had to fight to retain the museum's collections every day from nations who wanted their heritage returned. He was famous for saying, "There are no foreigners here; the museum is a 'world country.'" Sadly, it was not a view shared by everyone.

"Good morning, Sir Anthony," she said.

The Director looked at her with a slight start. "Ah Chelsea: back from Syria."

"Yes. I got deported."

"So I hear. What happened?"

She shrugged. "I stepped on some religious sensibilities."

He frowned. "Any lasting damage?"

Chelsea was momentarily put off balance. Sir Anthony appeared to know nothing of the clandestine work she'd been engaged in and was making no reference to it. She cleared her throat. "No, sir. The Syrian officer in charge of the dig and I had a tussle of egos…and I lost."

"Well, as long as you were not hurt…and there is no lasting reputational damage for the museum. Put a report in to the board about what happened. They ought to know." He looked at his watch. "Must dash."

"Goodbye sir," she said to his retreating back.

Five minutes later, she was deep in the bowels of the museum where Beanie had his technical laboratory.

The man himself was perched on a stool soldering something. His crutches were leaning against the end of the bench. Beanie pushed his protective eyewear up on his forehead. "Hi Chelse, what's up?"

Chelsea drew a deep breath and told him.

A few minutes later, he was rubbing his forehead. "Wow Chelse, are you sure you want to do this?"

She nodded. "I do. I bumped into Sir Anthony when I came in, and he made no reference to what we've been up to. I think all information about it stopped at Megan. That means there will be no repercussions from the Board. In fact, I think they would be pretty relieved to discover the hard drives were corrupted—if they knew."

Beanie nodded. "Well…if you're sure." He paused. "It was one heck of an adventure, though, wasn't it?"

"It was a nightmare."

Beanie nodded. "Do you get them too... you know…nightmares of what happened?"

She nodded.

For a while, neither of them said anything. Beanie gave a shudder, then said, "Give the hard drives to me and come back in two hours. Then we'll visit Megan together."

Two-and-half-hours later, the two of them were standing outside the office of Megan Caplan. They could clearly hear her voice coming from the other side of the door. "Don't give me excuses. Give me a way ahead. Have an outline on a single piece of paper ready for me first thing, tomorrow morning."

A few seconds later, a harried looking man Chelsea knew only vaguely, came out of the office. He did not look at them as he scurried past.

Chelsea knocked on the open door.

Megan looked up at her. She was sitting behind her desk and was not looking happy. However, when she saw Chelsea, her face brightened. "Oh, I'm so glad to see you. I didn't expect you both to come in for a few days. Come in. Come in, and shut the door. Tell me everything."

Megan's smile did not last for very long. She grilled both of them intensely.

Finally, she sat glowering behind her desk.

Chelsea found it hard to meet her eyes. Megan was a formidable woman, both in temperament and dress. Today she had kohl around her eyes and was wearing a white shirt and black slacks. Blue and gold Egyptian-style jewelry hung around her neck. She was handsome, statuesque, and intimidating.

"So there is no chance of rescuing the information from the hard drives?"

Beanie shook his head. "The information never actually got to them. The circuitry I embedded in the alloy must have lost a connection somewhere."

She glared at Beanie—her dark-rimmed eyes fixing on him like searchlights. Finally she sniffed. "I can't decide if your expression of guilt is because your scanner failed to work, or because you are not telling me the truth," she said brutally.

Beanie said nothing.

Megan tapped a finger on her desk. "Take me down to your workshop and show me the scanner."

Beanie spluttered. "Sure. But there isn't much of it that's still together."

"Why?"

"There's no way I wanted anything incriminating hanging around me. So I cut the clever parts into bits. They should now be on the municipal dump. I've still got the laser scanner if you want to look at that."

Megan glared at him.

"Hmph. Get out of here, both of you."

Chelsea and Beanie beat as hasty a retreat. Outside in the corridor, she leaned against the wall. "Whew!" she said, and didn't trust herself to say anything else.

Next morning, Tony was again at the gatehouse. Chelsea had asked him to come so she could give him the original 'battery' hard drives to dispose of. They were in the bag he'd given her, which was resting on the window seat. She was standing beside it, looking out of the window at the Cathedral. Tony doubted she was seeing any of it.

He stepped across and stood beside her.

Boys from the local private school were streaming underneath them, presumably going to morning chapel.

Shaken out of her reverie, Chelsea picked up the shopping bag and handed it to him.

When he looked inside, he saw that it contained the original battery hard drives.

She lowered her head. "I very much wanted to give you the new hard drives as well. I'm not sure I can trust myself to keep them. I just know that curiosity will get the better of me—particularly now I have Mahdi's tablets."

"Have you discovered what they are?"

Chelsea nodded. "I'm pretty sure they are tablets which contain the basic rules of grammar needed to translate Sumerian cuneiform into Eblaite. They all have Sumerian cuneiform on one side and Eblaite on the other."

"How many tablets do you have?"

"Twelve, and they are all teaching tablets." She cupped her elbows with either hand. "They're going to be of massive help in teaching us to read the 2,500 tablets or so unearthed from Ebla."

"What are you going to do with them?"

"I have to work that out. Technically, they're stolen artifacts from Syria, so the Syrians won't be too pleased to learn we have them."

"If they find out."

She nodded. "If…so I think I'll hang on to them for the moment."

Tony experienced a wave of misgiving. He was acutely aware that Chelsea had in her possession the cuneiform text of 465 tablets, and quite possibly twelve tablets that could unlock the secrets of what was written on them. If anyone had even a suspicion that she had either, it would make her very vulnerable.

He glanced at her. The idea of Chelsea being in any more danger appalled him. He weighed the shopping bag of hard drives in his hand. "Of course, if you did give me the other hard drives as well, it would mean we'd have to stay in touch."

She looked at him levelly in the eyes. "Yes, it would." She paused. "Do you live very far away?"

"As it happens, I don't. I live in Chatham, just twenty minutes away."

She expressed surprise. "Oh. That's extraordinary."

Tony continued on. "It would probably be a good thing if we could find each other if we need to. Would you be willing to allow us both to track each other's movements using the 'Find Friends' app on our phones?"

For a moment, she didn't respond. Then she nodded.

A short time later, he left.

Tony's official work responsibilities required him to study the organization that had employed him as their security consultant. His role was to analyze it and identity two things: those departments at risk from foreign pressure; and people at risk from foreign influence. He was invisible to most people within the organization and reported only to the Board.

Tony had not counted on being sub-contracted to escort a decidedly idiosyncratic technician to one of the most politically unstable places in the world—Idlib province in Syria.

Was he glad he took the job? There had certainly been nothing comfortable about it—but most of the missions he'd led had involved a great deal more hardship than this one. The job had certainly rewarded him with its challenges and dangers, but Tony no longer needed danger either to test himself, or to add spice to life. He'd relished such jobs in the past—partly because they proved to be a helpful antidote to his loneliness.

His heart gave a lurch—and prompted him to be more honest. *Yes*, he acknowledged. He was glad he had taken the job…and knew that for him, it was the most significant one that he'd ever taken. Chelsea was to blame. She was feisty, highly principled, courageous, and ridiculously beautiful.

He rubbed his forehead as he tried to navigate his way through new emotional territory. Finally, he could deny it not longer: he had to confess that he'd fallen in love. The delirium of love had breached his self-control. But with its heady sweetness, there was also pain. Whilst his heart was consummately lost, he was not at all sure that Chelsea felt the same.

Tony sighed a sigh that came from the depths of his soul, knowing that he would probably carry the regret of that for the rest of his life…for he did not for one moment put any faith in his ability to woo her.

But at least he could protect her for the next few weeks—which was just as well, as he very much feared she would need it.

First, however, there were things that had to be done. He had to destroy the original battery hard drives. There must be no record of them. Whilst he could dispose of them simply by throwing them into the River Medway, there was nothing so certain as seeing them destroyed.

He took out his phone and dialed a number.

"Hi Peter, Tony Patterson."

His friend, Peter, answered. "Tony. What can I do for you?"

"Same as before. I need to cook something. Where are you today?"

"At a farm on the edge of Wateringbury."

"Where's that?"

"Three miles west of Maidstone." Peter gave him the address.

Half an hour later, Tony drove his car into a farmyard. Peter's van was parked at the entrance of the stable block.

He walked over to where Peter was working. He was in the process of putting new horseshoes on a heavy horse. From the look of its arched neck, Tony thought it might be a Clydesdale.

The gentle giant stood patiently, tethered by a head-rope to a cringle on the wall of the stable.

Peter was wearing a divided leather apron that looked like cowboy chaps.

Tony watched him tap a leg of the giant horse. The horse allowed Peter to lift a feathered hoof and tuck it between his legs so the hoof was in front of him. Then, Peter set to work levering off the shoe and using pincers to remove the nails. It looked to Tony as if Peter was being rough with the hoof, but the horse took it all calmly, without complaint.

Peter then pulled a curved knife from the pocket of his apron and began cleaning out the sole of the hoof. "Are you still with the unit?" he asked.

"No. I'm freelance, now."

"I'm surprised it took you so long."

"Why?"

"You had a troublesome gentle streak."

Tony laughed. "Says him who is now a farrier shoeing horses."

Peter used a giant pair of nippers to clip the hoof wall before rasping the hoof flat with a file. He then walked over to the portable furnace set up in the back of the van and removed a red-hot horseshoe from it. After putting it on the anvil beside the doorway, he started banging and shaping it with a hammer. When he was satisfied, Peter lifted the animal's hoof and placed the shoe into position.

The hoof instantly smoked.

Peter removed the shoe and gave the hoof another rasp. Then he refitted the shoe.

"Wait 'till I've sized this shoe," he said. "It's the last one."

Tony nodded. "Do you miss it…the old life?"

Peter reached up and ran a hand down the flank of the Clydesdale.

"No."

When Peter saw what it was that Tony wanted to destroy in the furnace, he said, "Put your stuff on the anvil."

Tony did so.

Peter took a spike and hammered it through each battery hard drive. "That's just to make sure they don't explode." He pointed to the back of the van. "Put the bits on that ceramic tray, and clean it up when you've finished."

Tony stepped over to the furnace and turned the propane fuel fully on. Peter had told him, when he'd used the furnace once before, that it could heat up to 2,600 degrees Fahrenheit—just enough to melt steel.

In just a few minutes, there was nothing left of the four battery hard drives other than a puddle of alloy and a lingering acrid smell.

Chapter 13

C helsea was always reluctant to draw the blind down over the window at night and hide the magnificent view of the cathedral, but privacy was important to her.

She was at her desk in her pajamas working on the report for the museum's Board. It had to be pitched just right. It needed to be honest, yet give the Board confidence that its reputation had not been sullied overly much. She also took the opportunity to give a detailed report on the devastation she'd encountered at Ebla, and the remediation work that was being done. She included a list of the new discoveries that had been made. It didn't amount to very much. Most of what had been found was limited to the 465 clay tablets that the world was not allowed to see. She felt it propitious at this stage to make no mention of Mahdi's tablets, as their ownership was a gray area. Did they belong to the Syrian government, or to the rebels who notionally had control of Idlib province? She shuddered. She certainly wouldn't trust them to the Jihadist forces that had shown such scant regard for their nation's heritage.

It was now very late, but writing the report had left her feeling wired. With only the light from the smoke detector on the ceiling to guide her, she walked to the kitchen bench and made herself a hot chocolate. There wasn't quite enough light to tell her when the kettle had enough water in it and so she overfilled it.

Chelsea picked up her mug, collected her Kindle, and headed for bed.

She'd only just tucked her legs in when she heard the sound—a faint scratching sound. Incongruously, it was coming from the lock of the fire door beside her bedhead.

With horror, she realized that someone was trying to break in.

She leaped out of bed, grabbed her phone, and frantically dialed Tony's number, cursing herself for not having it on speed-dial.

Fortunately, the blessed man answered immediately. He didn't waste words. "What's the matter?"

"Someone's trying to pick the lock on the fire door."

"I can be there in fifteen minutes, but that will be too late. Chelsea, you've got to take the initiative."

"What…what can I do?"

"You live in a fortress; drop something on them." He paused. "Just make sure you can live with the consequences."

Chelsea instantly knew what she would do. She cut him off. "Got to go. Bye."

She ran over to the kettle, picked it up, and ducked through the doorway to the spiral staircase. In just a few seconds, she was at the door of the roof turret. It opened without much noise, but as she made her way along the low stone parapet, she had to walk over old clay tiles that creaked abominably. She desperately hoped she hadn't been heard…and that the intruders had not already broken in.

Finally, she reached the gabled end and peered over the edge.

Two men were on the fire escape immediately below her. There was enough ambient light from the streetlights for her to see that both were wearing balaclavas.

The man who had been crouching at the door stood up and pocketed what she assumed to be a set of picklocks and drew out a pistol from behind his jacket.

Any sense of reserve she might have felt instantly vanished. She flipped open the lid of the kettle and poured it over the heads of the men below.

There were instant howls of agony as the two men, still gasping in pain, groped their way for the stairs and stumbled down them at a run.

She watched with some satisfaction as they fled to the access gate in the wall. The men barged through without bothering to close it and disappeared.

Chelsea was alone and safe—at least for now. She shivered as the adrenaline began to dissipate and the reality of what she'd done began to dawn. The fact that she was on a roof in her pajamas on a chilly October night didn't help either.

She made her way downstairs, switched on all the lights, and re-locked the latch of the fire door—grateful that it was a modern lock that would not be easy to pick.

Chelsea lit the fire, threw a blanket around her shoulders, and curled up on the recliner. Taking a deep breath, she reached for her phone. Again, Tony answered straight away.

"Are you safe?"

"I...I think so."

"What happened?"

"I tipped hot water from the kettle over them." She paused. "One of them had a gun."

Tony gave a grunt of approval, or it may have been the briefest of laughs. "And how are you feeling now?"

"Shell-shocked, but no regrets." She chewed the bottom of her lip. "I just feel a bit vulnerable."

"I'm ten minutes away. Have you made yourself a hot drink?"

"Yes."

"Good. Put two extra sugars in it. I'll call you when I'm outside your door."

―――――――――

Tony ran one red light and broke the speed limit by at least 10mph. Finally; he pulled up outside the wall running down to the gatehouse. The first thing he noticed was that the gate in the wall had been left open. The two intruders had obviously been in a lot of pain when they left. The thought of it gave him some satisfaction. They certainly couldn't run to the police to complain.

He pulled out a rucksack from the back seat and did a quick reconnoiter up and down the street. As expected, he saw nothing to arouse his suspicion.

Tony made his way to the gate in the wall, closed it behind him, and walked over to the fire escape. Before he mounted the steps, he pulled out his phone and rang Chelsea.

"Hi," he said. "I'm coming up the fire escape, so you don't have to come down. Don't tip anything on top of me."

He heard her laugh. "Then you'd better knock politely on the door."

He did.

She opened the door, and there she was, pale and shaking. Tony shrugged the rucksack onto the floor and kicked the door shut without taking his eyes off her. A moment later, he'd wrapped his arms around her and drawn her to his chest.

She clung to him, pressing herself against him, and started to weep.

Tony gave her time to cry out her tensions. Without realizing it, he found himself stroking her hair as she nuzzled under his chin.

"You did well, Chelsea. Very well indeed."

Eventually, she calmed down to a point where she could disentangle herself from him.

"Would you like me to stay the night on the couch?"

She nodded. "I'll leave the fire on low. There's a heat exchanger on top of the roof, so you should stay pretty warm." She looked at him shyly. "I've already left a blanket out for you."

"Thanks. That'll be fine." Tony pulled out a silver foil-wrapped pill. "This is Temazepam. It will help you get off to sleep. Have you had your hot drink?"

"Yes."

He walked over to the sink, found a glass and filled it with water. "Here, swallow it down and get to sleep. I've got the watch."

She swallowed the pill and looked at him as if she wanted to say something, but didn't know how. Tony forestalled her.

"To bed." He smiled. "Sleep well. I'll turn the lights out."

"Thank you," she said, "…for everything."

Their eyes locked onto each other…and for a moment, nothing was said.

Eventually, Tony nodded. "You're welcome."

Tony elected to spend the night in the recliner with his rucksack close at hand. He wanted to minimize his reaction time. However, he was fairly sure nothing more would eventuate that night.

Occasionally, he cast an eye on Chelsea and was pleased to see that the Temazepam had done its job. Even tucked in the corner in relative shadow, he could see her face. It was framed in black hair that spilled carelessly across her pillow.

It was 9am before he saw signs of her beginning to stir. Tony got himself up and set about making breakfast, using one of the lights set under the wall cupboards so see by. He found a fridge behind one of the paneled doors and located an electric fry pan. Soon, four eggs and a tomato were spluttering pleasingly in the pan.

When he turned to check on Chelsea's level of wakefulness, he was surprised to discover that she was watching him.

"Good morning," he said. "Eggs and tomato on toast—nearly ready. I hope that works for you."

"It works very well. I'm ravenous."

"Then we'll add toast and marmalade to follow."

They ate breakfast together. Tony was acutely conscious of Chelsea's presence and luxuriated in the joy of doing simple domestic things with her.

She had donned a dressing gown, but her hair was still puffed up and disheveled. Chelsea showed no pretense—and still managed to look fantastic.

"What will you do today?" he asked.

"I've got to go up to London and hand up a report to the people in the museum. I'll do some work there, then…" she hesitated.

"You're not sure you're ready to come back here alone," Tony finished.

Chelsea lowered her head. "No." She rushed on. "But I realize you can't be around for ever."

"No. But I can help you Dynabolt some slots either side of the fire door that will let you slide in a crossbar. That should make you nearly impregnable."

He eyes widened. "You'd do that?"

"Of course. I'll visit the hardware store after breakfast, and we can have it all done before you head up to London." He paused. "Have you got anywhere you can stay tonight?"

Chelsea nodded. "I can stay with my sister, Ann. I'm well overdue for a visit." She smiled fondly. "She's my best friend in the whole world, and one of the wisest people I've ever met. Ann's a paraplegic—not that it slows her down much. She did a philosophy degree, but now works as an administrator at a children's hospice in Eltham. So it's not far from here."

Tony nodded. "She sounds interesting." He paused. "I'm glad you've got somewhere to stay, because I've got to catch a train today to South Wales—to the Brecon Beacons."

"The mountains?"

"Yes, just overnight. I'm helping with the selection of some service candidates. You'll be able to keep track of me on 'Find Friends,' although I probably won't be able to respond to calls."

"I thought you'd finished being a soldier."

He smiled. "You never completely cut the ties with my part of the service."

She nodded, and then yawned. "I'm off to have a shower."

Tony nodded. "Do you mind if I go up to the roof turret and have a look around to check security? When I've done there, I'll get along to the hardware shop."

"Of course not."

"Oh, and one more thing: Have you photographed Mahdi's

tablets and stored the images somewhere safe…and backed them up?"

"Yes, but just with the camera on my phone. I've backed them up on iCloud. It was one of the first things I did."

"Good. You should remove the images both from your phone and your personal computer?"

"Why?"

Tony did not give the full reason, but settled for saying, "Either can be stolen."

She nodded.

Tony slung his rucksack over one shoulder and headed for the door.

The view from the rooftop gave Tony a commanding perspective of the cathedral precincts to the north, and St. Margaret's Street to the south. He dropped the rucksack against the parapet and explored the roof turret. Two rusted U brackets were fixed to the back of it. Presumably they had once held a flagpole. Tony tested the strength of the lower bracket and found it was still solid.

He crawled back to his rucksack and extracted a coil of black climbing rope. Tony tied one end to the bracket and flaked the rope so that it would run freely. Next, he tied a long length of string to the free end of the rope. After weighting the end of the string with a piece of chewing gum, he dropped it over the edge of the wall facing the garden of Bishop's Palace. A huge beech tree, still with some of its leaves, hid the end of the garden and the gatehouse from anyone looking from the house.

Content with his work, he made his way back down the tiles to the door of the roof turret. There, he took out his phone and rang his old-time colleague, Peter, the farrier.

"Hi Pete. You said you were heading overnight to the old unit at Sennybridge later today. Is that still on?"

"Yes. Why?"

"I want you to take my phone on a holiday to the Brecon Beacons."

There was a moment of silence before Peter replied. "I suppose there's a good reason for this."

"There is. I'll retrieve the phone from you tomorrow evening when you come back through London. What time will you get to St. Pancras Station?"

Peter told him.

"Thanks mate. I'll buy you dinner."

Tony stood at the base of the gatehouse wall behind Bishop's Palace. It was 7pm, and he was in deep shadow behind the beech tree.

He found the string without much difficulty and gave it a gentle tug. Soon, the climbing rope came snaking down. Tony removed the string and put it in the rucksack he was carrying. Then, with a practiced economy of movement, he climbed twenty-five feet up the rope to the parapet of the gatehouse.

Once he'd hauled himself over the edge, he pulled up the rope and again flaked it out so it was ready to run free.

Tony crept down to the roof turret door and descended the spiral staircase. He let himself in to Chelsea's apartment, and with the aid of a pin torch, set about putting tiny pieces of hair across the joints of cupboards and drawers. Then, he took hold of the metal suitcase containing the clay tablets and hauled it up to the roof. Once there, he tied the rope to the metal handle of the suitcase.

He took his time inching the case up the roof tiles until it rested on the parapet behind the roof turret. Then, inch-by-inch, he lowered it over the side.

The case bumped and scratched its way down the wall. Tony had looped the rope around his waist and was belaying the case as he would a dead-weight climber.

Once the case reached the bottom, he tied a highwayman's hitch on the U bracket and threw the end of the rope over the edge.

Moments later, he had shimmied down the rope and was standing beside the case. A sharp tug of the tail rope soon brought all of the rope falling to the ground.

Tony coiled up the rope and packed it away in his rucksack.

From there, it was only a short walk to the ancient stone wall which ran along St. Margaret's Street. He found the gate in the back corner of the garden and let himself out. Once outside on the street, he pulled the metal case behind him to his car.

Tony drove across Rochester Bridge to Strood. After parking the car close to Strood station, he caught the 20:15 train to London. When he arrived at St. Prancras, Tony hailed a taxi that took him to the Grange White Hall Hotel.

He was in bed by 11pm.

The last thing he did was to text Beanie on his spare phone.

Beanie,

Join me for breakfast at the Grange White Hall Hotel. It's on Montague St. opposite the museum, just down from Russell Square.

Have the front desk page me when you arrive.

I've got something to give you.

Chapter 14

Chelsea bent over and gave her sister a tearful hug. "Oh, it's been so long Ann, and I've so much to tell you. My head and my heart are all over the place."

Her sister smiled, "Come on in. I'll put the kettle on."

Chelsea watched her sister as she wheeled her way expertly about the kitchen switching on the kettle and fetching plates for slices of cake. "How are you?" she asked.

"Oh, I'm fine. I've been having fun organizing and equipping a music and sensory room at the hospice. I think it's going to be good."

Chelsea looked at her sister fondly. She was beautiful, but as physically unlike her as it was possible to be. Ann had long fair hair and pale flawless skin; whereas she was dark and swarthy. Chelsea had fully expected to be the one supporting Ann after her accident, but in reality, it was often the other way round. Chelsea worried sometimes that she was living her life vicariously through her sister, borrowing her strength, her 'centeredness,' and meaning for herself.

The two of them were soon chatting away.

Chelsea shared a highly redacted version of the events that had occurred, so that she didn't betray anything confidential.

It was still enough to cause Ann's mouth to drop open with amazement.

"Wow!" she said. "You've really had a tough time of it. How are you feeling now?"

Chelsea sighed. "To be honest, I'm in a storm of emotions. Most of that is because of Tony." She looked at her sister shyly. "He's pretty special, and I'm afraid I've let him get under my skin."

"Alleluia! I think it's about time," her sister smiled.

Chelsea thought it wise to change the subject. "But I'm also heartbroken at all the wanton destruction, abuse, and desecration I saw in Syria. It's appalling. There's been indiscriminate bombing and shelling of civilians—and that's not to mention the vandalism of Syria's heritage by Jihadist forces. They've desecrated the ruins of Nineveh, bulldozed the Palace of Ashurasirpol II in Nimrud, vandalized the museum and library in Mosul, and destroyed the Temple of Bel in Palmyra." She threw herself back into her chair. "What is it about hard-edged Islam?"

Ann nodded her sympathy. "To be fair, they don't see it as vandalism. They have an ideological motive—a passion to stamp out polytheism and false gods."

"Do we have to turn to atheism for civility, then?"

Ann shook her head. "No. That would be disastrous. Atheism, whether it be in the form of Hitler's National Socialism, Communism, or the neo-Marxist ideologies that are currently on the rise in the West—can't help but remove all that is sacred from what it means to be human…and that paves the way for the vilest abuses that humankind can perpetrate."

Chelsea gave a bitter laugh. "That doesn't sound like something to look forward to—humanity collapsing back into the ways of the animal kingdom where nature is 'red in tooth and claw.'"

Her sister nodded. "No abusive regime can exist unless we allow our nation's opinion leaders to establish a philosophic climate that removes the sacredness of humankind." She paused. "Sadly, that's exactly what the UK is currently doing ."

Chelsea struggled to keep up with her sister's mercurial mind. "What's the answer, then?"

"Truth." Ann smiled. "It offers hope." She leaned forward and handed Chelsea some cake. "Now, tell me more about Tony. Where is he now?"

"Hang on, and I'll tell you." She consulted the 'FindFriends' app on her phone. "He's at a place called Sennybridge."

"Where's that?"

"South Wales."

"Oh." Ann paused. "Come on; spill the beans. Tell me about him."

So she did.

When she'd finished, Chelsea inquired tentatively, "Well, what do you think?"

Ann smiled. "I think you are transitioning."

"What?"

"Transitioning. You are no longer content to stake your claim in the world by being the best in a male dominated arena. You've grown up and don't feel the need to prove yourself any more." She smiled. "You are making room for the dangerous possibility of love. Congratulations."

⸻

Beanie hobbled into the hotel restaurant looking conspicuously out of place. He had his trademark beanie pulled over his rebellious red hair. It was lime green and orange today. His pullover looked as if it had collected most of the other colors of the artist's pallet.

Tony was pleased to see that he was now walking with the aid of a stick rather than crutches. That at least was a mercy.

Beanie spotted him sitting at a table and joined him. He sat down with evident satisfaction and craned his neck to look at the buffet breakfast. "I haven't had a slap-up breakfast in a posh place like this for ages. I'm going to binge," he said.

Tony smiled. "Tell me what you want, and I'll get it for you. How's the leg?"

"A small infection threatened it for a bit, but it's under control now. It's healing."

"Be patient. You may have only had a flesh wound but your system's still had a big shock."

Tony ferried food to Beanie, and the two of them set about eating.

"What have you got for me, then?" asked Beanie. "I'm all agog."

Tony took a while to reply. He leaned back in his chair and toyed with his coffee cup. Eventually, he said, "Beanie, I've seen enough of you to know that you are fiercely loyal and protective of those you care about."

Beanie gave him an interrogating look.

Tony continued on. "I suspect that you feel that about Chelsea. You are good mates."

"She's a great girl. What's on your mind?"

"Chelsea is in danger."

Beanie looked up with immediate concern. "What sort of danger?"

"A couple of men tried to break in to her gatehouse. We have to presume they wanted to steal Mahdi's tablets from her. If what she says about the tablets is true, their existence has international significance."

"Wow! Is she okay?"

"Chelsea's fine. She poured hot water on them from the roof."

Beanie raised he eyebrows and laughed. "That sounds like Chelse."

Tony continued. "The thing is; I suspect that these people will try again. Chelsea could be seriously hurt."

His comment caused Beanie to open his eyes wide in alarm. "What can we do?"

"I've already done it. I've stolen the tablets from her."

"You've done what?"

"I told you. I've got the tablets in a case up in my room. I want to give them to you for safe keeping."

"Wow!" Beanie scratched his hair. "What do you want me to do with them?"

"Can you scan them like you did the others and put the information on an external hard drive. Whatever you do, don't load the information on a computer that's linked with the Internet."

"Yeah, that's pretty easy."

Tony pressed on. "But that's not all. Could you then hide the tablets away so they can't be found?"

Beanie smiled. "I think so. I can hack the museum's computer and add them to an old set of artifacts that have already been stored." He shrugged. "The best way of hiding anything is to hide them in plain sight." Beanie paused. "You know, of course, that Chelsea will be distraught…and she'll have your testicles, mine too, if she finds out."

"I'm willing to risk that—at least until we know that Chelsea is safe, and we know a little more of what's going on. The thing is, Beanie: I'm asking you to keep this secret. But if you feel at any time that you need to reveal what's really happened, you must feel free to do so. I don't want to burden you with something that is not yours to carry."

Beanie grinned. "This is all so deliciously Machiavellian." He paused. "Do you think this will make things safer for Chelsea?"

"She's staying with her sister at the moment, so I've put out the 'welcome mat' for intruders to explore Chelsea's apartment, so they can satisfy themselves that the tablets are not there."

Beanie shook his head. "Crazy." He furrowed his brow. "The big problem is getting the tablets into the museum. Security has become very tight. Everything has to be signed in and checked off against a manifest." He scratched his head. "I'm reluctant to forge anything. It would be more than my job's worth."

"I wouldn't ask you to sign for anything, just add the tablets to an already existing incoming manifest—perhaps listed as Sumerian tablets from Nimrud."

"I can do that easy enough. But who will sign them in?"

Tony drew a deep breath. "I will."

"What?"

"As it happens, I'm the security consultant at the museum." Tony shrugged. "I work mostly out of sight reviewing the museum's systems." He paused and smiled. "I'm glad you appreciate my new security arrangements."

Beanie's mouth dropped open. "You?"

"Yes. I report to the Board, no one else; so I've got my own security pass."

"Well, I'll be jiggered." Beanie shook his head. "You're a dark horse." He paused. "I suppose your existence is fairly hush-hush."

"Yes, and I'd be grateful if it stayed that way."

Beanie held up his hands. "That's cool with me." He pushed himself back from the table. "Right. If you wait here, I'll head over to the museum and bring back your manifest. I'll be about an hour."

"Thanks, mate."

Beanie was a little longer than an hour, but he eventually returned and met up with Tony in his room. "Here you are."

Tony nodded his thanks and pointed to the case containing the tablets. "Don't lose them."

Beanie grinned. "If we lose them, it's not disastrous." He grinned. "I can feed the scans into a 3D printer and build you a whole new set."

Tony shook his head. "Just having the scanned information won't do. Chelsea is going to need these originals to prove authenticity when she eventually finds out she's still got the tablets."

Beanie grunted. "By the way, Megan Caplan has been trying to get hold of you. She wants a debrief about all that happened in Syria." He paused. "I take it she has no idea who you really are."

"No. To her, I'm just a jock contracted to make sure you got to Syria and back safely."

"Well, she's pretty keen to meet you. She's asked me to contact you. She says she's been unable to get through."

"I'll go and see her. Do you have her number?"

Beanie scrolled through his phone and gave it to him. As he did, he grinned. "Be careful. She eats men for breakfast. Actually, she eats anyone for breakfast. She's a *tour-de-force*. You'd better watch out."

Tony nodded. "I'll wheel the case over to the museum for you and sign it in."

"So you're Tony Patterson." Megan Caplan looked Tony up and down from behind her desk.

"Yes ma'am."

Megan nodded slowly. "You've had a high time of it in Syria, I understand."

"We got out safely, which was the main thing."

"Tell me, exactly, what happened."

"There's not much to tell. The place was more politically unstable than we were led to believe. We had to get out quick because we became engaged in a fire fight."

Megan tapped a finger on her desk. "More information, please."

Tony took a deep breath. "Beanie and I irradiated the tablets. It just took a day, and everything went without a hitch. We were to be driven to Khmeimim Air Base next day by the camp commander's adjutant. Unfortunately, he took it into his head to visit the house of a young boy who'd been acting as a servant for Chelsea. The boy claimed to have found some clay tablets that he was planning to sell. Evidently, the adjutant had been tasked with the job of collecting all such tablets from the townsfolk who had looted them."

Tony wondered how much more he should say. He continued on, cautiously. "Chelsea accidentally spoke of them within earshot of the adjutant. Beanie and the boy had developed a bit of a rapport by that stage, so when he saw the adjutant threaten the boy with a hammer, Beanie went for him. The adjutant shot Beanie, and I shot the adjutant." He paused. "I buried him in the cemetery and then drove everyone to the coast, where I implemented an exit strategy."

"Just like that?"

"Yes."

"You could have caused an international incident."

"Yes."

"Tell me about the camp commander." She looked at the notes she'd made on a piece of paper in front of her. "Major General Abbas Shamon, I believe."

"He watched us closely. It was evident that he didn't trust us at all. He was aloof, but competent at what he did. He looked to be a natural leader."

"A worthy opponent."

"We didn't oppose him, ma'am."

"Except by killing his adjutant."

Tony said nothing.

"Will they find the adjutant, do you think?"

"I doubt it. No one digs up graves during a MERs outbreak."

"Have you put in a report to the Board?"

"A brief one, yes."

Megan leaned back in her chair. "So, you're just a soldier."

"I'm more in the line of protection these days."

"You didn't see anything suspicious or odd when you were…er, irradiating the tablets?"

"No ma'am. It was all very straight forward."

"Well, if you recall anything, let me know." Megan smiled. "You'll find me very grateful."

She stood up from behind her desk and stretched extravagantly, stretching her blouse across her chest. "You'll find me very grateful, indeed."

Chapter 15

At 7:30pm, Chelsea's phone rang. It was Tony.

"Hi," she said. "How was Wales?" *Such a useless, inadequate greeting.* Her heart wanted to say so much more.

"Wales was fine. How are you?"

"I'm still with Ann." She paused. "She wants to meet you, by the way."

"To check that I'm a suitable and morally responsible... chaperone?"

"Something like that." *Nothing like that at all.* She clenched her free hand into a fist in frustration.

Tony continued. "I'm at St. Pancras having a meal with a colleague. My train leaves in ten minutes. I can get off at Eltham and say Hi, if you like. It's only a forty minute journey."

Chelsea's heart leaped. "Yes. I'd like that—very much. I'll meet you at the station and take you to Ann's. Then I can run you home in my car."

"Terrific. I'll see you in a bit."

Fifty minutes later, she watched Tony walk along the platform with his rucksack slung over one shoulder. His bomber jacket was unzipped showing the white tee-shirt underneath. He looked fit and dangerous. She watched him covertly for a few seconds, enjoying the sight, before she stepped from the shadows into his path.

"Hello stranger. Going my way?"

He grinned. "I hope so."

She led him to her car and waved an apologetic hand. "I'm afraid that's my car—the red, Fiat 500. I have no dignity."

"The chariot of kings."

Ann was waiting for them when they arrived. She'd positioned herself in her wheelchair at the entrance of the kitchen.

Tony shepherded Chelsea inside.

Acutely aware that Ann was seeing more than she was comfortable with, Chelsea said airily, "Ann, this is Tony."

Ann held out a hand. Tony took it between finger and thumb. Her hand looked small and pale next to his. For some reason, they held hands for a few seconds.

"Tony, at last we meet. I'm very pleased to meet you. Chelsea has told me a good deal about you." Ann paused. "Thank you for getting her out of Syria safely. And I understand that you are still keeping an eye on her."

"Yes. That's my..." he paused, "privilege."

"Is Chelsea in danger?"

"Yes. There are people who want some artifacts we brought back with us. Chelsea believes they may help establish who can lay claim to being the original occupants of Israel, so it's all pretty political."

Ann nodded. "You've been through a lot together." She looked at them both with a small smile on her face. "I think I can see how it is between you two."

Chelsea was appalled at her comment and tried to direct a surreptitious glare at her sister.

Ann remained completely unabashed. She spun round in her wheelchair. "Come and sit at the table. I've made a hot cheese dip for a late night snack."

Chelsea was surprised to see that Ann had not cleared away some concept drawings Chelsea had doodled earlier that day. She'd left them on the table.

Tony glanced at them and raised an eyebrow. "This looks familiar."

"Oh, it's just some ideas," Chelsea said.

"Hmm."

The sketches were of her gatehouse, showing plans for an upper room extension that incorporated the roof turret.

Chelsea rushed on to explain. "I think it may be possible to put a lightweight structure on the top and double my living area."

Tony nodded. "Tell me what you have in mind."

"I'd put an insulated zinc roof on top. That will tie it in with the cathedral's look—and I'd put in lattice windows above the stone parapet."

"Sounds great. What will the room be used for?"

Chelsea felt herself flush. "Um, a decent bedroom, a study, and more storage."

"Will you be able to get this through the planning people?"

"I think so. I'm not changing the essential fabric of the gate-house, and the extension will greatly assist in its maintenance. The parapet is currently quite dodgy."

Tony turned to Ann. "Have you seen Chelsea's apartment in the gatehouse?"

"No." She smiled. "My life is defined by stairs and acces-sible toilets. But I've seen it from the outside. It looks extraordinary."

"I could carry you up the fire escape. But I'm not sure what I can do about the toilet."

Ann laughed. "Perhaps. We'll see."

Conversation ebbed and flowed. Chelsea was pleased to see an easy friendship developing between Ann and Tony.

Finally, it came time to leave. Ann reached out and took both Tony's hand and Chelsea's hand in her own. "Such different hands...come together." She let both hands go and said to Tony, "You may kiss me on the cheek."

Tony smiled and obliged.

"Call me," she said, "if you need another cheese dip."

A short time later, Chelsea and Tony were squeezed side-by-side in the Fiat 500 and heading along the A2 to Rochester. For most of the time, they sat in silence.

"Where do you live?" Chelsea asked eventually.

"Westmount Avenue in Chatham, not far from your place. I'll direct you."

She nodded.

When she finally parked in front of Tony's flat, she rested both arms on the steering wheel and said, "You asked why I live in the gatehouse—a fortress."

"Yes."

She paused. "Because it's safe."

Tony gave her a questioning look. "And why is that particularly important for you?"

Chelsea tried to find the words to describe what she'd been unable to describe for many years.

Tony waited.

Chelsea finally blurted out. "Because I was adopted." Once she'd said it, the words came pouring out. "That's why my sister and I look so different. I was adopted; then Ann was born two years later. Our parents did their best to show equal love to both of us, but it was very evident that their affection was particularly directed toward Ann. I began to feel on the outer...and this feeling of vulnerability crept over me. It still haunts me."

Chelsea shook her head. "The irony of it all was that my parents bought Ann the horse that she'd always wanted...and it was the horse that bucked her off causing her to be a paraplegic. She was only fifteen at the time."

"But you are the best of friends."

"Oh yes. She never tried to parade the fact that she was a favorite, and always looked up to me as the big sister. We shared all our secrets...or most, in my case."

"She's a remarkable woman, your sister. She seems to see a whole lot more than you're aware of."

Chelsea nodded. "Yes. She sees what most other people don't, which can be a bit frightening...and she has a hope, which I envy."

Tony smiled. "Thanks for trusting me with your story, Chelsea."

He paused. "I can't pretend I know what to say." He shrugged. "Just know that I'm here for you—if you need anything."

Chelsea nodded and said, "I won't ask you if you've killed before." Her voice tailed off.

Tony nodded. "Thanks."

They were both quiet for a while.

Chelsea broke the spell by blurting out a question designed to put the brakes on the disturbing sense of intimacy that was developing. "Could you have stopped Beanie being shot, do you think?"

Tony rubbed his forehead. "Er, no. He was blocking the target. It was only when he spun away, that I had the kill shot."

Chelsea shuddered. "Are you always so clinical?"

"When I need to be."

"It must make you…difficult to live with."

He looked at her. "No one has seriously tried."

Tony was not surprised to have a hysterical phone call from Chelsea twenty minutes later.

"I've been burgled," she sobbed. "The clay tablets have been taken."

Tony tried to suppress a pang of guilt. Her despair and anguish reached into his soul, leaving him feeling wretched.

Chelsea continued on. "They've even taken the broken corner of the tablet Mahdi gave me—the Syrian stone. It was in the drawer of my desk."

This comment caused Tony to sit up with alarm. Those who had broken in may not have taken the Ebla tablets, but they now had incontrovertible evidence that Chelsea had links with them.

He pinched the bridge of his nose. The big question was: What did it mean?

Chapter 16

Abbas listened to the report from one of the field operatives detailed to watch Dr. Thompson's comings. He was sitting in a teahouse on the High Street having tea and scones...and wishing it was strong Arabic coffee and baklava. "Dr. Thompson has gone into the cathedral. She is sitting alone just inside, about four rows from the back."

Abbas pocketed the phone and pulled his greatcoat around him. He'd kept it on against the English chill. Moments later, he was striding under the arch of a gateway that stood over the lane leading to the cathedral.

A side door next to the great western door was open. He ducked through it and entered the cavernous interior. Stolid, round Norman arches flanked the nave, marching their way east to the rood screen, on top of which sat an impressive pipe organ. He noticed that the architecture of the cathedral changed at this point to feature the Gothic, perpendicular building style. It was a visual reminder that nothing in history stayed the same

For a moment, he allowed the peace of the surrounds to seep into his soul. Grand architecture, like that of Hagia Sophia in Istanbul, had always moved him. He remembered idly that the mosque, with its mighty dome, had begun life as a Christian cathedral. Such, indeed, were the vagaries of history.

The late afternoon sun was streaming through the stained glass above the western door leaving patterns of blue, red, and gold on the floor. Music filled the air. Someone was playing the organ—presumably practicing. From the mathematical precision of the tune, it was Bach. But he had not come here to listen to music.

He saw Dr. Thompson—Chelsea—such a nice name, exactly where he expected her to be. She was alone, and except for the occasional verger wandering here or there, the two of them were the only ones in the nave.

Abbas edged his way between the rush-covered seats and sat down, leaving just one seat between Dr. Thompson and himself.

Chelsea started out of her reverie and glanced round. When she saw him, her mouth dropped open in surprise.

"Good afternoon, Dr. Thompson." Abbas forced a smile. "We just keep dancing together, you and I."

Chelsea glanced around nervously, looking for a way to escape.

Abbas held up both of his hands, seeking to give reassurance. "Relax. You are quite safe. I just need to talk."

"What do you want?" She hissed.

Abbas looked at her dark eyes. They were fired up with passion. He felt a familiar wave of emotion. "Aah, Chelsea," he sighed. "It seems that we are forever on the wrong ends of the same stick."

"What are you doing here?" She whispered.

Abbas didn't answer straight away. He tilted his head back and listened to the music. Eventually, he said. "I have something that belongs to you."

"What's that?" she said crossly.

Abbas fished in the pocket of his greatcoat and pulled out the broken corner of a clay tablet. He saw the flash of recognition in Chelsea's face. "This, I believe, is yours."

"How dare you." She pointed accusingly at him. "It was you, or your men, who burgled my apartment and stole my tablets. That is theft; unconscionable theft. You have a nerve coming here to boast about it."

Abbas frowned. "What do you mean: 'We stole your tablets?'"

"Oh, don't get coy with me. You've stolen...everything."

An uncomfortable prickle of unease started to play on the back of Abbas' neck.

"You believe we have stolen the twelve tablets from Ebla?"

"Of course you have," she said crossly. Chelsea pointed to the broken piece of tablet in Abbas' hand. "That proves it."

Abbas turned the broken corner over in his hands, inspecting it on both sides. In reality, he was thinking furiously. One thing he was totally convinced of: Chelsea Thompson was telling the truth. She was no longer in possession of the twelve tablets he'd come looking for. Not only that, she believed him to be in possession of them. He sighed. That changed everything...and he didn't, for one moment, like the scenario it suggested.

His fears were confirmed by Chelsea's next comment. "Your goons tried to break in and steal the tablets the night before last, and would have if I'd not poured hot water over them."

"What are you saying?"

Chelsea rolled her eyes. "You know very well what I am saying. Your lot tried to break in two nights ago."

Abbas drew in a deep breath. "I assure you, we did not."

"Are you serious?"

"Yes."

Bach twiddled up and down his arpeggios.

Abbas, stretched his neck. So...there was another party who not only knew Chelsea had the twelve tablets, but also knew of their significance. Doubtless, they had them in their possession. He elected to play for time in order to sort out his thoughts.

"You, Ms. Thompson, are the common thread that links a good number of unsavory events, events for which you may be held accountable by an international tribunal."

"What do mean?"

"You stole twelve tablets that rightfully belong to the Syrian government."

Chelsea threw her head back. "Rubbish! Who do they belong to? Ebla is notionally under the control of Jihadists who have no regard for Syrian culture. And they certainly don't belong to you, or shouldn't do. You hide your archaeology from rest of the world. That's irresponsible and selfish."

Abbas lifted his chin. Chelsea was firing at her very best. It caused him to feel giddy. He needed to counter-attack.

"I have a missing adjutant, Hassan, whom I presume is dead." He paused before continuing. "I have a dead shop owner at Tell Mardikh who was the local dealer in stolen artifacts. He was executed by two shots, one to the chest, another to the head—after advertising the fact that he had your twelve tablets for sale."

Abbas had the satisfaction of seeing Chelsea sit back in shock.

"I know nothing about that," she stammered.

Abbas pressed on. "Crucially, I am in possession of a scanning device, deviously designed to record the images of all the tablets you kindly volunteered to irradiate. In other words, I have proof positive of the duplicitous, scandalous behavior of the British Museum."

He allowed time for the reality of what he said to fully impact her.

Chelsea seemed to deflate in front of him.

"What do you want from me?" she said.

Abbas could think of a number of things, but restricted himself to the matter in hand.

"I want to know who has the information on the 465 tablets you scanned. And I want the twelve tablets from Tell Mardikh that you stole."

"But, but I don't have them," she said. "You have."

Abbas looked at her dispassionately. "I assure you that I do not. They were not there when we, er, inspected your apartment." He paused. "We only found this." He handed her the broken piece of tablet. "That's proof that you were once in contact with the tablets. You will therefore find them and have them returned to me." Abbas dropped a business card on the seat that lay between them.

"But how can I? I said I don't have them," she protested.

Abbas shrugged. "That is your problem."

Chelsea threw her head back. Her eyes were filled with tears.

"But I can't do the impossible. I don't know anything." The despair in her voice was palpable.

"Then I suggest you ask that Rottweiler you have with you, Tony Patterson."

Chelsea frowned. "Tony? What would he know? He's just a security man."

Abbas laughed. "I think he is a lot more than a security man. My information is that he is the main security consultant for the British Museum."

Chelsea reared back in shock. "What?"

"You heard."

Abbas decided to press in and take full advantage of Chelsea's confusion.

"My sources also tell me that no information concerning the scanned tablets has yet been stored on any computer in the British Museum. He shrugged. "You also will need to convince me that they never will have that information."

"And why should I do that?"

"I can think of a number of reasons, one being to preserve the reputation of the British Museum."

"Pah! The Museum is custodian of world culture. It ensures transparency and fosters knowledge."

Abbas pressed on. "And the other reason is, I have your little servant, Mahdi, in my custody. He's currently in my house in Damascus." Abbas shook his head. "I would hate for anything untoward to happen to him."

Mahdi didn't remember much about how he came to be in the new house. He just knew that it was a place he'd never been before. But it was nice. The comforting sounds of normality could be heard— trucks revving and growling along the road, and motorbikes puttering along, occasionally squawking their horns. He could even hear children chattering and laughing as they went to school.

He tried to recall everything that had happened. A man had

spoken to him about Miss Chelsea. He had a message from her. Then he'd been grabbed. He didn't like that…and there was a prick in his arm.

After that, there were lots of engine noises. They seemed to go on forever. At one point he soiled himself. But when he woke up again, he was clean.

Eventually, he woke up without hearing any engine noises, and he found himself—wonder of wonders—on a mat in a laundry. But this laundry had a tiled floor and was bigger.

The laundry was part of the servant's quarters of a rich man's house. It had a front courtyard with a fountain in the middle that worked. Four paths from different directions led to a pond where the fountain was. He'd played in it once using the curving husk from a date palm as a boat.

The servants, and a soldier who was always on guard at the gate, controlled his new life. There were three servants: a gardener who came only on some days, a cook, and a man who lived in the servant's quarters who did the cleaning and supervised everything. The man was Mr. Salib. He lived with his family in the servant's accommodation. Mr. Salib was stern…and his wife was very fat. She spent most of the day doting and fussing over their son, Nabil. Nabil was also fat, and was one year younger than him.

Initially, Nabil wanted nothing to do with Mahdi. He was rude and occasionally lashed out at him with his fists. Over the course of a few days, however, a sort of truce was declared. This was largely brought about because of Nabil's love of playing marbles.

Mahdi was very bad at marbles—which helped their relationship greatly. He always lost.

In the mornings, Nabil would be dressed in a crisp white shirt and dark blue shorts in readiness for school. He would be back home at lunchtime. It didn't take long for Nabil to discover that Mahdi was a great asset when it came to doing homework. Even Nabil's mother approved of him helping her son.

It was a good arrangement for Mahdi. He was hungry to read anything he could get his hands on. His real love, however, was television…and the Salib family had one in their quarters.

Mahdi began to work out a scheme that might allow him to watch it some of the time.

As far as he could make out, Mr. and Mrs. Salib were responsible for cleaning the main house and keeping everything in order. He decided to volunteer to help with the cleaning in the mornings. The big house had a lot of brass things in it that had to be kept shining bright. Mr. Salib showed him how to use the cleaning material, and soon Mahdi's work was as good as his. In fact, Mahdi secretly thought his was better.

It was when he first worked inside the big house that Mahdi had a shock. There, sitting above the mantelpiece in the main room was a photograph of the camp commander at Ebla, Mr. Shamon. He was standing next to a pretty woman and two girls. Finally, he knew who owned the house, although he had no idea why he was there.

As time passed, Mr. Salib entrusted more and more of the cleaning to Mahdi. In return, Mahdi was allowed to watch the Salib's television, provided he sat outside the doorway.

Mahdi was delighted.

Chapter 17

Sir Anthony Spiers, Director of the British Museum, sat glowering behind his desk. "Bad business. Very bad. This killing of a Syrian soldier—most regrettable."

Chelsea felt constrained to say, "It was either that, or the museum being responsible for the death of one of their senior technicians. Syria is in chaos. It's one big killing field."

Sir Anthony grunted. "Well, hopefully, the Syrians won't find out and will at least be grateful that we irradiated their tablets for them." He sighed. "Who knows, they may even show their appreciation by letting us look at some. Okay, Chelsea. Thanks for the report." He paused. "I'm glad you got out of Syria in one piece."

Chelsea stood up and made for the door.

As she opened it, she was shocked to see Tony outside about to knock on the door.

She shut the door behind her and said stiffly, "I need to speak with you."

Tony nodded.

As they walked down the corridor, she continued speaking. "I've seen Abbas Shamon."

Tony looked at her sharply. "What! Major General Abbas Shamon, the camp commander at Ebla?"

"Yes. He bailed me up in Rochester cathedral, of all places… and he told me some horrible news…which I really don't know how to respond to."

Tony took Chelsea's elbow and drew her to a halt. He reached out for her hands, but she put her arms up and stepped back from him.

"Abbas also told me things about you, which you being outside Sir Anthony's office would seem to confirm."

"What things?"

"He told me that you are the chief security consultant for the British Museum."

Tony nodded slowly. "I am, but it is not a role the Board wants to be generally known. I work in the background."

"Spying."

"Watching. Learning." He shrugged. "Adapting protocols. Seeing points of vulnerability."

"And escorting museum personnel to war zones."

"That was a special contract. I was tapped on the shoulder because of my military experience in that part of the world."

Chelsea leaned back against the wall. "I don't know whether to trust you, Tony. I'm just not sure who you actually are."

Tony rubbed his forehead. He was putting on a stoic face, but she could see a stricken look in his eyes.

"What did Shamon have to say that was so distressing?" he asked, eventually.

"He found our scanning machine and knows what we've done. Abbas will publicly shame the museum if I can't assure him the museum doesn't have the information." She drew in a deep breath. "He also wants me to deliver Mahdi's twelve tablets to him."

"How does he know you've got them?"

"He gave me Mahdi's broken corner piece which his men stole from me the night before." She paused. "The thing is, he assures me he didn't take the tablets. Someone else stole them before he got there." Chelsea shook her head as if trying to rid herself of the memory of the conversation. "I told him about the attempted robbery the night before, and he denied it was his people."

"Do you believe him? You don't think he's just trying to get leverage on you?"

"Yes, I believe him. Someone else is in this game, and I've no idea who it is." She tilted her head back and blinked back some tears. "So, I have to get the tablets back from people I don't even know exist…"

"Or else?"

She started to sob. "Abbas has kidnapped Mahdi. He has him in his home in Damascus. There's no way we can get to him."

Even through her tears, she could see the look of shock on Tony's face. Seeing his grief, she momentarily forgot herself and allowed Tony to put his arms around her to comfort her.

However, almost immediately, she pushed him away. It was a fairly half-hearted push, but she finished the push by pummeling his chest with her fists. "Just who are you, Tony Patterson? I'm not feeling very safe…and I've no idea what to do."

"We'll work something out." Tony gave a tired smile. "After all, that's my job." He stepped back from her. "I can either stay here and let you hit me again, or you can let me buy you a coffee in the Coffee Lounge."

The Coffee Lounge was a café on the first floor at the south side of the Museum. It sold surprisingly good coffee. However, its main feature was its view of the museum's magnificent domed Reading Room.

When they were settled with their drinks, some sort of normality began to penetrate Chelsea's guarded stiffness.

"How did you get this job here?" she asked. "What do you know about archaeology?"

"I know a lot about security."

She shook her head. "But everything here centers on archaeology."

He smiled. "Why don't you teach me?"

"Would you really want to know?"

Tony inclined his head. "Anything that would help me understand more would be useful. From what I'm discovering, archaeology is a lot messier and a lot more political than I ever imagined."

Chelsea coughed a laugh. "You don't know the half of it. Archaeology may have its disciplines and protocols, but in reality, it is bedeviled by ideologies, world-views and preconceptions."

"What do you mean?"

For a long time, Chelsea said nothing. Then she pushed herself back in her chair. "Come, and I'll show you."

She led him to the south stairs, and then up to the third floor. There, they passed through a corridor of ancient Greek and Roman exhibits until they came to rooms 57 - 59, 'Ancient Levant.' The display room had pale green walls and a domed glass ceiling. Glass display cabinets with orange backing lined the walls.

Chelsea pointed to a small stone cylinder in one of them. "Do you see that cylinder? When you roll it over wet clay, it leaves a picture imprinted on it." An image of the imprinted picture was on display next to it. It showed a man and woman sitting either side of a tree which had fruit on its lower limbs. To the left of them both was a serpent.

"What do you think that story depicts?" she asked.

Tony answered straight away. "It's the Adam and Eve story."

"So some believe. That's why it is known as the 'Adam and Eve cylinder seal,' or the 'Temptation seal.' It's thought to date from about 2200 to 2100 BCE. Most archaeologists, however, now see no connection with the Adam and Eve story, and simply see it as a conventional example of an Akkadian banquet scene."

Tony rubbed his chin. "But all the elements of the Adam and Eve story are there—it would be churlish to deny it. It's difficult to imagine it can just be co-incidence. There has been some cross-over of influence." He turned to her. "But if there is, then the question I suppose, is: Which one came first? Which one influenced the other?"

"Precisely. Archaeology is not always straightforward. And there's another delicious controversy currently brewing over the chronology of ancient Egypt. It also seems to be largely driven by preconceptions."

"What's that?"

"Well, this particular hand-grenade has been lobbed by the British archaeologist David Rohl. Rohl is an agnostic and has no interest in trying to re-date Egypt's chronology to make it fit into the biblical narrative. But he's nonetheless open to thinking that the ancient texts have historical relevance. He actually suggests re-dating Egypt's chronology for good archaeological reasons."

"Really? Such as?"

"He says that the traditional historical markers used to date Egypt's chronology, before the sacking of Thebes by the Assyrians in 664 BCE, are highly questionable. Rohl suggests that if Egypt's chronology is unshackled from these anchors, it can be moved forward, so that it is younger, by 350 years. He believes it should be moved forward because of an ancient reference to a near-sunset solar eclipse observed in the Syrian city of Ugarit during the reign of Pharaoh Akhenaten." She rushed on. "According to archaeo-astronomy, the only time this eclipse could have occurred during the second millennium BCE was the 9th May 1012 BCE, 350 years later than the conventional dates for Akhenaten." Chelsea leaned back in her chair. "If the dates are revised as Rohl suggests, the whole story of the Jewish enslavement and exodus from Egypt falls into place." She paused. "Needless to say, atheists and liberal theologians hate the idea, but the orthodox Jews love it."

Tony shook his head. "What a mess." He cleared his throat. "Can I change the subject?"

She wondered briefly if Tony had taken in anything she'd said. "Yes," she said defensively.

"Can you organize to stay at your sister's place tonight?"

"Why?"

"I want to watch the gatehouse tonight to see what might happen when you are absent from it."

Chelsea shivered. "You think I might be burgled again? Good grief; I thought my place was a fortress."

"I don't know. I just want a chance to see who else may be 'in play,' as you say. Have you got your computer with you?"

"Yes."

"Good. You don't want it to be stolen." Tony rubbed the back of his neck. "Do you mind calling your sister right now?"

Tony was glad he didn't have to drive very far. He was sweating inside his ghillie suit. The shaggy, green camouflage suit made him look like something out of The Lord of the Rings. To preserve the sensibilities of anyone who might glance into the car—despite it being 10pm, he'd thrown a rug over his shoulders. It only added to his discomfort.

He pulled up outside the gate in the wall running down to Chelsea's gatehouse.

After waiting to see that no one was about, he reached behind into the back seat for the FX Wildcat. The Wildcat was an air-gun that could fire a lead pellet at 1,000 feet per second. It was deadly. Its power came from a compressed air bottle that doubled as the rifle's stock. The whole unit was just twenty-nine inches long. However, its main advantage was that it was completely silent.

A few seconds later, there was a faint tinkling, and the streetlight near the gate in the wall stopped working.

Tony waited a few more minutes, then got out of the car and jammed a credit card into the latch of the gate. It opened, and Tony pushed his way into the garden where Chelsea's fire escape was. The old stone garden wall hid him from anyone's sight. It was eight feet tall and ran down the side of the laneway to the gatehouse. He walked down to the place where ivy grew in thick profusion over its top.

The rain that had been threatening to fall throughout the evening, finally decided to do so.

Tony did not mind. Rain kept the guileless and the innocent inside.

He threw the hood of the ghillie suit in place and heaved himself up the wall so he could just peer over it. No one was about. The good patrons of the Coopers Arms pub a hundred yards away had all made their way home.

As quick as a cat, Tony pulled himself on top of the wall amongst the ivy and lay flat along the top of it.

Despite the cushioning from the ivy, he found his position both precarious and uncomfortable. It was, however, in deep shadow, and it afforded a clear view of Chelsea's front door as well as the fire escape.

The rain continued to fall for the next two hours.

Tony did not move.

They came at midnight—two men and a woman. The woman, he thought, was a nice touch. She could be a lover kissing her partner by Chelsea's front door...or simply one of a couple sheltering from the rain. Clever.

He could see another man standing guard, looking north along St. Margaret's Street. Tony very much suspected that someone else would be keeping watch to the south from a car further down the laneway.

Under the archway, the man and woman busied themselves at Chelsea's front door.

It only took two minutes before the couple let themselves inside. If they were from the same organization that had tried to burgle Chelsea's apartment last time, this time they'd sent a very much more professional team.

Tony couldn't help but reflect that Chelsea's fortress was not so fort-like. She'd do better putting a turnstile at the front door. It wasn't good. He resolved to replace the lock on the door and install a security alarm as soon as possible.

Twenty minutes later, the couple were back outside. The man further down the road immediately walked off in one direction whilst the two who had exited the gatehouse walked arm in arm in the opposite direction.

"This is an opportunity of a lifetime for you." Megan Caplan lifted her chin and was looking her regal best as she spoke to Chelsea from behind her desk.

Chelsea, however, was in a storm of emotions and full of misgivings—the reasons for which, she couldn't divulge. She felt trapped.

Megan continued. "You have been an elected member of the World Archaeological Congress for over a year now, and it's high time they heard from you." She tapped a pen on the desk. "The international Congress will be in Jerusalem. As these conferences occur only once every four years, I want you there."

"But there are things I have to attend to here," protested Chelsea.

"Rubbish. You are going. I want you to deliver a paper on everything that has been going on at Ebla. The world needs to know, and no one else is in as good a position as you to tell them."

Chelsea tried one more protest. "It doesn't give me much time to work up a paper."

Megan waved a hand. "I've already read your report to the Board. It's a comprehensive report. All you need to do is adapt it for the conference." She pointed at Chelsea. "Professor Yoseh Shalev from the Hebrew University of Jerusalem will be your host. He's asked that you also make yourself available to give a few lectures to his students."

Chelsea knew when she was beaten. Her mind was racing. She wanted to stay in England and untangle the impossible dilemma of Mahdi and the missing twelve tablets. But the more she thought about it, the more she knew there was very little she could do. Perhaps being away in Israel would buy her more time from Abbas Shamon. As she thought it through, the more convinced she became that it was the only route open to her. However, it was a route that only offered hope if Tony was with her. For all his mysteries and secrets, he was able to steady her in a way that no one else could.

She sighed. "I'll go on one condition."

Megan rolled her eyes. "I don't want conditions. This is a golden opportunity I'm offering you for international exposure."

"One condition," repeated Chelsea. "I want Tony Patterson to go with me."

Megan shook her head. "No way. You won't need him chaperoning you in Israel."

Chelsea played the last card she held. "I do. The trauma of everything in Syria has left me feeling very fragile and vulnerable. I don't think I'll be in any shape to present anything at a high-stress international conference without tangible support from someone…" she swallowed, "I trust."

Megan glared at her and said nothing for a long time.

"Oh very well then," she said. "I'll ask the Board."

Chapter 18

Tony walked along the path beside the stone parapet, which was all that separated him from the River Thames. He was in the Victoria Park Gardens in London. Its manicured lawns were covered with leaves. Some children, watched by their mother, were running through them and kicking them into the air. The London plane trees along the path still held on to a few leaves, as if reluctant to part with the optimism of summer.

He glanced across the river at the tourist boats that were moored there. Beyond them, traffic was streaming across Lambeth Bridge.

Tony spotted Mr. Carlisle sitting on a bench seat beside the path. He walked across and sat down beside him.

"How are things?" Carlisle asked, without preamble.

"Complicated, and I need your help." Tony went on to explain the situation concerning Mahdi and the boy's relationship with Chelsea. He necessarily had to tell him about the twelve tablets from Ebla.

"So we have a hostage situation," finished Tony. "Some of my old unit are over in Damascus, but I'm in no position to authorize anything." He paused. "But I'm guessing you can."

Carlisle leaned back and surveyed the view in front of him. "I'm bound to say that it is unusual for a political hostage to be held in someone's private residence. It rather suggests this affair has a personal element to it, or that Shamon doesn't want his political masters to know what he's up to. Interesting."

Tony wasn't greatly concerned with what Carlisle found interesting. He just wanted some action to be taken as quickly as possible.

"My suggestion is that Mahdi be snatched and taken to Amman in Jordan. I happen to know that we have a safe house there." He paused. "From there, it's only a forty mile trip across the Israeli border to Jericho."

Back in his flat, Tony massaged his temples as he paced up and down the floor, trying to think of anything else he could do. After doing a mental inventory, he decided that there was nothing. This left his mind free to return to its default position—ruminating on the disturbing frisson that had developed between him and Chelsea. The real trouble was, he didn't see how he could have behaved any differently given the circumstances. But that didn't matter. Whilst Chelsea exhibited enormous resilience in some areas of her life, in others, she remained extremely fragile. She thought he had willfully deceived her...and that had brought their developing relationship to a shuddering halt.

He shook his head. When relationships like this had presented such challenges in the past, Tony's response had been to simply let them go. However, the thought of not having Chelsea in his life was impossible to contemplate. She shone a light on the gray sterility of his existence—and exuded life and passion.

Tony forced himself to sit on the end of his bed. Almost immediately, he got back to his feet.

Finally he could bear it no longer. He took out his phone and rang Chelsea's sister, Ann.

She answered almost immediately.

"Hi," he said. "I was wondering if you were putting together another cheese dip tonight."

Ann laughed. "I could do, easily…or maybe swap it for a chocolate fondu."

"How do you stay so slim?"

"I don't have many visitors."

"Can I come over? I'm in a bit of trouble with Chelsea, and I don't want to lose her." He paused. "I thought you might be able to help straighten out my thinking, so that I avoid the worst of the landmines."

"Hmm. It sounds as if you need to talk. Come straight over."

"Thanks Ann."

Half an hour later, he pulled up in front of Ann's flat and rang the doorbell.

Ann answered the door and took him through to the kitchen.

True to her word, chocolate was warming on a spirit burner. Marshmallows lay on a plate in front of it.

Ann pointed to it. "Morale food. Take a skewer and help yourself."

Tony obliged, but his heart wasn't really into eating.

"Tell me what happened," said Ann.

Tony told the story. He ended by shrugging his shoulders. "I feel her slipping away from me, Ann, and I don't know what to do. I've only just discovered her."

"You're not asking me to be an advocate for you, are you?"

Tony shook his head. "No, that would be unfair to you. I'm quite prepared to carry my own responsibilities. I…I just want a wise head to check my thinking. I'm…not all that great with the whole relationship thing."

Ann cocked her head. "Tell me about your family. How do you get on with your parents?"

It took a moment for Tony to catch up with Ann's mercurial mind and the new direction the conversation was taking.

"Um…my father died of cancer, and my mother remarried when I was 17."

"Were you an only child?"

"Yes."

"And how do you get on with your stepfather?"

"He's American, and he took my mother back to the States with him." Tony paused. "He's not real comfortable having me around."

"So you joined the army, and it became your family."

Tony didn't know what to say.

Ann continued on. "Do your mother and your stepfather have children of their own?"

"No. He was a widower who already had two children from his first marriage."

Ann nodded. "So you feel a bit displaced, maybe even abandoned?"

Tony shrugged. "I haven't really thought about it."

She looked at him with her head slightly tilted—as if inquiring about something. Tony had the uncomfortable impression she was seeing rather more than he would wish.

"Well Tony, I'm not surprised you're not great with relationships. I think in large part it is because you don't actually know who you are." She waved a finger at him. "You don't know who you are, or why you are. It's hard for anyone to have confidence and be at peace with themselves if the only meaning they have pursued comes from running off and playing war games."

Having his military career dismissed in such an off-hand way could have rankled, but he knew that Ann was not actually deriding the military. She was addressing something altogether more personal—his very identity and meaning. He experienced a sense of disorientation.

"I've never really thought...about these sorts of things."

Ann waved her hand. "You are a thin plank, Tony. And now you are contemplating asking someone, my sister actually, to walk that plank with you. I think that's grossly unfair."

Tony blanched. "I just, sort of...thought that life...everything... came about by accident—and we just have to make the most of it?"

"If you claim that everything came from nothing as a result of nothing, you are not being rational. The only factor known to humankind that has ever been responsible for the extraordinary order we see in the universe is 'mind.'"

Tony laughed harshly. "You mean God? Because if you do, then I'm not sure he's made things at all clear."

"Oh, it's been my experience that he has—if you want to see it."

"How?" he retorted.

"He's hung his business card in the cosmos; showed us his purpose in Scripture, and come to us in person as Jesus." She shrugged. "That's a pretty comprehensive revelation."

Tony drew his head back. "I've never really…looked into it."

"Then it's high time you put your big boy pants on, and did." She paused. "Do you love my sister?"

"Yes."

"Then you need to be more than a toy soldier. You need to have substance, and you need to know where you're heading."

For a moment, the only sound came from the ticking of the carriage clock on the mantelpiece.

Ann leaned back in her wheelchair. "I told Chelsea the other day that she was transitioning into another phase of life." Ann pointed at him. "I think you are too. You are transitioning away from a world of danger…and now wanting more. I suspect you are seeking purpose. I also think you are no longer comfortable with the relational sterility of your life."

Tick, tick, tick.

"Seek truth, Tony, and go where the evidence leads." Ann gave a dismissive wave. "And don't worry about Chelsea. She loves you well enough. She just needs time to know you and trust you."

A gloved hand covered Mahdi's mouth.

Mahdi woke up immediately and tried to scream and kick his way free.

Red light from a small torch flicked momentarily onto Mahdi's scarred forearm. Mahdi had time enough to see an impression of a beard and a blackened face. However, the man smelled English. He smelled of soap.

"Relax, matey, relax," said a very English voice. "I've come to take you back to Miss Chelsea."

The man continued to speak. "My name is James, and I'm a friend of Mr. Tony and Miss Chelsea." He paused. "Do you understand?"

Mahdi nodded.

"I've not come here to harm you in any way. I've come to free you from here."

Mahdi stopped kicking and opened his mouth to speak.

However, he never got the chance to say anything. In just a few seconds, sticky, webbed tape had been wrapped around his mouth, and he was hoisted into the man's arms.

Mahdi had the presence of mind to grab for his canvas knapsack as he was swung into the air. He clutched the bag against his chest, knowing that it contained all that he owned in the world.

He was carried out into the courtyard to the front gate. Madhi eyes were wide with terror. He saw the soldier who was meant to be guarding the gate apparently asleep, slumped against the wall.

Moments later, he was bundled into a car and driven away.

There were three men in the car; two in the front seats, and the man called James with him in the back seat.

After ten minutes of driving, Mr. James peeled off the webbed tape from Mahdi's mouth. It hurt.

"Are you okay, kid?"

Mahdi struggled to find his voice. "Where are we going?" he said eventually.

"We're heading south down the M5 to Amman in Jordan. Mr. Tony has organized for you to cross the border into Israel and has promised to meet you with Miss Chelsea near Jericho." The man paused. "Would you like something to eat?

Food always interested Mahdi.

"Yes."

James handed him a muesli bar.

"Who are you?" asked Mahdi.

"I'm a soldier, a friend of Mr. Tony. He's asked me to come and get you."

Mahdi frowned. "But I don't need rescuing. I liked where I was. It had television."

"Kid. There are things going on that you know nothing about. Believe me, son; you don't want to stay where you were. Things were actually due to become pretty ugly." He paused. "Don't you want to go to the UK and join Miss Chelsea?"

"Miss Chelsea is the nicest person in the world, and I love her," Mahdi said simply. "But England is not my home. Can you take me back?"

The man called James, rolled his eyes, turned round, and faced the front. "Oh boy," he said.

Abbas threw his phone into the pillows of the sofa and sat with his head in his hands. It couldn't be possible. Chelsea's little servant boy had been snatched from his very own home in Damascus. He had seriously underestimated Tony Patterson's ability to move and act so quickly. There was little doubt that Chelsea had recruited his services.

He clenched his fists. Whatever else he needed to do, he needed to keep the pressure on Chelsea.

Chelsea, Chelsea...his mind began to wander.

With a savage jerk, he pulled himself back to reality. He made himself take his wallet out of his jacket pocket and extract a well-worn photo. It was a picture of his late wife and two daughters.

A familiar wave of grief rose up within him. He stared at his wife. She was looking stiffly formal. Abbas was under no illusions. His relationship with her could at best be described as 'dutiful,' perhaps even 'faithful.' He shook his head. It was certainly not like his earlier love—the impossible one.

Then he looked at his two daughters. They were the ones who broke his heart. He traced a forefinger lightly over their image. *Where were they now?* he wondered. Would he see them again? Had they lived a life virtuous enough to qualify for Paradise? He shook his head.

For a long while, he did not move. Then, half blinded by tears, he put his wallet away.

He forced himself to return to the matter in hand, Chelsea Thompson.

Whatever else he needed to do, he had to keep the pressure on her.

He felt behind him amongst the pillows, found her number, and phoned her.

Chelsea answered. "Chelsea Thompson speaking."

Abbas affected a lazy drawl. "Major General Abbas Shamon, at your service."

"How did you get my phone number," she said crossly.

"What? No 'how do you do?' No friendly banter?" He smiled in spite of himself, picturing her arcing up and flashing with indignation. "We need to meet." He said.

"Why?"

"There have been some developments that are very relevant to your well-being and that of the British Museum."

"Such as?"

"I'll tell you tomorrow. Shall we say 2pm?" He paused. "Let's meet in the crypt of Rochester cathedral. It's often where the dead lie, isn't it?"

Chelsea walked past the medieval perpendicular column near the north transept. It was, in fact, anything but perpendicular. It leaned at an angle Chelsea thought was alarming. Still, she reasoned, it had managed to stay upright for a good few years. It must be safe.

She made her way down the steps of the crypt into the unknown.

Chelsea had always thought that the crypt of the cathedral was surprisingly pleasant place. It had a low vaulted ceiling, and the it had a 'light' feel. This was largely due to the ground-level Gothic windows in the walls.

In recent years, a modern altar had been placed toward one end of the crypt. It was simple, unpretentious, and added to the peace of the place.

She found herself chewing her lower lip. Chelsea couldn't help but feel that the sense of peace would soon be at odds with the threats she felt must shortly come from Abbas.

The man himself was lounging in a chair by one of the windows. Light played on the strong features of his face. She had to concede, he was a handsome man.

He pointed to the vacant chair he'd pulled up opposite him. It was an imperious gesture.

Nonetheless, she sat.

He began without ceremony. "As you no doubt have heard, the little servant boy of yours has been snatched from my keeping. I have little doubt you had a hand in it."

For a moment, Chelsea was disorientated.

"I beg your pardon?"

Abbas snapped. "Don't come the innocent with me. As you know full well, I no longer have your servant boy in my custody." He paused. "You must feel very pleased with yourself."

Chelsea was euphoric. Tony. All this had to be Tony's doing. Oh, she could hardly wait to see him, and…she didn't let the thought progress. The truth was, she hadn't seen Tony for a few days, and it was taking a terrible toll on her emotions. She seemed to be dragging her feet wherever she went. Occasionally it would all become too much, and she would see where he was on the Find Friends app on her phone. He was usually in London. On two occasions he was actually in the British Museum when she was also there. It was ridiculous.

The one saving grace was that he always rang at night. He never said much; just asked if she was okay. She could never think of anything to say until after he'd rung off. And then she wanted to say everything.

Abbas sniffed. She wondered briefly how a sniff could sound so arrogant. It was enough to bring her back to the brutal reality of the present.

"I've called you here to say that the boy's release changes nothing. If I don't get an assurance the British Museum will never have the information from the scan of my tablets…" he paused, "and if you don't give me the twelve tablets from Tell Mardikh, I will publicly humiliate the British Museum and end your career." He sniffed again. "I will see to it that your name is advertised prominently as the person around which this whole tawdry affair has hinged. You will be a pariah in the academic world. Your career will be finished." He used his fingers to simulate a newspaper headline. "'Dr. Chelsea Thompson, the person who sank the reputation of the British Museum.'" He laughed unpleasantly.

Chelsea glared at him. Her mind was working furiously.

"Ah, your anger; how well I remember it…The flecks of gold in your eyes—exquisite." Abbas paused. "You are beautiful when you are angry—when your feathers are ruffled. Do you know that?" He leaned back and smiled, apparently pleased with what he'd said.

Chelsea refused to be cowed by this man. She resolved to fight him with every fiber of her being.

She lifted her chin. "If the museum hasn't got the information, they can simply deny everything you say. You will be seen to be making ideologically fueled, unsubstantiated allegations." She pointed to him. "You will not come out of this well. And if the Museum ever does get the information…" she paused for effect, "I can't believe your political masters will be very pleased. Your career will be over. You might even be shot."

Abbas shrugged. "That is why I have nothing to lose. My family is dead. All I have is my career, and I will do anything to protect it. If I preserve the honor of Syria in the process, so much the better."

Chelsea protested. "What you ask is also unreasonable. I am an archaeologist, not a detective able to search for stolen artifacts. I don't have the ability, the time, or the resources."

"You haven't got the time? What could be more important to you right now?"

"I don't. I'm going to the conference of the World Archaeological Congress in Jerusalem in a couple of weeks."

Abbas nodded slowly. "Well, isn't that a coincidence. So am I. That would be a perfect place for you to bring the tablets to me."

"But I haven't got them…" She threw herself back in her chair in exasperation. "And I don't have the first idea who has."

"Then I suggest you and, more particularly, your friend, Mr. Patterson, find out."

"Tony? He's not a magician. He has a regular job to do."

"Find a way."

"It's impossible." She pointed at him. "You know, don't you, that if you corner a wild cat, it will attack you. Desperation can drive people to do extreme things, which can be deeply wounding." She let her hand drop. "I would want to spare you that."

"My, my; Chelsea Thompson is showing me her soft side." Abbas smiled. "I like it." He reached out to touch her hair, but she pulled back. He sighed. "I'm not sure I have a soft side anymore, so you will forgive me if I am not impressed by your threat. But I am impressed that you made it." He paused. "You never give up, do you?"

Chelsea didn't answer.

Abbas put his hands into the pockets of his overcoat and pulled the coat around himself. Then he leaned back and stuck his legs out in a manner that bordered on insolence. "Will you be giving a paper at the conference?"

"Yes."

"About the recent findings at Ebla?"

"What little I've been allowed to see of them, yes."

Chelsea wondered where Abbas was going. She didn't like the tone in his voice.

"I'm sure your paper will go well. It will complement the information at the display stand the Syrian government will put up in the conference hall." He smiled. "You see, I plan to have a stand there."

A terrible sense of apprehension pressed down on her like a heavy weight. She braced herself for what she was about to hear.

"Prominently on display will be the scanner you and the British Museum used to steal information from Syria. The display will include big picture boards and the story of your deception in big text."

Abbas paused to let the full import of what he said sink in.

"Your career, and the reputation of the British Museum will be finished."

"Unless…"

"Unless."

He got up to go. At the foot of the flight of steps out from the crypt, he turned round. "Do you know: I actually look forward to these chats with you. Strange, isn't it?"

Chelsea hunched herself over in her seat and let her hair fall over her face. "I wish I could say it was mutual."

Chelsea massaged the sides of her temple. The guilt, and responsibility she was feeling, threatened to crush her. She was acutely aware that she'd set in motion a chain of events that had brought herself and the British Museum to a point of crisis. If only she'd…Chelsea tried to find the right words, …'behaved normally,' none of this would be happening. But it was too late now. She was trapped in an impossible situation, and the consequences of her actions were going to be dire.

She was sitting in the museum's Coffee Lounge, spinning out a cup of coffee that was now cold.

Finally, she dragged herself to her feet, determined to seek out company that might give her some distraction and relief. That meant a visit to Beanie in his workshop.

As she made her way between the tables, Megan Caplan's secretary waylaid her. "Ah, Chelsea. You're in today. I think Megan wants a quick word with you."

Chelsea nodded. "I'll pop in and see her before I go. I'm just going down to see Beanie."

She found him in his lair, busy tinkering with something on a circuit board. He pulled off his goggles and sat back. "You look as if the devil is chasing you," he said with brutal candor.

Chelsea sat herself down on a stool. "I think he is."

"Whassup?"

"I think we're in trouble Beanie." She shook her head. "And it's all my fault. I'm so sorry."

Beanie waited for her to say more.

"I've been speaking to Major General Abbas Shamon. He's here in England."

"What? The camp commander fellah?"

"Yes."

Beanie folded his arms. "What's he want?"

"He's somehow got hold of our scanning machine, and he is planning to expose our…trickery to the world at the World Archaeological Congress in Jerusalem in a few weeks."

"Wow."

"Yeah, wow."

Beanie suddenly slapped his forehead. "Oh no. If this Shamon fellah puts our scanner on display and causes a media fuss, Megan will find out, and know that I lied about dismantling the scanner." He put his head in his hands and groaned. "I haven't got the strength to get into a fight with Megan Caplan. Anyone but Megan." He paused. "I wonder if London council needs a technician to overhaul their aged computers. Or maybe I could mend fairground rides at Blackpool. It would be further away from London."

"Beanie, I'm so sorry. I should never have got you into this mess."

For a while, nothing was said.

Traffic growled its way along Bloomsbury Street.

Beanie eventually lifted his head. "Should we give the scanned information to the museum?" He shrugged. "Then at least they'd get something out of all this."

Chelsea shook her head. "No. The museum needs to be able to truthfully say it knows nothing about it. They won't be believed, of course, but at least they can have the hurt pride of knowing that it is true."

"Then, what options do we have?"

"I've no idea."

"Perhaps we could emigrate to Australia. Do they have the death penalty in Australia?"

"Seriously, Beanie. What options do we have? How can we stop Abbas carrying out his threat?"

Beanie became thoughtful. "What if we could give him something he wants?"

"He wants the twelve tablets from Tell Mardikh."

"But that doesn't guarantee he won't put the scanner on display at a later stage after he's got them."

"But if the agreement is for a swap…"

Beanie scratched his hair. "How could we pull off something like that? We've no experience in these sort of…clandestine things,"

"We know someone who has."

"Tony?"

Chelsea nodded.

"Yes. Having Tony would…change things."

Chelsea rested her head back in her hands. "But it's immaterial. We haven't got the tablets."

Beanie pulled the beanie from his head and began twisting it between his fists.

"What's the matter?"

"Oh, nothing. Nothing."

"Beanie. What's up?"

"I…I just need to go to the toilet. He avoided looking at her and hobbled for the exit."

When he came back, he was holding his phone.

"Who have you been calling?" she demanded.

"No one."

Beanie resumed his seat on the stool by his workbench. "What options do we have that don't involve giving Shamon the twelve tablets…we, er…don't have?"

"I suppose we could steal the scanning machine from him." Chelsea had intended her comment to be flippant, but she was alarmed to discover she half meant it.

"Steal it?"

"Yes."

"Is that even possible?"

"Tony might be able to help."

Chelsea shook her head. "I don't want him involved. He would lose his job if things went wrong—which, if we do anything at all, is highly likely. Besides, we wouldn't just need to steal the scanner, we'd need to steal pretty much the whole Syrian display stand—their information boards, the lot."

Beanie shook his head. "Wow. That would put the cat amongst the pigeons. There would be hell to pay. The Syrians would cry foul and point the finger at the British Museum yet again." He paused. "And if anyone in the international community caught sight of the original Syrian display, they could bear testimony to the real display's existence."

"That at least may not be such a problem," said Chelsea. "If I know Shamon, he would want a big reveal—a fanfare, a revelation with flourish. He won't reveal his hand until the opening morning when the display stands are open to delegates."

"So, you plan to go in at night to steal the display that's not yet there…and then what?"

A ridiculous idea suddenly came to her. "We replace his display with our own, a display that speaks of the close co-operation between Syria and the British Museum. We have replacement display boards, the lot."

Beanie laughed. "You're not serious about this are you?"

"Probably not." She became thoughtful. "But I'd be kicking myself if I had a chance to do something and wasn't prepared enough to give it a go. I can at least go to the conference carrying the stuff I need with me…in case," she finished lamely. Even to her own ears, she sounded pathetic.

"So, you're going to put together a series of display boards, with your own photos of Ebla on them, and your own text. Then you are going to set it all up for the first day of the conference…at the same time Shamon is putting together his display. And then magically make his display disappear so only yours remains…whilst Mr. Shamon remains cool and sits there, the model of equanimity." Beanie shook his head. "You don't feel that is a little bit…stupidly fanciful."

Chelsea again put her head in her hands.

Beanie laid a hand on her shoulder. "Look," he said, "I've got another idea…"

There was a perfunctory knock on the door of Beanie's workshop.

"Come in," he called.

Megan Caplan strode into the room.

Chelsea saw Beanie involuntary cover his mouth.

"Ah, Chelsea. My secretary told me you'd be here." Megan looked around the workshop, as if inspecting it. Seeing nothing to comment on, she continued. "I'm afraid that the Board have not given permission for Tony Patterson to accompany you to the WEC conference. They have budget stringencies, evidently." Megan smiled. "I'm sure you'll manage very well on your own." She looked at her watch. "I must go."

Moments later, she was gone, leaving an aroma of focused intent swirling in her wake.

Beanie expelled a breath of air.

Chelsea closed her eyes. It was all too much. She needed help, and there was only one person able to give it.

She pulled out her phone and rang Tony.

"Hi," she said. "Where are you?"

"At the museum."

"So am I. Can I meet you in the Coffee Lounge?"

"Yes. I'll see you there in five minutes."

She turned to Beanie. "So sorry, Beanie. Got to run. I'll catch up later."

———

Seeing Tony sitting in the café instantly began to steady her nerves. His legs were stretched out beside the table, and he was surveying the scene around him through half-closed eyes.

She suspected that he was seeing a great deal.

"Hello," he said. He got to his feet and pointed to the counter. "Let's order some drinks."

She nodded and led the way to where the pastries and cakes

were on display. Tony put in their order and paid, innocent of the fact that the girl behind the counter was trying to flirt with him.

When they'd returned to their seats, Chelsea told Tony that she'd been asked to deliver a paper at the World Archaeological Congress in Jerusalem.

Tony nodded. "I imagine that's quite a privilege. Congratulations."

She toyed with her teaspoon. "I asked if you might be allowed to accompany me, but the Board turned my request down."

Tony raised an eyebrow. "Who told you this?"

"Megan Caplan."

He looked thoughtful. After a while he said, "I...er, have access to funds that may allow me to go anyway."

Chelsea jerked herself upright. "Seriously?"

"Yes."

"Surely, you can't just take off from your work here?"

"As it happens, I can. My work commitments are very flexible, and I'm due for some leave."

Her heart skipped a beat. Suddenly, a whole new range of possibilities began to suggest themselves. The trouble was, none of the possibilities had definitive form. It was more a feeling of hope, the feeling that Tony was with her...and for the moment, that was enough. Her frazzled nerves clung to hope like someone about to drown.

Tony continued to speak. "Let me get back to you when I've organized a few things."

Chelsea suddenly remembered Mahdi. "Tony, I've had another talk with Abbas Shamon."

He raised an eyebrow. "Oh yes? What did he have to say?"

"He still intends to publicly humiliate the British Museum at the WAC conference, unless I can give him the twelve tablets from Tell Mardikh. And...he wants an assurance that the museum won't be given the information we scanned at Ebla."

Tony nodded.

"He also told me that someone has snatched Mahdi from his

custody, and he is no longer held hostage." She paused. "I suppose that was your doing?"

"I had a bit of a hand in it, yes."

She reached forward and laid a hand over his. "Thank you. From the depths of my heart, thank you."

Tony cleared his throat. "You're welcome."

Reluctantly, she withdrew her hand. "What's going to happen to Mahdi now?"

"We're still in the process of working that out. But I can tell you that he's safe and well."

Chelsea stared at her uneaten piece of cake.

Tony reached forward and lifted her chin. It was a curiously intimate gesture.

"I think you have a greater need right now," he said.

Chelsea laughed. She couldn't think of anything that was greater than the needs currently pressing in against her. "What's that?"

"Dinner. Can I take you to dinner?" He paused. "I'm not sure that just having an evening phone call…is working all that well for me."

Tony steered his car across Rochester Bridge acutely aware of Chelsea sitting beside him. He continued on to Higham, and before long, was pulling into the gravel driveway of Knowle Country House. The restaurant was an elegant two-story building with a steeply raked roof and prominent stone chimneys. It sat comfortably in a well-tended garden—at peace with the world. However, the last of the twilight was fading into night, so he couldn't see much of it.

Tony was pleased to see that there were a number of cars parked, but that the parking area was not crowded. He had inquired when making the booking whether this night would be a quiet night. Their website had told him that the place was a popular wedding venue, and he wanted to avoid competing with large noisy parties.

Chelsea nodded appreciatively. "I've always wanted to come here."

Tony smiled. "This place was built in the 1850s by the rector of Higham. He was a great friend of Charles Dickens, evidently. The website says that he stayed with Dickens at Gad's Hill whilst this house was being built."

"You've done your homework."

"I was a bit surprised. The house looks a lot older than nineteenth century."

"That's probably due to the Gothic style of its main windows. Someone's let the Oxford movement's church architecture spill over to the rectory."

Tony understood enough to nod.

When they got inside, they discovered a restaurant that had been tastefully decorated with cream and gold wallpaper and drapes.

A waiter escorted them to their table.

Chelsea was looking sensational. She was wearing a figure-hugging electric blue dress, over which she'd thrown a light-blue pashmina. Her hair had been left free so that it tumbled down to her waist.

Tony had elected to wear a thin woolen pullover under his jacket.

Chelsea looked at him almost shyly and said, "Tony, this is a lovely gesture." She paused. "But I'm not quite sure what it means."

"Why don't we find out?" He gave her a searching look. "Are you game?"

"I…I think I am."

Tony nodded.

Chelsea smiled. "So, tell me. Where are you at, these days?"

"Physically, I'm with you. Spiritually, I'm on a journey. Emotionally, I'm beginning something totally new."

She inclined her head. "With me?"

"Yes."

"Are you…scared?"

"I'm scared of hurting you." Tony searched out her eyes. "What are you scared of?"

"I'm scared…of losing you."

And there it was. It was said.

Tony expelled a breath of air. "Wow! I liked hearing that. I liked it very much." He reached forward, took her hand, and sandwiched it between his own.

"Chelsea, this is a journey I want to last." He glanced up at her. "Looking at you now, it would take very little for me, maybe…us, to ignite and burn ourselves out…"

"…with passion."

Tony swallowed. "Yes."

She nodded.

The waiter interrupted them. "May I get you both a drink before you order the meal?"

…and the spell was broken.

Chelsea was trying to work at her computer in the shared office she used at the museum. However, memories of the previous night with Tony continued to intrude.

It had been an evening of both agony and ecstasy that had ended on a frustratingly muted note. He'd taken her home and parted company with her, with just a brush on the cheek with his lips. The look in Tony's eyes had betrayed him, however, making it clear that it was not so much a kiss as a promise of things to come.

She clearly felt both his caution and his smoldering energy—which, for the moment, he was keeping ruthlessly under control.

Chelsea's heart, however, had raced. She was impatient. Her whole body was impatient. She wanted to be encircled by his arms, to lose herself in a kiss that would leave her heady and intoxicated—lost to all things sensible. As it was, she'd simply laid a hand on his chest, against the fine woolen jumper, and felt the hard planes of his muscles. She hoped that he'd felt through her hand the sentiments she found impossible to articulate.

Chelsea shook her head, cross that she'd let her mind wander yet again, and turned her thoughts to the task in hand.

In truth, it was a task she was frightened of, and she wasn't at all sure she should commit herself to it. It was a task involving an audacious theft.

Chelsea had ruminated for most of the last two days on the dreadful dilemma she'd placed the British Museum in. As she pondered the scores of different scenarios, one thing emerged as the top priority—and that was to somehow steal Beanie's scanner back from Shamon. Without the scanner, Shamon could only make allegations, which most people would simply dismiss as 'sour grapes.' He'd have no evidence to back up his claim. She sighed. Whichever way she looked at it, stealing the scanner was the project she had to commit to.

Chelsea tapped the end of her pencil on the desk. *How? How? How?*

The idea, when it came, shocked her. Who would have unfettered access to a man's hotel room—someone other than hotel staff?

There was only one answer she could think of: A wife.

Even as she thought about it, she felt her breathing rate increase. The idea was absurd.

But was it?

If she could impersonate Shamon's late wife whilst he was safely away at a conference function, she could have access to his luggage, which would doubtless include the scanner. Chelsea didn't believe for a moment that Abbas would entrust it to anyone else. He would keep it with him in his room and only reveal it to the public on the morning the display hall was opened to delegates.

What would she need to persuade the hotel staff she was Abbas' wife?

That would largely depend on where Abbas was staying for the conference. She swung back round on her chair. Chelsea needed to find out from the conference organizers where the delegates were billeted. Would they even tell her? She had no idea.

Chelsea opened up her computer, found the conference website, and left a message for the conference organizer inquiring where her

Syrian colleague, Abbas Shamon would be staying. She said that the British Museum needed to drop off some resources for his display stand.

Having made the request, she felt a degree of relief. Something had finally been set in motion.

Nonetheless, she was not prepared for the answering email when it came thirty minutes later. It was a succinct reply that advised her to contact Mr. Shamon personally via his email.

She rolled her eyes in exasperation…and before the frontal lobe of her brain could urge caution, she phoned the organizer direct.

A moment later, she was explaining to a helpful Indian man that she was hoping to be billeted next door to Abbas Shamon, as they'd recently worked at Ebla together and needed to liaise over a presentation.

"Hang on," he said, "and I'll tell you where he is staying."

A minute later, Chelsea had the name of the hotel.

What was the next step?

Ring the hotel. She looked at the time. Jerusalem would be two hours ahead of London. If she rang straight away, it would be just before lunch.

She put the call through, and was eventually passed through to the reception desk.

"Hello, I'm one of the delegates to the World Archaeological Conference in two weeks time. I just want to ask what the checking in procedure is in your hotel."

"Certainly madam. It's very straightforward. We take your credit card details and photocopy the front two pages of your passport… and you pay when you leave. Was that all you wanted to know."

"Yes. Thank you."

Chelsea ended the call with her heart racing.

What if she could provide them photocopied pages of her passport, but with the photograph of her replaced by a photograph of Abbas' late wife? If she could find a photo of Mrs. Shamon, it would be easy enough to do.

For the next thirty minutes, she explored the Internet, entering every permutation of names and occasions that might yield results.

In the end, she was rewarded with a picture of Abbas and his dark-haired wife at the ceremony when the rank of Major General was being conferred on him.

She looked at the woman standing beside Abbas and instinctively reached out to her, wanting to apologize for the deception she was contemplating that made such sore use of her memory.

As she looked at Mrs. Shamon, two things very evident. One of them shocked her. It was the fact that she looked so like her. Just three things were markedly different. One was the fact that she was considerably taller than Chelsea. The other was the hairstyle. And the final factor was that Mrs. Shamon had a birthmark on her neck.

Chelsea chewed on her lower lip. The birthmark was easy. A few seconds with a make-up stick would fix that. She sighed. For the rest, she would just have to hope...and wear a scarf.

A familiar voice hailed her from the doorway of her office. "Hello."

It was Tony. He was leaning against the doorframe, looking at her. "How are you feeling this morning?"

"Honestly?"

He nodded.

"Frustrated."

He smiled sheepishly. "Glad it's not just me."

She stood up, walked over to him, and took him by the lapels. "I'm not made of delicate crystal, you know."

For a moment, he didn't say anything. Eventually he said. "I needed you to feel safe." He rubbed the back of his neck. "You...in that dress." He smiled. "It didn't make me feel as if I wanted to be very safe."

She rose herself up on her toes and kissed him on the cheek. "Did it ever occur to you that the dress was worn in the hope that you might not be?"

Tony shook his head and glanced over her shoulder. He furrowed his brow.

"What are you up to Chelsea Thompson?"

She backed away from him and quickly tidied up her notes, passport and photocopied pictures.

"Nothing. Nothing at all. Just a project I'm working on…for the conference."

Tony shook his head. "Sorry. It doesn't wash. Tell me honestly: What are you up to?"

Chelsea sighed and sank back into her chair. "It's something very, very stupid, and I don't want you involved in it." It could go badly wrong."

Tony's answer was to drag a chair from the neighboring desk and sit beside her.

"Spill the beans."

Reluctantly, she did.

When she had finished, Tony didn't say anything for a long while. He just sat there with his eyes closed.

Then he sat himself up in the chair. "Sorry, Chelsea. But your plan is fundamentally flawed."

Chelsea couldn't help but feel slightly aggrieved. "Why?"

"The hotel will insist on seeing the original passport. Security is the sole reason they insist on it."

"Oh." Chelsea lowered her head and felt very foolish.

Tony went on. "But your plan is basically sound."

Her head shot up. "You think so?"

"Yes. But you need a bit of help?"

Chelsea shook her head. "No. I don't want you to get involved. It could go badly pear-shaped."

Tony reached out a hand and laid it over hers. "If you are involved, then I am involved." He shrugged. "I'm afraid it's that simple."

Chelsea couldn't help but feel a degree of relief. She sighed. "What do we need to do then?"

"What I need to do is to get you a Syrian passport."

She looked at him incredulously. "You can do that?"

"Probably." He got to his feet and smiled. "I'll get back to you."

Tony leaned against the wall of the museum corridor and put through a call.

"Mr. Carlisle, can we meet?"

There was a pause on the phone before Carlisle's distinctive voice came through. "May I recommend the Tate Gallery on Millbank? The Turner exhibition is exceptional. Look for his painting of Norham castle at sunrise. I'll see you there in an hour."

True to his word, Carlisle was seated on a bench in front of Turner's painting. He had his hands pushed deep into his overcoat pockets.

As Tony sat down, he spoke. "William Turner trail-blazed his own way. That's why many consider him to be the father of modern art. I think they're right. But what I particularly enjoy is his lack of clarity, the ambiguity of much of his work." He nodded toward the picture in front of him. "This picture is a classic example, and it's one of my favorites. It matches my own world—a world of mists and unknowns." He paused. "What can I do for you?"

"I need a Syrian passport with these details on it." He handed Carlisle an envelope. There's a picture of a woman in there that has to be on it."

Carlisle took the envelope without a word. "Is there anything I should know?"

"Not at this stage."

Carlisle nodded, got to his feet, and ambled away.

Chapter 19

Israel

Professor Yoseh Shalev eased himself behind the wheel of the car and smiled at Chelsea and Tony. "Welcome to Jerusalem, the most contested and fought-over city in the world."

Chelsea was not quite sure how to respond. "I'm not sure whether to say, 'it's a pleasure, or to commiserate,'" she said.

The professor's expansive belly jiggled as he laughed. "Here, you can do both. We live with ambiguity."

It was evening in Jerusalem, and therefore the view out of the car window was limited. Nonetheless, Chelsea could see enough to feel the wonder of being in a city that had such a rich and violent history. No less than three of the world's religions vied for ownership of its heritage.

Chelsea was sitting beside the professor in the front seat. She noted that the professor was wearing the traditional Jewish skullcap, the *yarmulke*, but was also wearing a silver crucifix around his neck. She asked him about it.

"Ah, Chelsea…may I call you Chelsea?"

"Of course."

"Please call me Yoseh." He paused. "I am a Messianic Jew—in other words, I am a Christian Jew."

She couldn't constrain herself from probing deeper. "Which one comes first?"

The professor waggled a forefinger. "Ah, you Westerners: you always want to pigeon-hole everything. You are in Israel now. The thinking here is more contextual and untidy. I am both a Christian first and a Jew first." He grinned. "That means I am doubly a child of the covenant."

The professor pointed out some key landmarks as they threaded their way through the city. Chelsea craned her neck, trying to catch what it was he was pointing to.

"I'm looking forward to learning more of the city's history while I am here," she said.

The professor's countenance became thoughtful. "Most of the world simply has an academic curiosity about history. But for us Jews, the issue is whether we will survive history." He paused. "So you will not be surprised to learn that history has great significance for us."

Not much was said for the next few minutes.

The professor broke the silence and spoke over his shoulder. "And what do you do, Tony? What is your interest in being here?"

"I'm here merely as Chelsea's assistant." Tony cleared his throat. "She had a pretty tough time of it in Syria, so the British Museum has sent me with her to do the fetching and carrying for her."

Chelsea winced at the implication she needed such help, but stayed mute, acknowledging there was more than a little truth to his statement.

The professor continued. "Well, I hope you take time to learn a little about our historical discoveries while you are here. They ought to be of significance to you."

"Oh. Why's that?"

"Because this country was the cradle for the Christian culture that has underpinned your English civility for centuries."

Tony laughed. "We've not always been very civil."

"It's relative. And we certainly haven't shown much civility here in Jerusalem, either. But if you look beyond religious denominations squabbling over ownership of gaudy sacred sites, and the peddling of superstitions and questionable historical claims, you will find true history here, and be enriched by it."

"And you think that's important?"

The professor stroked his beard. "Oh yes. Christianity is not a philosophy that has developed over the years. It is not, for example, one that has depended on someone's claimed revelations whilst meditating somewhere. It is something based on concrete historical events." He wagged his forefinger. "This is Christianity's great strength. But it is also something that makes it very vulnerable."

"Why's that?"

"Because if it can be shown to be factually incorrect historically —Christianity collapses like a pack of cards."

The professor pulled up in front of a white, sliding security gate. "You're both staying here at the Pilgrim Guest House in St. George's College." He smiled. "You'll find it very Anglican...very polite. They're heavily into interfaith dialogue, reconciliation programs, and guided pilgrimages."

Chelsea looked up at the soaring tower of St. George's cathedral within its grounds. It could have been transplanted straight from England. She was slightly more thoughtful when she saw the high stone wall with wire security fencing on top surrounding the site. It was a reminder, if she needed it, that she was once again in a volatile area of the Middle East.

Once they drove into the grounds, Chelsea appreciated the spacious, middle-eastern feel, and the genteel quality of St. George's College. A garden with paved walkways had been tastefully laid out, seeking to advertise a peace that was hard to find outside its walls.

The professor wheeled Chelsea's suitcase into the front foyer as he spoke. "St. George's is just ten minutes from the Damascus gate near the Temple Mount." He stood Chelsea's case upright. "If you walk to the Old Jewish Quarter of the city tomorrow morning, you'll have a wonderful view of the Temple Mount and our famous Wailing Wall." He smiled. "Right, I'll see you tomorrow at dinner. The campus of the Hebrew University you'll be speaking at tomorrow night is quite close by, so we'll eat there before you speak. I'll pick you up at five."

Tony took off his sunglasses, ostensibly to give them a clean. In reality he was using the pretext to stare at the reflection in them of the scene behind. A man's head poked out momentarily from the street corner. It was the third time Tony had noticed him.

Chelsea was standing beside him, blithely innocent of everything. She was standing at an iron balustrade looking over the Tyropoeon Valley to the Wailing Wall that marked the Western end of the mighty platform that had once formed the base for Herod's temple. Devout Jews were bobbing their heads in prayer as they stood in front of it.

"There used to be a saying: 'Those who have not seen Herod's temple have not seen anything beautiful,'" she said.

Tony was only half listening. But he did notice that Chelsea's voice had become quite husky. "There's certainly not much of it left now," he replied.

"No, sadly." She sighed, then smiled. "It was said that so much incense was used in the temple that it caused the goats for miles about to sneeze." Chelsea swallowed and coughed. "Have you got a throat lozenge?"

"No."

"My throat is feeling wretched."

At this point, Tony felt obliged to share his growing misgivings with Chelsea.

"Chelsea, don't panic and don't look round. But I think we are being followed. I'm a bit unsure of what's going on. Do you mind if we move on from here?"

She started with surprise. "Sure," she said. "Are we in danger?" Her voice was more of a croak.

"I don't know. Let's head back into the old Jewish quarter. It's a maze in there, and we may be able to shake them."

Tony led the way, walking purposefully but not so fast as to attract attention. Before long they were making their way down narrow laneways lined with ancient stone buildings with shuttered windows and air conditioning units displaying various degrees of rust. Everything was bewilderingly similar but ever changing. All of the buildings seemed to be built of limestone. The plazas were paved with limestone, and the alleyways were surfaced either with limestone or granite. Here and there, some trees had been planted in the plazas that dared to introduce some contrast to the pale white rock. Tony wondered how they survived.

He towed Chelsea down one alleyway, then another. Some of the alleyways had aerial walkways above them. Occasionally they had to step back and make way for a scooter whizzing past or a group of chattering children. He paused to give way to one group, and was in time to see not just one man following them, but two.

Tony grabbed Chelsea's hand and hauled her into a side alley. He was now hopelessly lost and running on instinct. There were steps, arches, domes, and ancient churches everywhere.

He dived into another alley, turned a corner, and found to his horror that it ended in a stolid building with a blue door, which was firmly shut. They were trapped.

The two men had now been joined by a third. All of them were wearing casual jackets with suspicious bumps at their hips as they came round the corner.

Chelsea was leaning on a buttress fighting for breath—obviously in some distress.

One of the men spoke. "I think we've all had enough of these fun and games, don't you?" He smiled, but his humor didn't touch his eyes. "We are from the government, and we'd like to have a little word with you." He paused. "We have a car not far from here. It will take us to a quiet place where we can talk. Then you'll be returned to St. George's College so you, Dr. Thompson, will be in time for your lecture tonight."

The car journey was brief. It pulled into the underground

garage of a featureless white, building. Two of the men opened the door for them and shepherded them inside. They were taken upstairs, along a corridor to a small conference room.

A man was sitting half way along the table. He was slim with graying hair and had a deeply tanned face. He could have been forty or sixty. He looked up when they arrived and said, "Would you like some tea?"

Tony answered for both of them. "No thanks." In situations like this, Tony always wanted to know what he was drinking. He couldn't help but feel, however, that Chelsea could use a drink. "Why are we here?" he asked.

The man leaned on his elbows and joined his hands together. "Not to talk to you, Mr. Patterson, but to talk with Dr. Thompson."

"What about?" said Chelsea huskily.

For a long while, the man said nothing. He steepled his fingers. "Let's just say that we are expressing a keen interest in your work, and in any discoveries you may have made." He gestured toward the chairs opposite him. "Please, sit down."

Tony and Chelsea did so.

"My government…"

Tony interrupted him. "By which you mean the Israeli government."

"Er, yes." The man drew a breath. "My government would be most keen to locate twelve tablets that were offered for sale by a dealer at Tell Mardikh a month ago." He paused. "We have reason to believe you might have come in contact with them."

Chelsea answered without prevarication. "Yes, I did have the tablets. They were actually secreted away in our luggage without us knowing. I still don't know the details of how or why." Chelsea's voice was barely a whisper.

The man looked over at one of the three men who had accompanied them to the room. They had remained standing. "For goodness sake, get Dr. Thompson a glass of water."

The man left and returned with a glass of water. It even had ice in it.

Tony watched Chelsea drink gratefully from it.

"Do go on, Dr. Thompson."

Chelsea shrugged. "There's not much more to say. The suitcase with the tablets was stolen from me the third night I was back in the UK. I now have no idea where they are."

"Stolen?"

"Yes."

A long silence ensued.

"Do you have any capacity to help these tablets become, er, unstolen?"

"What do you mean?"

"I do not wish to trifle with you Dr. Thompson, but on the face of it, your story sounds very lame."

Chelsea said nothing.

The man continued. "Do you know the significance of the tablets?"

She nodded. "They are grammar tablets which have Eblaite cuneiform on one side, and its translation in Sumerian cuneiform on the other. They would be of inestimable value in giving a definitive translation of the 2,000 tablets recovered from Ebla."

The man nodded. "And now even more have been found, I understand."

"Yes. Another 465."

"It's a pity the Syrians won't let us see them." He paused. "Do you suspect they might have taken your tablets?"

"I have spoken to Major General Abbas Shamon, the Syrian officer in charge of the dig. He assures me he hasn't got them." She paused. "He's just as keen to get hold of them as you."

The man nodded. "I have no doubt that he is." He leaned back in his chair. "I think that is all we need to talk about today."

"We are free to go?" asked Tony.

"Of course. You always were." The man held up a finger. "But let me say this: If you were to come by these tablets again, my government would respond with considerable gratitude if you were able to let us see them." He handed Chelsea a card with a telephone number written on it. The man had written his name underneath, 'Mr. Cohen.'

He stood up from his seat. "I hope everything is perfectly clear."

"Perfectly," wheezed Chelsea.

Mr. Cohen nodded to the three men standing at the end of the room. "Please take Dr. Thompson and Mr. Patterson back to St. Georges."

Chapter 20

Professor Shalev looked at Chelsea with alarm. "Don't say anything. Just rest your voice as much as you can before the lecture. Tony and I will do the talking."

Chelsea nodded, gratefully.

The three of them were in the staff dining room of the Hebrew University. The meal consisted of crème of celery soup, followed by a main course of fish. Ordinarily, Chelsea would have loved it. But her laryngitis—and she was in no doubt now that it was laryngitis, took the edge off it. And if that wasn't enough, the menthol throat lozenge she was sucking most certainly did.

She leaned back in her chair and let the conversation flow over her.

The professor turned to Tony. "The Department of Archaeology here was established largely due to the initiative of Professor Eleazer Sukenick. He was one of the first academics to recognize the importance of the Dead Sea Scrolls."

Tony was listening politely. "I can't imagine there are many more crucial places to do archaeology than Israel."

The professor leaned back. "I wonder if you are familiar with Sukenick's greatest discovery."

"What was that?"

"In 1941, he was working with his assistant, Nahman Avigad, excavating the tombs of the Kidron Valley beside the Temple Mount. They discovered a tomb that had been blocked by a large closing stone. When they explored it, they found eleven stone ossuary boxes containing bones of those who had died. Because of the war, the professor documented his findings, and the artifacts were stored away."

"What happened then?"

The professor smiled. "For some reason, Sukenick's findings were not made public until 1962. But when they were, it caused a sensation. The side of one ossuary box was inscribed with the words, 'Simon Alexander,' and below that, the words, 'son of Simon.' The lid of the same box was inscribed 'of Alexander' in Greek...and below it, in small Hebrew letters, a misspelling of the word 'Cyrenian.'"

Chelsea could see that Tony was trying to remember something. He was holding a knuckle against his forehead. "All of this sounds a bit familiar."

"It should do," said the professor. "Archaeologists have concluded that it is highly probable these bones were those of the son of the man forced to carry the crossbeam of Jesus' cross." The professor fished out a pocket copy of the New Testament and flicked over the pages. Then he read:

A certain man from Cyrene, Simon, the father of Alexander and Rufus, was passing by on his way in from the country, and they forced him to carry the cross.

He looked up at Tony. "That's in Mark's gospel, chapter fifteen."

Tony blew out his cheeks. "I'd no idea it was all..." he seemed lost for words.

"What?" prompted the professor.

"Historical," finished Tony.

The professor laid a hand on Tony's shoulder. "Now you are beginning to appreciate the importance of history here."

Chelsea had an impending sense of doom regarding her ability to deliver her lecture. As they walked over to the lecture hall, she tugged at Tony's sleeve, and hissed. "I can't do it, Tony.

I've almost completely lost my voice." She was barely audible, even to herself.

Tony came to a halt and rubbed his forehead. Then he looked at her and shocked her by saying, "No, I don't think you can. Let me do it for you. Give me your notes."

She shook him by the arm. "You can't," she whispered furiously. "The notes are really rough. You won't be able to read them."

He put a hand on her shoulder. "I'll be okay…and I've seen the visuals of your presentation. You showed me on the plane, remember?"

They were running late, and the lecture theater was more than two-thirds full when they arrived. The professor took Chelsea's memory stick to the projectionist then turned round and gave her the thumbs up.

Chelsea slumped back into a chair at the back of the auditorium, closed her eyes, and waited for the train wreck.

The professor walked down to the front and tapped her on the shoulder to warn her things were about to start.

She experienced a moment of terror and danced at Tony. He was standing in the aisle. Tony caught the professor by the arm and whispered to him.

The professor frowned, nodded, then continued his way to the podium.

"Distinguished guests; Ladies and Gentlemen. Welcome to tonight's presentation on the archaeological work being done at Ebla in Syria. The talk tonight was to be given by Dr. Chelsea Thompson, but sadly, she is suffering from laryngitis. As such, her able assistant has stepped in at the last minute…" he paused, "the very last minute, to give us our talk. Please welcome Mr. Tony Patterson."

Chelsea put her head in her hands.

There was some polite clapping.

Tony surveyed the audience and began to speak.

"In 1964 a young graduate of Rome University, Paolo Matthiae and his team uncovered the remains of an ancient city near Tell Mardikh, a town thirty kilometers south of Aleppo. It was a discovery that proved that the Levant was, at one time, the center of an ancient, centralized civilization that was equal to Egypt and Mesopotamia. Paolo had discovered the kingdom of Ebla, a kingdom that can justifiably be called the first recorded world power."

Chelsea frowned. This was Tony as she'd never heard him. Much of what he was saying wasn't even in her notes. How on earth…? She leaned forward and continued to listen.

"Paolo's team uncovered an ancient library of wooden shelves that had been stacked with clay tablets with a cuneiform writing, writing that had never been seen before. The shelves had long since collapsed and rotted away, but the tablets remained in their stacks, waiting to be understood." Tony paused as a new picture came up on the screen.

"Matthiae called in the help of Giovanni Pettinato, an Italian epigrapher who specialized in interpreting ancient inscriptions. He already understood Sumerian cuneiform, but he realized he was looking at an entirely new language that he called Eblaite. Eblaite is now recognized as the oldest known Semitic language. Let me tell you what was discovered."

Chelsea shook her head. Tony was unbelievable. His presentation was superb, far better than she could have imagined.

Finally, Tony brought his presentation to an end.

"Let me close by bringing you up to date with the findings of the World Archaeological Congress when it had a brief window of opportunity to revisit the site during a ceasefire between Syrian government troops and the Jihadists. I'm afraid the news is not good. There has been much looting and vandalism. But there has been another significant find. More clay tablets with Eblaite cuneiform writing have been found. These tablets have been taken to Damascus—a place not easy for international scholars to access." He paused.

"It is thought that the kingdom of Ebla was all but wiped out by the Akkadian King, Naram-Sim, in 2250 BCE, and completely wiped out by the Hittites in 1600 BCE. Let us hope that war and politics don't wipe out the last memory we have of them today."

At the finish, Tony received generous applause.

The professor returned to the podium beaming, thanked Tony, and bade everyone good night.

Tony made his way to the back of the auditorium. He looked at her sheepishly.

She mimed and gesticulated with her hands, "How did you do that?"

Tony shrugged. "I probably should have told you. I studied Ancient Near Eastern Studies at University College, London, before I joined the army."

"What?" She said hoarsely. "You didn't think to tell me this?" She frowned. "Was all your apparent ignorance in the British Museum just feigned?"

Tony held his hands up. "No, no. Most of what you told me was new to me—fascinating actually, and I was grateful to learn it."

"But you studied Ebla at college?" she whispered.

"A bit. But I mainly focused on Akkadian, Assyrian, and Babylonian culture, so there's lots I don't know." He put a finger against her lips. "Now rest your voice. Stop speaking. Hopefully, you'll feel better in the morning."

She shook him by the arm in exasperation. "Have you got any more surprises for me, Tony?" she croaked.

Tony was pleased that the next two days were fairly gentle for Chelsea. She stayed in her room for most of the time, presumably preparing for the conference. Just occasionally, she ventured out to the gardens of St. Georges.

Professor Shalev managed to get time off on the second day and volunteered to walk with Tony to the Damascus Gate, and on down Al-Wad Street to the Western Wall.

It seemed to Tony that Al-Wad Street was one long continuous bazaar. Store-holders sold everything imaginable under the archways and canopies of the stone-paved street. It made for a colorful and cheerful scene. Sometimes the laneway narrowed and buried itself under ancient buildings whose history Tony could only guess at.

Eventually, they emerged at the Western Wall.

The professor spoke. "I apologize I can't be with you very long and give you an extensive tour," he said. "I'll have to leave you here. Our first semester has only just started, so these first few weeks are bit busy."

"You have a different academic calendar to the West, then."

"Yes we do. We operate on a Jewish calender."

The professor pointed to what was left of Herod's temple platform. "Mount Moriah is under that platform. That was where God provided a sheep for Abraham to sacrifice, so he wouldn't have to sacrifice his son." He nodded, as if to himself. "Centuries later, God provided Jesus, the 'lamb of God' to die for the sins of humanity on the same spot." He paused. "It seems that God does nothing in the New Testament that he hasn't first prefigured in the Old Testament."

"I suppose that puts you in the box seat as a Messianic Jew. You can see things from both perspectives."

"Yes, I suppose it does." The professor smiled. "Are you confident you can find your own way back?"

Tony nodded. "I'll be fine. Thanks."

The professor waved goodbye and was soon lost in the crowds, leaving Tony to wrestle with the disturbing reality of history.

He didn't, however, give himself the luxury of dwelling on things metaphysical for very long. There were things to do. He walked south to the Dung Gate in the southern city wall and caught a taxi to an address in the Mekor Haim district, about two miles south of the Temple Mount. It was the address of a metal foundry that specialized in aluminum casting.

Chelsea looked at her watch. Tony would be away until lunchtime. That meant she had three hours to do what she wanted to do.

As she contemplated what she'd planned, she found it impossible not to feel a pang of guilt that she was doing something behind Tony's back. She chewed her bottom lip and reasoned with herself that the situation they were facing was entirely due to her actions. As such, she should take responsibility for it. The more she could distance Tony from events the better.

Feeling only marginally better, she took out the card Mr. Cohen had given her from her purse and rang the number.

It took some time before the phone was answered. When it was, Chelsea spoke quickly. "Mr. Cohen; this is Dr. Chelsea Thompson. Forgive me for whispering, but I have laryngitis." She paused. "Can we meet up? I have a proposition for you."

His answer was immediate. "Of course. When?"

"Now, if possible."

"Where are you?"

"At St. George's College."

"A car will come for you. I'll phone you when it's at the front gate."

Twenty minutes later, the phone call came through, and she made her way down the driveway to the white security gate. The guard on duty gave her a friendly wave as he opened it for her.

As she walked through, a man got out of the front seat of a black saloon car and opened the rear door for her. She recognized him as one of the men she had seen the day before.

She looked inside the car and saw Mr. Cohen already seated in the back seat.

"Good morning, Dr. Thompson. Where would you like to go so we can have a quiet chat?"

The question momentarily threw Chelsea off balance. "I don't much care where," she said. "I don't know Jerusalem well enough to make a suggestion."

Mr. Cohen nodded. "Then why don't I take you to Gethsemane." He smiled. "It is an apt place to wait and contemplate options before the main drama." Cohen seemed pleased with his humor.

Chelsea didn't share it.

The car burrowed its way through the morning traffic, and

before long was motoring up the east side of the Kidron Valley. From what she could see, much of the area below the road was given over to graveyards. It wasn't the friendliest of sights.

Mr. Cohen gave a command in Hebrew, and the car pulled into a parking area reserved for tourist buses. Many of them were already parked along the road and were disgorging their passengers. Seeing the brutal face of commercialism in a place of such religious significance left Chelsea with a vague feeling of disappointment. However, before she could interrogate her feelings further, Mr. Cohen issued another order, and the two men sitting in the front seat got out of the car. They lounged against the bonnet. One of them took out a packet of cigarettes.

Nothing was said for a while. Mr. Cohen seemed to be in no hurry and gave Chelsea time to order her thoughts.

After a minute or so, she turned and faced Mr. Cohen.

His face remained impassive. "What can I do for you, Dr. Thompson?"

Chelsea drew in a deep breath. "I can give you laser scanned, high quality images of the 465 clay tablets recently found at Ebla."

The man nodded. "And why would you do that?"

"I would give them in return for you confessing to the world that you obtained them covertly though your own, er...devices." She hurried on. "And in a gesture of good will, you have made this information available to the British Museum."

Mr. Cohen's expression did not change. "Tell me why my government would agree to say such a thing?"

Chelsea drew a deep breath. "Because I am also going to give you my personal photographs of six of the twelve grammar tablets from Tell Mardikh which you have been trying to get your hands on."

She was gratified to see a spark of interest finally penetrate Mr. Cohen's bland expression. "You have these photos?"

"Yes, but not with me."

Cohen nodded. "We came close to getting the tablets in Tell Mardikh, but the dealer was, er...uncooperative." He tapped a finger against his lips. "Why will you not give me photos of the other six?"

"Because I might need to buy your help again."

"That may prove very frustrating."

"You will still have enough information to help you make the greatest breakthrough in archaeology in decades." She paused. "At the moment, you have nothing."

"I may not agree to help you unless I get pictures of all twelve."

Chelsea shrugged. "Then, nobody wins."

Cohen remained silent. He joined his hands together and tapped his forefingers against his lips. Eventually, he said, "You have raised a very interesting proposition."

"I need an answer."

"I take it that the British Museum were actually the ones responsible for getting the illicit scans of the Ebla tablets."

Chelsea nodded. "It is probably more accurate to say that a branch of the British Museum operated independently to obtain them."

"Hmm. So you want to shift the blame from the British Museum to Mossad." He laughed quietly. "Israel is already a sworn enemy of much of the Islamic world, so I don't suppose that would change much."

Chelsea was watching Cohen closely for any signs of prevarication or deception—not that she was confident of being able to spot it if it was there. "Do we have an agreement?" she asked brutally.

Cohen folded his hands together, closed his eyes, and leaned back in his seat. He stayed like that for five minutes.

Chelsea wanted to scream.

Finally he opened his eyes and smiled. "I need to make some phone calls. Why don't you get out and admire the view?"

Chelsea nodded and got out of the car. She gazed across the Kidron Valley at the terracing rising up to the eastern wall of the Temple Mount. The gold dome of the 'Dome of the Rock' could be seen just peeking over the top. The Islamic shrine seemed to gleam its defiance against all things Jewish. She shook her head. This city had seen so much fighting and death—and it didn't look like ending any time soon.

It was a full thirty minutes before the back window of the car slid down and Mr. Cohen called out to her. "Dr. Thompson; let's resume our chat."

She got back into the car and waited for him to speak.

He didn't keep her waiting. "Yes. We have an agreement."

Chelsea slowly expressed a breath of air.

"Thank you. That is very helpful."

Cohen looked at her, his face again without expression. "But I suspect that is not all you want to ask me."

Chelsea was mortified that she was so transparent. "No it's not. There are a couple of other things I need your help with."

Chapter 21

It was a fresh November morning, but the sun was valiantly beating back the chill on what promised to be a splendid autumn day. Tony was ambling with Chelsea along the stone-paved walkways between the garden beds of St. George's College. Someone had left some plastic chairs outside in the sun beside a pseudo-Gothic colonnade. Tony pointed to them, and they both sat down.

"How's the voice?" he asked.

"Much better…and it needs to be. Professor Shalev has organized for me to give a presentation after lunch…" she smiled, "unless you want to do it for me."

Tony lifted up his hands in surrender. "Once is enough. Who are you speaking to this time?"

"It's a small select group…invitation only. He's pulled together all the specialists in Levant archaeology. Each one is a leader in their field."

Tony nodded. "It's going to be a busy day for you with all we've got planned—not to mention the official opening of the conference and reception tonight. Are you sure you're up for it?"

Chelsea leaned back and allowed the sun to play on her face. "I have to be."

Tony could see the strain in her face and wished he could do more to alleviate it. "You don't have to go through with this, you know. I do have another option…another plan."

"Will it result in us getting the scanner?"

"Probably. Possibly."

Chelsea shook her head. "If it's just probably, we have to run with the plan we've got."

Tony stared moodily at a blue jay that had parked itself on a garden bed wall. Somewhere in the background a warbler was singing. He envied the bird its optimism.

In truth, he was in torment wondering whether he should admit to the fact that he had Mahdi's twelve tablets, and that they could be traded with Abbas Shamon in return for the scanner—if he was agreeable to the swap. He sighed. The trouble was, there were too many 'ifs.'

Chelsea had nearly been told of the tablets a few days ago in London. Beanie had rung him in the British Museum to say that he was on the point of telling her about them, but had missed the opportunity. He'd asked Tony to tell her instead, saying that he feared Chelsea's wrath.

Personally, Tony wanted the tablets to be in the custody and care of the British Museum. It was difficult to think of any organization that had proved itself to be as responsible with its care of artifacts and was truly international in its outlook. It sat above brawling children like a benevolent parent. Even as he had the thought, he winced. He was glad he didn't have to voice his convictions out loud. It would be difficult to do so without sounding patronizing or as if he were advocating for some form of imperialist colonialism. He shook his head. Real life was complicated.

Tony stretched his legs out in front of him and decided to play for time. "What will you be talking about after lunch?"

Chelsea stopped nibbling at her bottom lip. "I think it's time to end all this secrecy. It's causing, or has caused, too much drama."

She looked up at Tony. "I want to tell people about Mahdi's twelve tablets and enlist their help in trying to track them down."

Tony raised his eyebrows and managed to say nothing.

Chelsea continued. "As good as my photos are, they are not the real thing." She shrugged. "Photos can be doctored…and when it comes to deciphering cuneiform writing, every scratch and fleck of clay needs to be super clear to give confidence that the right translation has been given."

Tony wondered idly what sort of definition the laser scans would give of the tablets. Beanie had assured him that every grain of sand and silt in the clay would show up. He hoped it was true.

"Will you tell them that you have photographs of the tablets?"

Chelsea shook her head. "Not yet."

"Why?"

"I want to leave them with the maximum motivation for finding the tablets."

Tony smiled. "There's a sneaky side to you, Chelsea Thompson, that I'm only just beginning to appreciate."

She managed a grin.

After lunch, they were again in a lecture theater at the Hebrew University, but this one was very much smaller.

Tony watched Chelsea from a seat in the back row as she gave her presentation.

He smiled. Chelsea certainly cut an imposing figure. Energy and passion seemed to radiate from her as she spoke about the research and discoveries at Ebla. She was also beautiful to look at. Tony very much suspected that the men in the audience were captivated by her personality and looks every bit as much as by her words. He smiled, and knew himself to be a lucky man.

Chelsea finally brought her presentation to a close.

"Somewhere out there, are the twelve looted tablets which could provide the key to unlocking the secrets of the Ebla tablets." She paused. "They could provide the biggest archaeological break-through we've had in decades." Chelsea allowed time for the full import of her words to sink in. Then she reached down to a bag she'd placed by her feet and pulled out the broken corner of one of Mahdi's tablets.

"All I've got of the physical tablets is this." She lifted up the stone for all to see. "It's all I've got to give me hope. I call it my 'Syrian stone.'"

She then invited those present to come up and examine it.

After everyone was settled again. She said. "So keep your ears and eyes open. Let's agree to share any information that may come our way concerning this. All of you in this room are key players in the Levant archaeological world. One of you is bound to come across the tablets at some stage."

Tony dropped his head. She had no idea how true her statement was.

As he pondered the rich ironies of life, Tony came to a decision. He would wait a few days and see how things played out. There was always the option of producing the tablets if the need became dire, and he had gone to some lengths to organize things so that this would be possible. The one thing he wanted to avoid was for Chelsea to be hurt because people thought she had custody of them.

Then, of course, there was the small issue of confessing to Chelsea that it was he who had stolen the tablets. He sighed. How would that affect their budding romance?

Abbas felt distinctly odd flying into Ben Gurion Airport. It was a few miles southeast of Tel Aviv, and just 28 miles northwest of Jerusalem. It seemed that nowhere was very far from anywhere in Israel. He was entering the land of a people he'd been taught to hate—and he had, except for one notable exception.

Abbas reflected on the vagaries of history. Despite its diminutive size, Israel had dared to triumph and thrive. The tiny nation had grown to become a thorn in the side of Islam. He wondered how God had let that be possible.

Abbas tried to remember where the antipathy between Jews and

Islam had begun. The Qur'an indicated that Mohammad had become increasingly hostile toward Jews during his lifetime—even allowing 600 of them to be beheaded after the Battle of the Trench in 627. The charge against them was that they had behaved treasonably. Abbas rubbed the side of his nose. They probably had.

The plane landed with a squeal of tires and taxied to the terminal.

Inside the terminal building, security was intense. Israel Police, Israel Defense Force, and Border Police were all in evidence. Abbas was not greatly surprised. The airport had been the target of several terrorist attacks. He looked around him, hoping to find something to criticize. Sadly, the arrival hall was built to impress. Striated columns soared upward into the high ceiling, making the hall look like an ancient temple. Abbas still managed a sniff of derision.

As he stood in the queue waiting to clear customs, he reflected on his next meeting with Chelsea Thompson and what might transpire.

Chelsea, who looked so much like Sara, it was bewildering—or was it just his grief? His wife had also looked a bit like Sara. That was probably why he'd married her.

He rubbed his chin. Would Chelsea play ball? Was there a chance he could rescue his career if it became known that people other than Syrians had the information on the 465 new tablets?

Abbas turned his thoughts to Tony Patterson. What did he know about the tablets? He suspected that Patterson knew a great deal more than Chelsea realized. The man was dangerous. His instinct told him that.

Finally, it was his turn to be processed by customs. An officer examined his passport and then summoned another officer across.

Abbas groaned inwardly. The last thing he wanted now was difficulty with the customs.

The new officer called him across to a table and asked him to open his cases.

Abbas did so, with ill grace.

The man pointed to the scanner nested in one of the cases. "What is this?"

"It is a radiation unit used to sterilize archaeological artifacts. This unit is going on display at the conference of the World Archaeological Congress in Jerusalem."

The man nodded and asked for the keys.

Abbas handed them to him.

After turning to talk to a colleague, the security man relocked the cases and returned the keys to Abbas.

A short time later, Abbas walked through the exit gate. It had the words 'Welcome' written above it in both English and Hebrew.

'Welcome.' He shook his head. Impossible. This was Israel.

As he waited for a taxi, he put a call through to Chelsea Thompson.

When she answered, he didn't bother to introduce himself. "Have you got the tablets?"

"No. But I want to talk with you."

Just hearing her voice made him feel heady. But he needed to be brutal. "Why?" he demanded.

"To reason with you."

With a sinking feeling in the pit of his stomach, he heard himself say, "There will be no reasoning; no talking."

"Please," Chelsea pleaded.

Abbas spoke over the top of her. "No, no no. There will be no talking, Dr. Thompson. I'm going to bring hell down upon your ears. Do you hear that? Hell. I'll be talking to the press at 9am tomorrow, unless you arrange for me to have the tablets."

He ended the call, cutting her protestations off in mid sentence.

His free hand was balled into a fist, and he wanted to throw his phone into the gutter. But after weighing it in his hands, he put it in his pocket.

Abbas was cross with himself. He knew he'd let his anger...or more accurately, his emotions, run ahead of him without adequate control. Chelsea Thompson seemed to have that effect on him. He sighed. But it was too late now. The die was cast.

Once he was settled in the back seat of his taxi, he took out his phone again and placed a call to *The Jerusalem Post*, and then another to the *Haaretz News* in Tel Aviv. Finally, he rang the Arab newspaper, *Al-Ittihad* in Haifa. Abbas asked them to be present at 9am next day at the Syrian stand in the display hall of the WAC conference. He promised it would be worth their while.

Chelsea closed her eyes and leaned back against the headrest of the car. She was already exhausted having given her presentation. It was not a good omen, for she had yet to play her part in the main action planned for the day.

Tony had hired the car and was driving her from the University to the conference center.

"I'm not sure I'm up for all this," she said.

"Then don't do it. I've got another plan."

She waved a hand, irritably. "No. I've come this far. I have to go through with it now."

"Only if you're sure." He paused. "Just remember; you've got a number of jumping off points."

She forced a smile. "And I've got you."

He nodded. "Yes you have. I'll never be far away."

Tony dropped her at the conference center, and went off to park the car.

She made her way to the display hall. People brushed past her with a preoccupied air as they put the last touches on their displays stands. She sought sanctuary with her colleagues at the stand being used by the British Museum. Their display featured the discovery of an untouched 4,400-year-old tomb at Saqqara in Egypt. It looked good. However, she had not come to the hall to view the exhibits of the British Museum. She had come to scope out the Syrian stand.

With a sense of unreality, she made her way through the hall until she spotted the Syrian stand. Two men, presumably local Arabs, were putting up the basic elements of the display. There wasn't much on show, just the black, white, and red flag of Syria with its two green stars in the middle and some photographs of Ebla. Nothing controversial was on display...yet.

She breathed a sigh of relief, but knew that the respite was temporary. The empty display boards stared at her threateningly. Abbas was, as expected, planning to put his posters up in the morning. One of the bare display boards had a table in front of it. It was not difficult for Chelsea to work out why. She shivered.

The Syrian stand had been crafted to look like a Bedouin tent. Under normal circumstances, she would have thought it was quite sweet.

She smiled at the two men working on the stand and searched around the tent for any sign of a case that might contain the scanner. All she saw was a large tubular carry-case that had been left at the back of the stand. It was locked with a tiny padlock. Chelsea had no doubt that it would contain slanderous posters that shrieked the duplicity and deceit of the British Museum.

Chelsea could see no sign of any case that might hold the scanner. She was not surprised. Abbas would keep that with him in his hotel room.

She waved farewell to the two men on the stand and headed out to the foyer.

Tony was lounging against the wall waiting for her.

Just seeing him, helped steady her nerves. She decided to make the most of the little surge of confidence and took out her phone.

The receptionist at the hotel Abbas Shamon was staying at, answered.

Chelsea moved herself close against Tony, feeling his strength, and spoke.

"Hello. My name is Mrs. Shamon. My husband is staying in room 414. I've had an appointment canceled that has allowed me to join him for the WAC conference. Will there be any problem with me booking in to join my husband this evening?"

"Not at all, Madam. We look forward to you staying with us. What time will you be arriving?"

"About 6pm."

"That will be fine, Madam. Have a good day."

Chapter 22

Chelsea returned to St. George's College and changed into a kaftan, headscarf, and a wide-brimmed hat. It was a slightly idiosyncratic combination, but a necessary one.

She was now back in the car with Tony, parked sixty yards away from the hotel where Abbas Shamon was staying.

"All set?" he asked.

She nodded, not trusting herself to say anything.

"Here's your passport."

Chelsea slapped her forehead. If it weren't for Tony, she would have left it behind in the car's console. She looked at its cover. It was dark blue like the British passports and was labeled 'Syrian Arab Republic.' in three languages. Underneath was the Syrian symbol— an eagle with spread wings.

She opened the passport to the front page. An image of a woman she had never met stared back at her. Chelsea looked at her guiltily and shut the passport quickly.

Tony got out of the car, opened the boot, and handed Chelsea her luggage. It was simply a lightweight hold-all containing a partly blow-up plastic swimming ring, and a large shoulder bag.

"Try and make it look heavy," he said. Then he leaned forward and kissed her on the cheek. "I'll be here waiting."

Before she could persuade herself to do otherwise, Chelsea squared her shoulders, and walked toward the steps of the hotel entrance.

Everything then seemed to take on a surreal, dreamlike quality. Only her rapid breathing reminded her that what she was doing was real.

She approached the reception desk, smiled, and handed over her passport. "Good evening. I rang earlier. I'm joining my husband in room 414."

"Certainly, madam. If you could just fill in your details here, that will be all." The young man handed her a form that asked for her personal details. Chelsea experienced a moment of panic. She forced herself back under control.

"May I see my husband's form? I want to check what bank account he is using."

The young man hesitated, and then nodded. "Of course." A moment later, he passed Abbas' form across to her.

She tried to keep her handwriting steady as she copied the details onto her own form.

The receptionist smiled. "Thank you." He handed back Chelsea's passport. "And here is your access card."

Chelsea nodded her thanks and turned to go.

The young man called after her. "Oh. One more thing."

Chelsea wanted to run.

"I presume you will be having breakfast with us."

"Yes. Yes, of course."

She headed toward the lifts.

The receptionist again called after her. "We can carry your luggage for you, Madam."

Chelsea waved a hand. "Don't worry, I can manage." She headed determinedly toward the lifts to forestall further conversation.

Make the bag look heavy.

In the lift, Chelsea experienced a few seconds of respite.

However, Tony had warned her that lifts also contained CCTV, so she needed to act the part at all times and ensure that her hat was always pulled well down on her head.

All too soon, the lift stopped at the fourth floor. Chelsea took a deep breath, levered herself off the wall of the lift, and stepped into the corridor.

Room 414 was just twenty yards away. This was a point of potential danger. There was a small chance Abbas had chosen not to attend the opening conference reception. If he had not, she reasoned that she could simply say she'd come to reason with him.

Chelsea knocked on the door.

There was no response.

She pressed the access card into the slot and pushed the door open.

Immediately, she could smell him. It was a very faint odor, but quite distinct. She hadn't consciously realized that he had a smell before. It was odd.

There was an open suitcase on a bench. It didn't look as if Abbas had unpacked much. She looked around anxiously for the other suitcase, the one Mossad had described to her. It was nowhere to be seen.

Panic started to rise up in her gullet. She forced herself back under control and opened the doors of the built-in wardrobes.

And there it was: sitting demurely at the bottom of a wardrobe.

With a sigh of relief, she tugged it into the room and unlocked it with the key given to her by one of Mr. Cohen's men. When she asked how he'd got it, the agent had been evasive, saying only that they'd managed to get a copy of it at the airport when Mr. Shamon arrived.

The big question was: Would the duplicate key work?

It did.

Chelsea eased back the lid and stared at the scanner nestled inside the case.

She saw that the alloy hood had been neatly cut in half. Beanie's circuitry and the workings for his hidden laser were laid bare for all to see. She gulped. It was brutally incriminating.

Chelsea lifted the unit out and placed it in the large shoulder bag she'd pulled from the hold-all. Then she deflated the plastic swimming ring and squashed it, together with the hold-all, into the shoulder bag as well.

To her eyes, the bag now looked way too full. She sighed. She would just have to brazen things out.

After everything was put away, she hoisted the bag over her shoulder and did a visual check that everything had been left as she'd found it.

Moments later she was back at the lifts.

The shoulder bag looked ridiculous. She shifted it to the other shoulder, the one that would be most hidden from the reception desk. Then she lectured herself as the lift descended. *Make the bag seem light. Make the bag seem light.*

The lift doors opened, and she headed resolutely for the main entrance.

No one challenged her.

Two minutes later, Tony was lifting the shoulder bag from her and stowing it in the trunk.

She wanted to hug him, to sing and dance…but Tony had told her of the importance of acting naturally.

But she'd done it. She lay back in her seat and gave a contented sigh.

"You're at a jumping off spot, Chelsea. This can be the point where you go no further, or you can…"

"…continue on," she finished.

"So, how are you feeling?"

"Wired. Scared. Elated."

"Ready to continue?"

After a short pause, Chelsea answered. "Yes."

Tony nodded. That meant he had to help keep her adrenaline up. Chelsea needed to be concerned enough so that she did her best, but not so scared that she felt overwhelmed. It was a delicate balance—and the point of balance was different for every person. He acknowledged that if the last twenty minutes had demonstrated anything, it was that Chelsea had both courage and the ability to think on her feet. He would have told her so if he didn't need to keep Chelsea focused and on edge.

"Use the adrenaline you're feeling," he said. "Let it keep you sharp. You've got two phases of this operation to go. Both are dangerous."

"Boy, you really know how to cheer a girl up."

"Are you scared?"

"Yes."

Tony nodded. "Good."

Chelsea rolled her eyes. "Good! Is that all you can say?"

Tony didn't let himself smile. "Get changed," he said.

For the next few minutes, Tony had his sensibilities challenged by Chelsea stripping herself of her kaftan. She pulled it over her head. Underneath it she was wearing an emerald green, slim fitting, cocktail dress. For a moment, it rose up her thigh.

Tony gulped.

Chelsea restored her modesty, commandeered the rear-view mirror, and began applying lipstick—bright red. It was the right color for Chelsea. It matched her personality.

Then she removed the birthmark on her neck.

When she'd finished, she slumped back into her seat.

Tony drove the car to the entrance of the venue where the delegate's reception was being held. No parking was allowed, so he was only able to drop her off.

He turned to Chelsea. "You are not badly late—probably only two champagnes behind everyone else." He paused. "All you need to do is to be seen. Don't try and do anything clever. Keep it simple."

Chelsea nodded. "What will you do?"

"I'll park nearby and have my phone ready." He allowed what he hoped was a reassuring smile. "I won't be far away."

Chelsea laid a hand briefly on his shoulder, then stepped out of the car.

Chelsea attached herself to a party of people in the foyer and slipped into the throng of delegates in the reception hall.

It was as well she did because she caught sight of Abbas standing fairly near the entrance. Fortunately he had his back to her and didn't see her.

After she judged she was far enough into the room, she turned and made her way back toward the entrance, making no effort to conceal herself.

This time, Abbas saw her. She saw his jaw stiffened as his eyes fixed themselves on her.

She lifted her chin, in what might have been a challenge.

Abbas then, very deliberately, turned his back on her.

Chelsea was relieved. The last thing she wanted was to have an argument with Abbas in a public place...or at all, if she was honest.

She melted back into the crowd.

A few minutes later, the MC called for order and introduced the city mayor, inviting him to give his speech of welcome.

After the speeches, the guests began to dissipate. A few stayed on, determined to make good use of the wine and champagne.

Chelsea put through a call to Tony.

"All's well so far. Shamon saw me, but we didn't speak."

"Excellent. I'll come to the door. I'm parked about two-hundred yards away. Give me five minutes. I'll come and walk you to the car."

When they both eventually arrived at the car, she saw that Tony had parked it under a tree, well away from any streetlights.

As she got in, Tony said, "You are at another jumping off spot, Chelsea. How are you feeling?"

She answered without hesitation. "I'm ready for more." Abbas' arrogance had irked her.

Tony nodded.

Chelsea removed her make-up and wriggled back into her kaftan. She handed Tony a make-up pencil. "Here, give me a birth-mark." She pointed to the spot on her neck.

Tony obliged. "I preferred you in the green dress," he said.

She couldn't resist a smile, but didn't give herself the luxury of dwelling on his comment.

Chelsea took out her phone and dialed the number of the conference organizer.

"Oh, hi," she said. "I'm with Major General Abbas Shamon from the Syrian delegation. Some of our material for the display stand has only just turned up. May I have permission to put it up right now?" She paused. "I do apologize. It is late, and I know the hall is closed."

"Yes madam, the hall is closed. You'll have to check with the security staff on duty. They may, or may not let you in. It depends how disruptive it is to their rosters and whether they can spare staff to supervise you."

"Thank you," said Chelsea. "I'm heading over to the hall now. Would it be possible for you to ring them and let them know I'm coming?"

"I suppose I could do that for you. Yes." The woman paused, then added. "Good luck."

"Thanks."

"Whew!" Chelsea threw herself back into her seat. She turned to Tony. "Are you planning to walk me to the display hall?"

"No. That might be dangerous. I'll shadow you."

Chelsea wasn't quite sure what that meant, but she nodded all the same. "Wish me luck."

Tony shook his head. "Luck is a treacherous companion. Do your best not to need it."

"Are you saying that to keep me wound up?"

"Yes."

She managed a smile and got out of the car. After pulling a tubular carry-case from the back seat, she walked toward the display hall.

A few minutes later, she was knocking on the door. She could see two security officers sitting at their booth just off the foyer. One of them answered the door.

"Hi," she said. "Did the conference office ring to say that I was coming over?"

The man nodded. "Yes, they did."

Chelsea showed the security officer her Syrian passport. "My husband is Major General Abbas Shamon. I've come with material that's just turned up for the Syrian stand. It should only take fifteen minutes to put up. Can you let me in?"

"Wait here," he said, and returned to his booth.

A few minutes later, he returned. "You're not a delegate here, ma'am. I'm not sure I can let you in."

A wave of anxiety washed through her. "No, but my husband is Major General Abbas Shamon. He is a delegate."

"It's most irregular, I'm not sure…"

At that point, their conversation was interrupted by a car speeding into the car park behind her. It came to a halt with a jerk. Three men got out of the car and walked toward the door of the display hall. Chelsea recognized two of them. They were Mr. Cohen's men.

The men showed the security officer their identification. When he saw it, the officer visibly shrank.

"What seems to be the matter here?" asked one of the men.

The security man bobbed obsequiously. "This lady is the wife of one of the Syrian delegates. She wants to come in and finish setting up a display stand. But she is not a delegate."

The Mossad agent scowled. "Oh, for goodness sake, man. Let her in. The last thing we need is to cause unnecessary drama with Syria. Use your common sense." The agent paused. "We are here to do a security sweep of the hall. This is an international event, and we can't afford for anything to go wrong. We shouldn't take long."

The security man returned to his booth where he switched off an alarm. Then he led them to the entrance door of the hall and turned on the lights.

"Thank you very much," said Chelsea.

The three Mossad men walked into the hall without a word and proceeded to inspect the stands on either side of the aisles.

Chelsea busied herself with pinning her posters onto the empty display boards at the Syrian stand. It did not take long, and she was pleased with the results. The posters spoke of the co-operation between the British Museum and the Syrian government in ensuring the newly discovered tablets were free of the MERS virus.

She made her way back to the foyer.

A few minutes later, the Mossad men joined her.

"We're finished," one of them said. "Please lock the place up, and let no one else come in until the morning. Is that clear?"

The security officer bobbed up and down. "Yes. Of course."

Chelsea had the Syrian tubular carry-case under her arm. "Thank you very much," she said, and made for the door. She was feeling euphoric. Five steps to go, before freedom. Four, three, two… A moment later she was outside.

A shadow detached itself from the shrubbery nearby, and a moment later Tony was at her side.

They walked together to the car.

"Whew!" said Chelsea, as she sat herself in the front seat. "What happens next?"

"Tony started the car. "We go to the offices of the British Consulate-General. I've got access to a safe there where we can store the scanner and the Syrian posters."

"What? At this time of night?"

Tony nodded. "I've got permission…and some of their staff are still on duty. It's less than a mile from St. Georges, so it's very convenient."

"And then what?"

"Bed."

"But I'm not ready for bed. I feel like partying." She danced her arms in the air.

Tony looked at her with a smile hovering on his lips. "Trust me. You're going to feel a horrible adrenaline let down in twenty minutes, and you're going to want to sleep."

Chapter 23

His children were calling him, their hands outstretched...but another invisible hand was drawing them further and further away. Abbas was banging his fists on the top of a coffin, screaming in protest.

With a snort, Abbas jerked himself awake.

It took a moment for him to realize that the banging still continued. Someone was knocking loudly on his door.

He blinked sleep from his eyes and groped for his watch. It was 6:30am. Who on earth would be banging on his door at this time of the day?

He got to his feet, blundered his way to the door, and swung it open.

Two stern police officers and a man in civilian clothing stood facing him.

"What is the meaning of this?" Abbas demanded.

The man in civilian clothing looked at him levelly. "Sir, we have reason to believe that you may be in possession of some stolen property."

Abbas scoffed. "That's absurd. You do realize that it is 6:30 in the morning? How dare you come barging in like this."

The man in plain-clothes answered him dryly. "We're quite aware of the time, sir. If you could step out of our way…" he pointed to the chair, "…and perhaps remain seated there. We'll do a quick search." He made no attempt to smile. "If we find nothing, we'll leave you in peace and be on our way."

Abbas waved his hand. "Search all you like." He plumped himself down on the seat and glowered at the policemen as they began searching his room.

One of them pulled out the case containing the scanner. "Do you have the keys for this, sir?" he asked.

Abbas got up, found his trousers, and fumbled in the pockets. "Here you are," he said, handing over the keys. He sat back down and massaged his forehead.

The policeman opened the case.

Abbas was mentally rehearsing what he would say to explain the significance of the scanner.

"Well, well," said the officer. "What do we have here?"

The officer's comment caused Abbas head to snap up. He stared at the case. For a moment, he experienced a moment of unreality, a moment of total confusion. Abbas furrowed his brow.

There, in the center of the case, lay the corner of a clay tablet with cuneiform writing on it. He recognized it instantly.

"I'm afraid, sir," said the plain-clothed man, "that we will have to take you in for questioning. Please get dressed and come with us."

Abbas sat in the police interview room. Its starkness was oppressive. He'd been there for nearly two hours, and in that time he'd only been given a cup of instant coffee and a sandwich.

The full import of what was happening dawned on him as he waited. He paced up and down the room in a lather of fury.

Finally, the plain-clothes man and a uniformed police officer entered the room.

Abbas looked at them both with ill-concealed exasperation.

"Finally. It's about time. You do realize that I have to be at a press briefing at nine o'clock?"

"That may have to wait, sir," said the plain-clothed man.

Abbas threw back his head and groaned. "Have you spoken to the hotel staff and viewed their CCTV footage?"

"We have." The policeman paused. "We have also been shown a booking-in form that was filled in by your wife."

Abbas' eyes opened wide. Then he said through gritted teeth. "My wife has been dead for six years. What are you talking about?"

"I'm sorry to hear that sir." The policeman looked down at the notes. "We'll have to check that of course." He tapped the end of a pencil on the table. "Has anything been stolen from your room?"

"Yes," said Abbas. "I've been trying to tell you. A radiation unit. It was in the case."

"Do you have any proof of that, sir?"

Abbas threw himself back in his chair. "No."

The officer nodded. "I'm sure you appreciate our position. We want to show the utmost courtesy to the Syrian government. After all, this could blow up into a nasty international incident." He smiled. "I think we both want to avoid that. But if we are to do so, we need to double-check the facts, and that will take a number of phone calls—some of them international. It may take time." He got up to leave.

"But I don't have time. I have to get back to the conference," said Abbas, getting to his feet.

"For your press conference?"

"Yes."

The interviewing officer shook his head. "I'm afraid you're going to miss that sir."

"No," Abbas screamed. "I can't miss it."

The officer frowned. "Please don't make this more unpleasant than it has to be. On the face of it, a stolen artifact, one of some value, we are told...has been found in your luggage. We would be derelict in our duties if we did not investigate it thoroughly."

"But the woman..." Abbas spluttered.

"We are investigating that too. But I'm bound to say that we have no clear image of her on CCTV." The interviewing officer paused. "Can I ask…" he paused, and then continued. "Is it possible that you have a…how can I put this delicately…a lover?"

Abbas wanted to explode. He knew very well who was behind all this. The broken corner of the tablet bore eloquent testimony to the culprit—Chelsea Thompson. Somehow, she'd managed to be in two places at the same time…and plant the piece of tablet in his luggage. More significantly, she'd managed to steal the scanner. In every way, she'd outsmarted him. He now had nothing to show the press.

He put a hand over his face and groaned.

"You did what?"

Chelsea looked at Tony guiltily. "I've been in contact with Mr. Cohen."

"The Mossad agent?"

"He didn't actually say he was Mossad. We've just…sort of assumed it."

"They don't have a policy of advertising such things, but I think it's a safe bet."

"Well, all I can say is that he was, after only a few phone calls, able to speak on behalf of the Israeli Government, so he carries some clout." She shrugged. "I simply decided to make use of it."

Tony and Chelsea were in the dining room of St. Georges College, eating breakfast. It was early, and they were some of the first people in the dining hall. Although there was a delicious smell of bacon and eggs in the air, Chelsea felt unable to eat much. She nibbled at some toast and poured herself a succession of coffees.

True to Tony's prediction, she'd fallen asleep the night before, almost before she lay on her bed. Her eyes still felt puffy now, and the rest of her felt lethargic. In short, she was in no mood to hear any remonstrations from Tony. She did, however, feel an obligation to let him now know what she'd done, as it was relevant to what she had to do that morning.

With a sigh, she confessed everything.

When she'd finished, Tony, bless him, did not react beyond showing initial surprise. He simply sat there for a long while, rocking his teacup round and round on its base, obviously deep in thought.

"Did I do the right thing?" she asked eventually.

Tony left his teacup alone, folded his arms, and gave her a thoughtful look. "I think you did brilliantly."

"You do?"

"Yes." He paused. "The downside is: you've painted a target on yourself. There are going to be some very angry people we may have to contend with." He pursed his lips. "It's difficult to know how they will react. You'll need to be doubly careful. And you've thrown the discoveries at Ebla to the four winds…and it's difficult to predict where they will land."

Chelsea took a deep breath. "What I haven't told you is that I plan to stir the hornets' nest a bit more this morning…and I may need you to be on hand…in case things go wrong."

Tony nodded slowly. "You'd better tell me what you have in mind."

Tony fingered the day pass that hung around his neck. Chelsea had organized for him to have one, even though he was not a delegate. It gave him access to the display hall but not to the main sessions. He was sitting in a booth diagonally opposite the Syrian stand. It belonged to Greece. A young man with a thick accent was trying to share his excitement at the discovery of a *Homo sapiens* skull that was 210,000 years old. It had been found in southern Greece, evidently, and was the earliest example of *Homo sapiens* found outside of Africa.

Tony's main attention, however, was focused on what was going on across the aisle.

The press had gathered around and were talking excitedly to each other, so much so, that even the Greek archaeologist gave up speaking and began to watch curiously. He looked at Tony and shrugged, as if to say, 'I have no idea what's going on.'

It wasn't long before he found out.

Chelsea came striding along the aisle and stopped just outside the knot of reporters. She cleared her throat.

"Good morning, ladies and gentlemen of the press."

Those gathered immediately turned and thrust various recording instruments in her direction.

She lifted up the delegate's tag hung round her neck for all to see.

"My name is Dr. Chelsea Thompson. I'm from the British Museum. You've been invited here this morning for two reasons. The first is to draw your attention to the close cooperation that exists between the British Museum and the Syrian government. The second is to enlist your help in finding a set of twelve clay tablets that originally came from Ebla. It is thought that they could be highly significant in helping us decipher all the clay tablets that have been unearthed there."

Chelsea went on to talk about the 465 new tablets that had recently been discovered.

"These can now be added to the original 2,000 tablets that were unearthed at Ebla in 1964. These earlier tablets have been stored in museums in Idlib, Aleppo, and Damascus. As such, they are very vulnerable, and their current status is uncertain." She paused. "The 465 tablets found recently have all been taken to Damascus. Hopefully the Syrian government will allow the international archaeological community access to them—particularly given the British Museum's partnership in irradiating the tablets for them."

She turned round and fixed them all with a smile. "However, what we'd particularly like from you is your help in tracking down the twelve tablets that hold the key to deciphering the others. They have cuneiform writing on both sides, measure thirty by thirty-six inches, and show evidence of having being burned. Because of this, they will be rock hard."

Chelsea then brought the press briefing to a close.

The press wandered off without any great evidence of excitement. If it wasn't quite the scoop they'd hoped for, Tony reasoned that they could at least be satisfied that they were helping the world of archaeology in their search for lost tablets.

Chelsea came across to him.

"How did I do?"

Tony didn't answer directly. "Is anyone staffing the Syrian stand?" He pointed to the display Chelsea had put up. "Have you had any reaction?"

Chelsea grinned. "No. The two young Arabs that were helping yesterday arrived first thing today, but when they saw everything was in place, they left."

Tony nodded. "Well, you have been about as visible and public as you can possibly be." He drew in a deep breath. "You've sown the wind. Let's hope you won't have to reap the whirlwind."

Tony rubbed his chin and did a mental inventory of what he needed to do that morning. This was the morning Chelsea was delivering her paper, so it gave him the opportunity to dispose of the scanner and the Syrian carry-case of posters.

He dropped Chelsea off at the conference hall.

"Wish me luck," she said.

He smiled. "Luck is a treacherous companion..."

She laughed. "I know. 'Do your best not to need it.'"

"Seriously, Chelsea. You don't need it. You'll be fine."

He was still smiling at the memory of her laughing when he drove into the car park of the British Consulate-General. They had an incinerator there dedicated to the destruction of sensitive documents.

Tony retrieved the scanner and the tubular carry-case containing the Syrian posters. He didn't bother opening the case; he simply threw the whole thing into the fire chamber of the incinerator. It flared up, momentarily burning brightly, then died down as if with a sigh. Minutes later, there was only ash.

He carried the scanner unit back to his car, and drove to the metal casting company in Mekor Haim to dispose of it.

Forty minutes later, Tony was staring at a puddle of aluminum as it was poured into a rectangular mold. He was glad to see it. It was all that was left of the scanner that had caused Chelsea so much angst.

The cheerful metalworker who poured it smiled and said in Russian-accented English. "You want the metal?"

Tony shook his head. "Thanks for your help." He'd spun a story about a nephew who had been using the machine to project pornographic images onto the sides of civic buildings. "It's good to see it destroyed."

"Serve 'im right, eh."

"Yes."

After paying generously for his services, Tony left.

Chapter 24

It was the morning of Chelsea's presentation to all the delegates at the WAC conference. This was her first exposure to international scrutiny by the best archaeologists of the world. As such, she knew it to be a key moment in her career.

Chelsea was programmed to deliver the session immediately before lunch. The trouble was, her heart was still in turmoil regarding the audacious things she had done in neutralizing the attack Abbas had planned on her and the British Museum. She was unsure of what would happen next and couldn't shake off a sense of impending dread.

On the positive side, she'd already talked so much about the discoveries at Ebla that when the time came for her to deliver her paper, she breezed through her talk. Her presentation was passionate, persuasive, and poignant...and the applause at the end was more than mere politeness.

She put her hand over her heart and bowed her thanks to the audience.

Sadly, Tony could not be with her to share the occasion. He was not a delegate. He'd chosen to use the morning to get rid of the scanner and the Syrian display posters. She was glad of that, at least. Chelsea knew she wouldn't be unable to breathe freely until both had been destroyed.

Nonetheless, she wished that Tony were with her. His very presence seemed to settle her…and she loved his company. His smile and warmth left her heady. Tony's love was a delicious warm blanket she could wrap around her and delight in. Her soul had flown free from a place where it had been caged for a very long time. She smiled. Love had crept up on her, leaped, and possessed her. She now knew herself to be helpless in its grip. The sense of being loved, of being amazed and absurdly proud of Tony, was wonderful.

As she walked back from the podium to her seat in the front row, the MC for the conference session delivered some notices and dismissed the delegates for lunch.

She was in no hurry to eat, so she stayed in her seat, allowing the adrenaline surge of the moment to dissipate. A few people walked past and congratulated her as they filed out of the hall.

Someone came up to the conference MC and handed him a note. He nodded and came down the steps of the staging to join her in the front row. "Well done, Dr. Thompson. It was a great presentation to end the morning."

Chelsea nodded her thanks.

The MC glanced at the piece of paper. "I've been given a note for you." He adjusted his glasses and read. "A Mr. Tony Patterson and Professor Yoseh Shalev are waiting for you at the gate of the car park. They are wanting to take you out for a celebratory lunch."

Chelsea's heart leaped, and she was unable to suppress a grin. "Thanks."

She packed her papers away in a folder and hurried out of the hall into the car park. When she looked, there was no sign of Tony.

Suddenly, she felt something press into her left kidney.

A man growled in her ear, "You will be shot dead if you don't do exactly what I say."

At the same time, a car speared forward and screeched to a halt in front of her. Without ceremony, she was bundled into the back seat.

She was dimly aware of the car swerving and accelerating away and of needing to brace herself from being tumbled about.

It was only when she settled herself that she realized that Abbas Shamon was sitting next to her.

Chelsea sat in the back seat of the car with a sense of sickening disbelief. Her movements were wooden, as if her body could not quite keep up with what her mind was having to process. She closed her eyes in anguish. How could she have allowed this to happen? She was furious with herself…and also afraid. What would happen next?

She glanced at Abbas. He was looking grim. The veins in his neck were standing out, and his jaw was clamped shut. Every now and again, he would twist round in his seat and stare out the back window, presumably to see if anyone was following.

She risked asking a question. "Where are we going?"

Abbas ignored her, and began speaking to the two men in the front seat in Arabic. The men's voices became raised. Some sort of argument or debate was going on.

Chelsea glanced outside. They had left the outskirts of Jerusalem and were heading east along Highway 1. The road snaked its way through the desolate Judean wilderness. There seemed to be no vegetation at all to soften the rugged, sandy-colored hills. Chelsea shivered. Its bleakness matched her mood.

Her thoughts turned to Tony. What would he do? More disturbingly: What pressure would Abbas put on him now she had been captured? Would whatever Abbas planned be bearable? Would she and Tony even survive?

She lowered her head. She'd only just lost her heart to Tony. The idea that she might lose him now was unbearable. Tears came to her eyes, and she brushed them away irritably.

Her movement caused Abbas to snap his head around. He stared at her and sniffed.

"You should have thought about tears before you carried out

your foolish actions." After staring at her for a few moments longer, he returned to his conversation with the men in the front seat.

From what she could deduce from the gesticulations and the few Arabic words she knew, the men were worried that they might be stopped some place up ahead. After a few minutes, the men seemed to come to a resolution, and Abbas sank back into his seat.

He stared at her stonily.

"You impersonated my wife."

"Yes."

Abbas ran his eyes over her, and for a long while, seemed to be lost in thought. Then he shook his head and frowned, as if suddenly returning to reality.

"That was a particularly nasty thing to do."

"It didn't give me any joy to do it. For what it's worth, I am sorry if my actions opened up old wounds."

Abbas laughed harshly. "Your actions…" he paused, as if lost for words, and then tried again. "Your actions…have made me look a fool, and been a gross insult to the Syrian government." Abbas' neck was flushed red.

Chelsea had little doubt that what he said was true—almost. And it was that 'almost' that decided her to push back. If she could put him off balance, she might learn something.

"But do you know what I think?" She didn't wait for an answer. "I think that the Syrian government actually know very little about what you planned to do here in Jerusalem. I think you are operating on your own initiative—largely, I suspect, to protect your own skin."

For a long while, Abbas said nothing. Then he lifted his chin and said, "And I will continue to operate on my own initiative." He paused. "You will be taken to Syria, and you will be exchanged for the twelve tablets from Tell Mardikh."

A sickening feeling rose in the pit of Chelsea's stomach. "But we don't have…"

Abbas cut her off and leaned forward and gabbled in Arabic as he pointed to the left.

The car swung off the highway and made its way down a narrow, twisting road that wound its way alongside a deep canyon.

She'd seen the canyon occasionally from the highway. It seemed to have accompanied them for most of the way since they'd left Jerusalem.

"Where are we going?" She asked.

Abbas sank back into his seat. "To Jericho by a back route, then through Jordan to Syria."

Chelsea's heart sank.

After a few minutes, the road dropped from the top of the canyon and wound its way to the bottom where it ran alongside a small stream that splashed and swirled its way along a bolder-strewn riverbed. They had to slow down at a corner to make way for a tourist bus coming in the opposite direction that was laboring its way up the hill. The bus told Chelsea that whilst they may be on a back route, it was a route tourists used. That had to mean that it wasn't completely isolated.

Every now and again, she saw evidence of the road having been recently repaired. Someone had put a priority on it. Perhaps there was civilization ahead…and where there was civilization, maybe there was a chance to escape.

The car rounded a corner, and Chelsea could see a car park with two tourist buses parked on it.

Almost before the plan had formed in her head, she said, "I need to go to the toilet. Can we stop here please? It's urgent."

Abbas shook his head. "No."

Chelsea took him by the arm and shook it. "It's urgent. Do you want me to soil the car?"

Abbas looked at her disdainfully, then barked an order at the driver. The car pulled into the car park and nosed its way towards an ugly public toilet made of cement blocks. She was able to see that some local Bedouins had set up trestle tables at the other end of the car park by the buses. They appeared to be selling jewelry, colorful shawls, and oranges. Some donkeys were also milling about, being tended by their owners—most of them, just boys.

One of the men in the front seat got out and walked around the toilet block, and then went inside. When he came out, he nodded at Abbas.

Abbas took Chelsea firmly by the wrist and led her to the toilet. He pushed her inside. "Be quick, or I'll come in and get you."

As she expected, no one else was in the toilet. There was no one she could appeal to for help.

Chelsea entered a cubicle and locked the door. She searched round looking for anything that might give her hope.

A louvered window with opaque glass sat high above the toilet. If she were to escape, that was her only chance.

She stood on the toilet and examined the window. Tentatively, she gave the lowest pane of glass a push. It moved in its slot until the lower lug at one end holding it in place was exposed. Gritting her teeth, she gripped the lug and tried to bend it. Reluctantly, it moved. She twisted again and managed to move the lug further so that it was free from the edge of the glass.

Perhaps there was hope.

Her fingers started to spasm from their exertions.

She shook them loose and repeated the process on the other side of the window.

When that lug was also been bent out of the way, she slid the pane of glass out of its slot, stepped down from the toilet, and placed the glass gingerly on the floor.

There were two more panes to go.

In a few minutes, they too were lying on the floor. Unfortunately the top pane had cracked, leaving a jagged piece of glass protruding from the edge. Despite her best efforts, it remained jammed in place.

Realizing there was no time to lose she hoisted herself up through the open window, and pulled herself through headfirst. For almost the only time in her life, she was grateful for her small size. She wriggled and squirmed...and suddenly, plopped on the ground on the other side. Chelsea managed to cushion her fall slightly with her arms, but she had not escaped unscathed. The protruding piece of glass had given her a bad gash on her upper left arm, and it was bleeding profusely.

She ignored it and looked around frantically. There was no way of escape to the sides. Abbas and his men would see her and catch her straight away. The only way open to her was straight down.

She looked over the cliff edge and gulped. Whilst it wasn't quite vertical, it was very steep and rocky. Stubby shrubs and tufts of dead grass grew only where they could find a foothold.

Chelsea lay down on her stomach and began to descend feet first. It was a tortuous, scratchy descent.

Suddenly, she slipped. Rubble and rocks fell with her as she desperately clawed at the cliff face for a handhold.

Chelsea fell in an undignified heap onto a paved walkway.

Badly winded, she forced herself onto her hands and knees and fought for breath.

When she was finally able to look up, Chelsea found herself staring at a donkey. She noticed, idly, that it had a white nose and very long ears. A startled boy was standing beside it.

"You okay?" asked the boy.

Chelsea lowered her head to try and clear her thinking. "What is this place?" she wheezed.

"This St. George's Monastery. You want to have a look?" Then the boy shook his head. "But maybe too late. It closing." The boy helped her to her feet and pointed across the ravine to the massive cliff wall on the other side.

Chelsea looked to where he was pointing. She was amazed by what she saw.

A monastery had been built into the cliff face. In some cases, the cliff even overhung it. Chelsea couldn't believe how anyone could have constructed it.

However, she didn't have time to dwell on the view. She needed to escape. The problem was, she could barely walk.

"I need to get to that monastery. Can you take me?" she asked.

"Sure. It cost 110 shekels."

Chelsea had no purse. She took off her watch. "Here, take this instead."

The boy took the watch, examined it briefly, and smiled. "Sure, lady."

He helped Chelsea get onto the donkey, and then sent the

donkey on its way with a slap so that it began clip-clopping its way down the winding path. The young boy ran beside her.

Chelsea only had enough strength to grip the reins and hope she could stay on. She was, however, able to see the view.

The path was protected from the ravine below by a low stone wall. As they went down it, the monastery across the other side of the canyon loomed closer. It seemed to be built in many layers. Steps going to little rooms and buildings had been built everywhere. The highest steps led up to a tiny stone cubicle that was built under a cliff edge. Chelsea found it hard to believe anyone could live there. They would need nerves of steel.

She could see that the main building was built of stone. Three tiny balconies hung on its edge overlooking the gorge. Chelsea couldn't help but think that the view from them must be amazing. She also noticed that a large bell tower with a turquoise dome had been built beside the monastery entrance on the eastern end.

Before long, they reached the bottom of the gorge, and she found herself in a terraced garden of olive and cypress trees. The peace of her surroundings seemed to reach out to her, but Chelsea's desperate circumstances didn't allow it to touch her.

They crossed over a stone bridge and began to wind their way up the path until they came to the monastery forecourt in front of a severe looking gatehouse. It was built like a fort.

A monk, dressed in black, wearing the black stovetop hat of the Greek Orthodox church, was closing a small door set within the huge entrance gate.

Behind him, someone was ringing the bells in the bell tower.

Chelsea slid off the donkey and stumbled toward the door.

The man who was closing it, paused and watched her, frowning. When she got close, he shook his head and said in thickly accented English, "No, no. It one o'clock. All tourists go. You go now."

He must have seen the desperation in her eyes for he frowned, as if uncertain. Then he noticed Chelsea's blood-soaked arm.

He beckoned to her to come through the door.

But she was now light-headed. Everything was strange and moving. She stepped forward, staggered…and fainted.

Chapter 25

C helsea woke to see a large black jackdaw moving in front of her. She blinked, and the black jackdaw resolved itself into a bearded cleric. He was dressed in a black habit.

He leaned over her.

"Ah, awake at last. That is good."

She had a brief impression of kindly eyes. But before she could focus properly, he had turned away to wring out a blood-soaked cloth above an enamel bowl.

Chelsea turned her head to inspect her arm. It had been firmly bandaged.

She looked around her. A vaulted ceiling had been carved out of the rock. She was in an alcove of a larger room. It seemed to operate as some kind of medical dispensary because she was lying on an old-fashioned medical bed.

The man continued to speak as he cleaned things up.

"Jesus told a parable about a good Samaritan who walked the very road you have crossed over to get here." He turned round and smiled. "I am not a Samaritan, but I too am bound by God's love to care for the wounded." The cleric wiped the last of the blood from Chelsea's arm.

"I hope you realize that it is no small thing, you being here. The last woman allowed in the monastery outside of tourist time was a Byzantine noblewoman. She claimed the Virgin Mary had directed her here to be healed of an incurable illness." He squatted down beside her and inspected the bandage. "You, however, are curable. I've put some myrrh on your wound. It's a good antiseptic and also acts as an analgesic."

"Thank you," she said weakly.

"You are American?"

"No. English."

"Ah, that is good. I like England."

"Your English is very good."

He smiled. "That's because I spent my early years as a novitiate in England, studying under Metropolitan Anthony Bloom. He was Russian Orthodox. I was on exchange there." He lifted his head as if trying to recapture the memories. "He was a remarkable man."

Chelsea had no idea who he was, but nodded anyway. "Forgive me, but who are you?" she asked.

"I'm sorry. I should have introduced myself. My name is Father Makarios. I'm the abbot here."

"This is Greek Orthodox, I presume."

"Yes."

Seemingly satisfied with the inspection of his handiwork, Father Makarios stood up. "The rest of our community is currently attending a service. I should be there too, but it seems that God has ordained otherwise." He smiled. "We have two churches here, the 'Church of the Holy Virgin' and the 'Church of St. George and St. John.' Both are beautiful."

"Please," said Chelsea. "I need to get an urgent message to someone who can fetch me."

The cleric nodded. "All in good time. You must rest…and perhaps let this place speak to you. Much happens when you allow quietness."

"But I need to send a message. It is very important," she pleaded.

"I have no doubt it is. But sending a message from this place is not a straightforward process. As you no doubt saw, we are buried under the cliffs of a wadi...and we only have one phone." He smiled. "Mine, as it happens. When someone needs to use it, we send them up the path to the top where the reception is better."

"Oh," she said. "I'm not sure I'd be able to manage that."

Father Makarios nodded. "Don't worry. I'll send one of the brothers instead. Tell me who you want to contact, and what the phone number is."

"His name is Tony. He's my...assistant."

The cleric's eyes twinkled. "Assistant?"

She blushed. "And a very dear friend."

The cleric nodded. "Now," he said. "We need to get you away from the common areas to a place where you can recuperate in private. It would not be helpful if you were seen by the other monks." He smiled. "...not least because you are very beautiful. But I'm afraid it will be a bit of a climb. How are you feeling?"

"I'm fine now. But perhaps I could hold on to your arm."

The cleric nodded. "Of course. Let's get you to the isolation room."

He offered his arm and began to steer her through the monastery complex. She had a vague impression of vaulted ceilings and lofty, richly decorated architecture. Gilt and gold seemed to be everywhere.

Father Makarios continued to talk as he walked.

"This monastery dates back to the 4th century when a group of Syrian monks sought solitude here. The monastic movement had taken over much of the Christian church by then, and Christians were going everywhere to seek God in remote places. They chose this place because this is where Elijah once lived in a cave. Then, in 480AD an Egyptian called John of Thebes built a chapel that became the monastery."

"Why is the monastery called St. George? It sounds very English."

"It was named after Saint George of Choziba, a Cyprian monk who lived here during the 6th century. Very little of that monastery remains. It was destroyed by the Persians in 614 when they came here to massacre the monks."

Chelsea shook her head at the savagery of history. "It's beautiful now," she said, looking around her.

"Yes it is. A Greek monk called Kallinikos began restoring the monastery in 1878. He didn't finish until 1901."

"Wow. I can't begin to think how he did it."

The cleric smiled. "It is our home, and we are, usually, very pleased to be here. We are more comfortable than our predecessors. They slept in the caves just east of here."

He guided her up a succession of stairs until they came to the roof plaza. However, the steps did not stop there. They went on and up, past small rooms that hung onto the rock face.

She ventured to ask, "Where are we going?"

Father Makarios pointed upward. "Not far now."

She looked to where he was pointing.

"I don't believe it," she said. A steep set of stairs led up to a tiny building that seemed to be suspended under a cliff overhang. It was the tiny building she'd seen from the other side of the canyon. Fortunately, the steps had a metal railing. The downside of that was that she could see straight through it. Chelsea had to battle vertigo as she made her way up the dizzying steps.

"Is this the highest part of the monastery?"

"Oh no. One hermit cell is only reached by a ladder. The monk that lived there hauled things up in a basket."

Chelsea shook her head and held on tight to the cleric.

When she finally stepped inside the tiny building, she could see that it contained very little other than a bed, a chamber pot, and a chair.

"Lie down here and rest," he said. "I'll go off and fetch you some water and a bowl of nuts." He shrugged an apology. "We eat very simply here. But I'll find some lime juice to put in the water."

Chelsea lay down gratefully, but couldn't stop herself from saying, "Could you send the message as soon as possible?"

The cleric looked at her calmly. "I can see that you are

distraught, but I believe it is no accident that God has brought you here." He paused. "Be still and try and find out why."

Twenty minutes later, the cleric returned carrying a jug and a bowl of nuts. Father Makarios poured her a drink and handed it to her.

"Brother Petros has made your call. Your friend, Tony has said he will be with you in just over an hour."

Chelsea closed her eyes. "Thank you so much," she said, closing her eyes. Tony would soon be with her. Wonderful. She could finally relax.

After an hour's rest, Chelsea was escorted from her eyrie, down the dizzying stairs and through the monastery—then across the concourse to the gatehouse. Father Makarios opened the small round-topped door set into the main gate and ushered Chelsea through.

When she stepped outside, she was greeted with the incongruous sight of a cleric in a black habit, sitting on a quad bike.

Father Makarios pointed to it. "Brother Petros will take you up to the car park where you can meet your friend." He paused, and then added, "Whatever happens to you in the future, know that you will leave this place with something very powerful."

"Oh. What's that?"

"You will go with our prayers."

She nodded her thanks and climbed onto the quad bike behind Brother Petros.

The quad bike puttered down to the bridge. It had stone arches at each end. Chelsea had barely noticed them when she was on the donkey. She glanced down at a small stream running underneath. It was difficult for her to believe that such a small stream had, over the course of history, carved such a mighty canyon.

The bike began to make its way up the winding path on the other side. The sun was now well down. Golden light and deep shadows were highlighting the cliff face. However, she was unable to give it the attention it deserved because of her excitement at the prospect of seeing Tony again.

Brother Petros slowed down to round a hair-pinned bend when suddenly two men stepped from the side of the track into his path. Both were holding guns. One of them was Abbas Shamon.

Brother Petros jerked on the brakes, and they came to a stop.

"We just keep meeting each other, don't we," said Abbas, harshly.

Chelsea sat where she was, horrified, unable to process the shock of what she was seeing.

Abbas ordered Brother Petros to get off the bike and return to the monastery.

The monk didn't move.

Abbas fired his pistol over the monk's head.

Brother Petros got off the quad, briefly laid a hand on Chelsea's shoulder, and with commendable dignity, started walking back down the track.

Abbas took Petros' place in the driving seat, whilst the other man climbed aboard the luggage rack behind her.

The quad bike jerked forward, forcing Chelsea to hang on to the waist of the man who had become her nemesis. She wanted to weep.

Tony looked at the flat tire and had to battle to stop himself from screaming in frustration.

He was pulled to the side of the road on Highway 1, only about five minutes out from Jerusalem.

The professional side of his brain began asserting its control, and Tony was soon busy jacking up the car and swapping the flat wheel for the spare. Nonetheless, he had to fight to keep from being overwhelmed with anguish. Chelsea had rung for help from a monastery just outside of Jericho. How on earth had she managed to get there? The brother from the monastery who rang him was unable to tell him any details other than that Chelsea had been hurt and needed him to pick her up.

There was no scenario he could think of that didn't cause him huge concern.

He got back in the car, started the engine, and stamped on the accelerator.

Ten minutes later, he saw the signpost to Wadi Qelt. He swung the car left and piloted it down the winding road that led along the edge of a canyon. The road twisted and turned, and demanded all his attention—particularly at the speed he was driving.

He eventually came to the car park Brother Petros had told him about. It was late in the day, and his was the only car in it.

Tony parked the car and ran to the paved path that wound its way to the bottom of the canyon. He paused momentarily to take in the sight that greeted him. Tony stared in disbelief at the monastery that seemed to defy gravity and hang under the cliffs on the other side of the wadi. However, he couldn't allow himself the luxury of dwelling on the spectacle. He set off again at a run.

Seven minutes later he had crossed the bridge, run up the other side, and was banging on the door of a formidable looking gatehouse.

The small door in the main gate opened almost immediately, and Tony found himself staring at a monk dressed in black, wearing a strange black hat. Before he could explain himself, the monk said. "You are Tony, yes?"

"That's right."

The monk beckoned him to come through. "I am Brother Petros. Come; let me take you to see our abbot, Brother Makarios. He is waiting for you."

Brother Petros let him across the Monastery's forecourt, then in through the main entrance by the bell tower. Brother Petros spoke as he hurried along the corridors. "I'm taking you to the chapel of 'St. George and St. John.'"

Tony didn't care where he was going. He just wanted to see Chelsea. He was dimly aware of corridors with arches and icons everywhere. Moments later, he was led into a church. It was richly decorated, and the walls were painted with biblical scenes. The church had a lofty arched ceiling and a high domed cupola above the windows. The last of the day's sun shone through the glazing giving the church an ethereal feel.

A man dressed in a black habit was kneeling in front of the main altar on the tiled floor.

Brother Petros came up behind him and coughed.

The kneeling man lifted his head.

Tony could see that the man was quite old. Instinctively Tony stepped forward and helped him to his feet. In truth, he had been humbled by the man's piety.

The old man spoke. "You must be Tony. I am Brother Makarios." He paused. "I'm afraid we have bad news."

The abbot invited Brother Petros to recount all that had happened.

As Tony listened, a sense of dread pressed down on his heart. He tried to make sense of what he was hearing. After a few clarifying questions, there was little doubt as to what had happened. When brother Petros recounted the words he'd heard: 'We just keep meeting each other, don't we,' there couldn't be much doubt.

Abbas Shamon had kidnapped Chelsea, but somehow, she'd managed to escape to the monastery...only to be recaptured. She would have been taken across the border into Jordan by now. He groaned. Things couldn't be worse.

The abbot looked at him, concern evident in his eyes. "I am so sorry," he said. "We were going to call the police, but decided to wait for you first. I hope we did the right thing."

Tony nodded. "You did. Thank you. I'm afraid this business is tied up with relationships between nations, so it's very political. Things will have to be handled delicately. It is as well that the police are not involved at this stage."

"Well," said the abbot. "I have no idea what you are talking about. All I know is that Chelsea has been captured by people at gunpoint." He paused. "You should probably also know that Chelsea has sustained a nasty cut, which I have treated. Ideally, it needs to be stitched."

Tony nodded. "Thanks for looking after her."

For a while he was quiet. All he could hear was silence…and something he didn't expect; the sound of peace. Could peace be heard? It was strange.

"What will you do now?" inquired the abbot.

Tony had little doubt about what would happen next. He sighed. "I will wait," he said. "I am fairly confident that I will be called before very long and will receive a series of demands."

"Demands that will secure Chelsea's release?"

Tony nodded. "Until then, I'm not sure we can do anything."

"Will you be able to meet those demands, do you think?"

"Probably."

The abbot nodded.

"I should get out of your hair," said Tony.

"You are not 'in our hair.' No one comes here by accident."

The abbot led him back through the monastery complex and across the forecourt to the gatehouse. When he stepped through the gate, he saw Brother Petros sitting on a quad bike.

The abbot waved him off the bike, saying that he would drive Tony back to the car park personally.

When they arrived at the car, the two of them turned and stared at the monastery on the other side of the ravine.

The abbot pointed to it. "The main cupula you can see, painted blue like the dome on the bell tower, is actually the dome at the top of our main church." He turned to Tony. "Fix the picture of it in your mind, and know that I will be praying under that dome for you both."

Chapter 26

The phone call came at 7am next day.

Tony was in his bedroom at St. George's College.

With a sense of impending dread, he answered it. "Tony Patterson, speaking."

The voice of Abbas Shamon savaged what little remained of his sensibilities.

"As you will be aware, we have Dr. Thomson in our custody. Whether or not you see her again will depend entirely on how you respond to my demands."

Tony decided to be as compliant as possible and not give offense. It wasn't easy. He wanted to rave about the evil of Shamon's actions and tell him that he would be hunted down to the ends of the earth if he hurt Chelsea in any way. Above all, he wanted assurance that Chelsea was alive and well. But he took himself firmly in hand and said evenly, "If your demands are reasonable, I probably will."

There was a pause before Abbas came back at him.

"I am not naturally a violent man, but in this case, I have not only been driven to violence, but I welcome it. Both you and Dr.

Thompson have dishonored my country and very nearly ruined my life. I shall not hesitate to kill. Do you understand me?"

"Yes, I understand." He paused. "What is it that you want?"

"If you are to see Dr. Thompson again, you will bring me two things. You will bring me the twelve tablets from Tell Mardikh. Secondly, you will bring me the scanner that Dr. Thompson stole from me."

Tony kept his voice calm. He desperately wanted to avoid a slanging match of threats. "I hear your demands. But of course, there can be no transaction unless I have proof of life. I need to hear from Dr. Thompson to check that you have her and that she is well."

"You want to hear from her? Well…it so happens I have her here with me."

There was a scuffling sound in the phone, and then Chelsea's voice. "Tony, Tony…she started to cry. But through the tears she managed to say. "I am well, Tony. Please make sure you stay safe. Please…please."

There was the sound of the phone being ripped away from her. Abbas' voice cut in sharply. "You've heard she is alive. Now, my demands…"

Tony interrupted him. "One of your demands I can comply with. The other is an impossibility."

Abbas shouted him down. "Do not play games with me. I will not hesitate to kill. You will accede to both my demands."

Tony could detect the beginnings of hysteria in Abbas' voice. With a feeling of desperation, he forced himself to sound measured. "The scanning machine was taken to a metal foundry and melted down into a pool of aluminum. It no longer exists." He paused. "I cannot negotiate the impossible."

Abbas started to yell.

Tony interrupted him. "Mr. Abbas, I am going to end this phone call and give you time to think. I can give you the twelve tablets…" he paused, and was able to hear Chelsea in the background scream. Tony realized that he must have his phone on speaker mode so Chelsea could also hear.

Chelsea screamed. "Tony, you can't do the impossible. Please don't put yourself in danger."

Tony rubbed his forehead in frustration. "It's okay, Chelsea. Trust me. I've got this."

"No, Tony. It's impossible…"

There was a yelp from Chelsea…and Abbas was suddenly the only voice he heard.

"I want the scanner. Do you hear?"

Tony replied in a carefully modulated voice. "I'm going to end this call, because there is no benefit in continuing. The scanner no longer exists. Until you accept the reality of that, there can be no progress." He paused. "Call me back when you think you can proceed." Tony ended the call.

The next five minutes were the longest Tony had ever experienced in his life. He tilted his head back and closed his eyes in anguish.

The phone rang again.

Abbas did not waste words. "Patterson…" Abbas spat out the word with venom. "I am prepared to believe the scanner no longer exists, but you will bring the twelve tablets to me, or…"

Tony interrupted him. "Yes I will. Just tell me when and where."

Abbas was silent for a moment, as if put off his stride. Then he came back. "You will bring them to Mt. Nebo. We will do the exchange in the car park at 6pm after the tourists have left."

Tony furrowed his brow. "You are talking about Mt. Nebo in Jordan?"

"Yes. It's only three hours from Jerusalem."

Tony spoke over the top of him. "But you need to add on the time it may take to get through the border crossing…" but Abbas had rung off.

Tony sat down on his bed. He felt weary to the soul.

However, before he began to find his equilibrium, the phone rang again.

Not knowing what to expect, he answered.

With relief, he heard the voice of James, who was still in service with his old unit.

James did not waste words. "Hi Tony. We have a situation here." He paused. "I've got to offload Mahdi as soon as possible."

"I understand, James. When?"

"Today, if possible."

Tony had nothing else scheduled for the day.

"Yes. That's possible. Where?"

"At the Allenby Bridge border crossing."

"Time?"

"Midday."

Tony did some rapid mental calculations. "Yes," he said. "I'll be there."

Mahdi looked at the ugly bridge. It was made of concrete. Even the low diagonal struts holding it up were made of concrete. But it was quite a long bridge. He'd never seen one as big before. It crossed over a thick ribbon of trees, bushes, and rushes...and a small river that he felt was far too small to warrant a bridge as big as the one he saw.

A few minutes later, Mr. James had parked the car at a place where soldiers were milling about holding guns.

He didn't like them and sank down in his seat so he wouldn't be seen.

Mr. James glanced at him. "Don't be frightened, matey. This is just the border crossing between Israel and Jordan." He pointed to the cars parked on the other side of the building complex. "Mr. Tony will be waiting for you somewhere over there. But first, you need to be cleared by the border officials. It's purely routine, so don't be scared."

Mahdi was only half persuaded. He did manage to get out of the car and stand behind Mr. James in a queue of people.

Eventually, it was their turn to speak to the man sitting behind a computer at a desk. Mr. James spoke to him briefly.

"And who are you, young man?"

Mahdi looked at him defiantly, trying to pretend he wasn't scared. "I'm Mahdi Daher or Mahdi Dayan. Take your pick."

"Do you have a visa?"

Mr. James handed a piece of paper to the man.

The official spoke to him. "Wait behind that line, sir."

Mr. James stepped back, leaving Mahdi standing alone by the counter.

The border officer tapped away at a computer. Then he furrowed his brow as he peered at the screen. After a moment, the man picked up a phone and made a call. When he'd finished, he beckoned him to come through the gate.

Mr. James made to follow him, but two soldiers with guns stepped in his way.

"Wait behind the line, sir," they said.

Madhi suddenly found himself alone. Instinctively he reached back for Mr. James, but he couldn't reach him.

His heart began to pound.

One of the soldiers told him to sit on a seat.

Mahdi held his haversack to his chest and sat down.

He had to sit for a long time. Mahdi couldn't even see Mr. James from where he was sitting.

In the distance, he heard the sound of a helicopter. The shuddering beat of its rotors became louder and louder. It was not a sound Mahdi liked. He was haunted by memories of things he couldn't remember. He cowered down in his seat.

The helicopter noise became frighteningly loud, then died away.

A man came into the border security building and spoke briefly with the officer who had told him to sit down. The officer pointed to Mahdi.

The other man walked over to Mahdi and without saying a word, picked him up—squeezing him tight in his arms, and carried him out of the building.

Mahdi screamed in protest and began to kick and flail as best he could, but the man held him secure. He turned his head this way and that, trying to work out what was happening.

With a shock, he realized that he was being taken to the helicopter.

⸻

Tony watched the Bell 206 helicopter land without much interest. It was painted white and blue and it made an elegant landing on its metal skids. Two men got out of it and walked over to the border crossing building.

He was distracted from seeing more by his phone ringing. When he answered it, James' voice came through with a hint of urgency.

"Tony, I don't know what's happening, but the officials here have taken Mahdi and won't let me cross over with him. Something's going on that's not in the script. You better stand by and be ready."

Tony answered instinctively. "Roger that. Standing by. Out."

When he looked up again, he was amazed to see a man carrying a child toward the helicopter. The child was yelling and kicking. With a shock, Tony realized it was Mahdi.

Concern and anger flared up within him. Perhaps it was his frustration at not being able to protect Chelsea that sparked his action. But one thing Tony knew: he was not going to lose anyone else. He sprinted toward the helicopter.

As he ran, he heard the helicopter's engine rise in pitch and volume.

With despair, he saw the helicopter lift from the ground.

Tony did a desperate lunge and then leaped into the air. His hand gripped on the skid of the helicopter.

Almost immediately a boot came down on his hand. Someone was trying to stamp on his fingers.

But he held on.

Moments later he was whisked through the air at a height which meant instant death if he fell. The buffeting he'd felt from the downdraft of the rotors was now augmented by the wind blowing at him from the forward motion of the helicopter. It was brutal.

Tony tried to heave himself up onto the skid, but when he tried, a boot kicked at his hands.

In desperation he let go with one hand and felt for the knife he kept concealed in his boot. He brought it up and tried to stab the foot that was kicking him.

However the foot simply lifted itself out of the way, and it wasn't long before Tony was forced to drop the knife and hang on with two hands.

Falling off now meant death. He glanced below and was dimly aware of a thick ribbon of trees either side of the river. They were flying south over the Jordan River.

Tony's muscles were tiring. Panic rose up within him. How long could he hold on?

Even as he thought it, the helicopter began to slow and descend.

Moments later, it was hovering just above the river.

A voice shouted out at him from the open door of the helicopter. "Time to let go, mate." Tony looked up and saw a man holding an Uzi submachine gun.

He didn't argue. Tony let go of the skid and fell ten feet, landing on the water inelegantly on his back.

When he spluttered to the surface, the helicopter was already well away.

He glanced around and saw terraced concrete platforms with curved iron railings lining the riverbank. Bizarrely, there were people dressed in white robes standing in the river.

He swam to some concrete steps and hauled himself out of the water.

A group of people dressed in white watched him incredulously. One of them spoke to him in an American accent.

"Man, that's got to be the most interesting baptism I've ever seen."

Tony looked in bewilderment. "What is this place?" he asked.

The man swept his arm around. "This is where Jesus was baptized." He paused. "Surely, you knew that."

Tony rolled his eyes and silently cursed the pilot. He had a warped sense of humor.

"How far is it to Allenby Bridge?" he asked.

"About three miles. Go up there and turn right."

Tony nodded his thanks, and began walking. His boots squelched, and water dripped from him. He judged that he would be dry by the time he reached his car.

As he steamed gently in the sun, he tried to make sense of what had happened. But try as he might, he couldn't do so.

A wave of anguish swept through him. He fervently hoped he would do better managing Chelsea's exchange than he had managed Mahdi's.

Chapter 27

Jordan

Tony was way too early, but he couldn't help himself. Sitting alone, fretting over Chelsea and going over what he'd planned for the thousandth time, was driving him mad. He'd driven from Jerusalem in the early afternoon and headed east to Jordan.

After being cleared to enter the country at Allenby Bridge, Tony crossed the Jordan River. For the next twenty minutes, he skirted round the edge of irrigated fields before turning southeast into the Jordanian wilderness.

As he drove, he felt his body gradually tighten in anticipation of what lay ahead. Tony made himself breathe deeply. He then plugged his phone into the car speaker system and selected a playlist from Brahms. Tony was in need of his soft melodic genius to soothe his jangled nerves.

He piloted the car 2,700 feet up the rugged hills until he came to Mt. Nebo. At the top of the mountain, he saw a couple of cafés seeking to capitalize on the tourist trade, and a large car park. It was almost deserted. The last tourist minivans and buses were leaving.

Tony parked on the far side of the car park, and for a while sat there drumming his fingers on the steering wheel. Then he reached into the back seat for a knapsack, slung it over his shoulder, and got out of the car.

It was about a five-hundred yard walk to the Memorial Church of Moses on top of Mt. Nebo. Tony took his time because there was an hour to spare before his meeting with Abbas Shamon. He didn't go into the church, but made his way to the plaza on the far side of it. For a long while, he simply took in the view. It was impressive. Tony could imagine Moses standing here, looking west over the Promised Land that he and the Jewish people had been journeying toward for forty years. He'd read the story as part of his preparation for the day and learned that Moses had died on this mountain without realizing the fulfillment of his journey. Tony fervently hoped that the same wouldn't happen to him. So much hinged on what would happen in the next hour.

His main priority was Chelsea's safety. He would do anything to secure that. As to who got what in terms of archaeological artifacts, he didn't greatly care. At the moment, he was heartily sick of the archaeological world's wrangling, subterfuge, and politics. But even as he thought it, he knew his jaundiced view was not one he normally held. In truth, he found the archaeological world captivating. It opened the door to the drama of history, and perhaps even taught the lessons of history—lessons that the wise might learn from. Sadly, however, the political affairs of men seemed incapable of escaping the never-ending cycle of ambition; killing; hubris; self-protection; defeat; and death.

Tony glanced up at the striking metal statue standing at the edge of the plaza, quite possibly at the very place Moses had stood. It depicted a snake writhing around a cross—a nod to the time when Moses constructed a similar monument so that the Hebrew people suffering from snakebites could look at it and be healed. The imagery had since been adopted to represent the medical profession around the world. This thought led him to think of Brother Makarios who had promised to pray for him, a stranger he barely knew.

Tony furrowed his brow. Why? He wondered. Even as he

thought about it, he had the sneaking feeling that love was behind it. He glanced at the statue. Maybe it was the love of someone prepared to take on the vile abuses, injustices, and unkindness of humanity…and kill it off by dying with it. If the statue meant anything, it was that love was found in self-sacrifice. He knew that there was a truth there somewhere that teased and beckoned to him.

Tony glanced at his watch. It was time to return to the car park and face whatever was waiting for him.

There was another car parked about forty yards from his own. Other than that, the car park was deserted.

As Tony walked across to them, two men got out of the front seat of the other car, opened the back door, and hauled Chelsea out so that she was standing between them.

When Chelsea saw Tony she immediately tried to run toward him. The two men either side of her pulled her back savagely. One of them put a pistol to her head.

Tony lifted his hands to show he was unarmed and continued to walk until he was twenty yards away. Then he stopped.

The back door of the car opened, and Abbas Shamon stepped out. He looked at Tony with a cold glare of contempt.

"Have you brought the tablets?" he asked.

The man believed himself to be in total control. Tony decided to put a dent in his equilibrium.

"Someone will probably die in the next few minutes." Tony deliberately adopted the demeanor of a pessimist in an attempt to forestall the threats he felt sure would soon come from Abbas. He hoped to make it clear that he was already aware of the dire situation he was in.

Abbas frowned briefly. "It doesn't have to be like that," he said. "Not if you've got the tablets."

Tony mentally sighed with relief. Abbas was seeing the possibility of people emerging unscathed from their meeting. That meant he could be negotiated with.

Abbas continued to speak. "But Dr. Thompson will die if you haven't got what I want. That is a certainty. She has been a constant thorn in my side" he shrugged, "and I have nothing to lose."

Tony nodded. "How do you want to be remembered, Shamon? Do you want to be known as the man who murdered a distinguished British archaeologist? Will you be known as the one who brought shame on his nation because he let foreigners have politically dangerous information about its heritage? Is that the epitaph you want?"

Abbas breathed in a lungful of air. "After I have killed Dr. Thompson…"

Tony interrupted him.

"Chelsea. You mean, after you have killed Chelsea. She's the woman who worked alongside you at Ebla. You know her, so make it personal. Make it honest. Call her Chelsea."

Abbas swallowed. "After I have killed…Chelsea…"

Tony knew that he had successfully wrested some control of the conversation from Abbas. He interrupted him again.

"But you don't have to kill Chelsea. I can give you two things. I can give you detailed laser images of all the tablets you recently found at Ebla. Your scholars can study them at their leisure, knowing that if the originals are destroyed or are under threat like the earlier tablets found, you still have the information. Would you like that?"

"But the British museum would also have it." Abbas yelled. "They would have our information—ours. They will have stolen it…stolen it from me."

Tony shook his head. "No. They will have preserved it from the ravages of war, and made it available to Syria in a form that can't be destroyed—and made it available to the world. Syria's story is part of the world's story."

Abbas shook his head. "No, no, no." He lifted up the edge of his jacket, took a pistol out of its holster and aimed it at Tony. "Have you brought the twelve grammar tablets from Tell Mardikh?"

Chelsea suddenly screamed and lunged forward again. This time, she caught her captors unaware and broke free. She ran to a point that was just five paces from Abbas and spun around, shielding Tony from him.

"If you're going to shoot anyone, shoot me," she yelled.

Abbas' gun wavered. He frowned. "You would die instead of him?" he asked incredulously.

"Of course."

"Why?"

"It is what…" she paused "…love does."

Abbas nodded. "Love, eh." He sniffed. It was an attempt to appear disdainful, but Tony didn't think he quite pulled it off.

Tony spoke out. "It's okay, Chelsea. I've got this. Please move aside."

The impasse was solved by Abbas. He stepped forward, spun Chelsea around, and put an arm around her neck. Then he ground the end of his pistol into Chelsea's temple. "Stay still, he growled." He then turned to Tony. "Do you have the twelve tablets from Tell Mardikh?'

"Sort of."

"What do you mean, 'sort of?'"

Tony held out a hand to placate him. "I'm going to tip the contents of my knapsack onto the ground, so stay cool. There's no trickery here."

With slow deliberate actions, Tony took the knapsack from his shoulder and lowered it to the ground. Then he bent over, took the bottom of the bag, and tipped it up. Four hard drives spilled out onto the asphalt.

He stood up, stepped back, and pointed to them.

"These are four hard drives with high definition, three dimensional scans of your Ebla tablets."

Abbas nodded slowly and then spoke rapidly in Arabic to one of the men behind him.

The man came forward, picked up the hard drives, and retreated to the front of the car.

Tony saw him open up the top of a laptop computer.

Five minutes of silence ensued. For Tony, it seemed like an eternity.

Then the man climbed out and nodded to Abbas.

Abbas turned to Tony,

"It seems that they are good. But they are not what I demanded. I want the twelve clay tablets." He made a show of pushing the pistol into the side of Chelsea's head, forcing her to bend sideways.

Tony held up both hands, again, seeking to placate him. "Well you can…in a very safe form. I have their pictures on a hard drive in my top pocket." He paused. "I'm going to take it out with one finger and thumb and lie it on the ground. So again, stay cool."

Tony picked out the hard drive and laid it on the ground.

"Now you have the complete set. You have everything. Let Chelsea go."

"No," yelled Abbas. "I want the physical clay tablets. That was what I demanded."

"Well, you can't have them without first releasing Chelsea. I must see her drive my car to the entrance of the car park while I stay here with you. She will then take the tablets out of the trunk and leave them at the car park entrance."

"No," screamed Chelsea. "You have to let Tony come with me."

Abbas shook his head and shifted the aim of his pistol until it was pointing at Tony. However, his attention became distracted by the noise of some high revving engines. They were coming closer and closer. He frowned and looked over his shoulder.

Tony was able to see them before Abbas. Two cars swept into the car park and sped across to where they were standing.

Abbas hauled Chelsea back against the car, seeking to use it as a shield.

Three men emerged from the cars. All of them were armed with Galil sniper rifles.

The three men spread out and dropped to the ground. They then pressed the stocks of their rifles into their shoulders and took aim.

Abbas screamed. "Keep your distance, or Dr. Thompson dies."

Two more men got out of the cars. They both carried Uzi machine guns. They stood unsmiling by the car as an older man got out holding onto the arm of a young boy.

Tony recognized the boy straight away. It was Mahdi. The man holding him was Mr. Cohen.

The Mossad agent smiled. "Well, well. What drama do we have here?"

"Stay back, or I'll shoot," yelled Abbas.

Mr. Cohen shook his head. "No, I don't think so. What is more, I don't think you will die today Major-General Abbas Shamon."

Abbas furrowed his brow. "What?"

"You have too much to live for...unless, of course, I deem otherwise."

Chapter 28

Chelsea's mind was in a whirl. As she looked at Mr. Cohen, hope, glorious hope, began to spring up within her like a fountain. But even as she allowed herself to believe it, her mind was working furiously.

She glanced at Tony. He'd tried to engineer her escape, whilst he remained to face the wrath of Abbas. How little he knew her. There was no way she would have driven off without him.

She also realized that Tony must have taken photos of the twelve tablets if he was able to put them on a hard drive for Abbas. She wasn't sure how he'd managed to do it, but she had no doubt that he had.

She glanced at him. He was alive and well, and was speaking to Mr. Cohen. She heard him say, "How did you know I'd be here trading Ebla's tablets for Dr. Thompson?" he asked.

"Let's just say we have made good use of technology."

"You mean surveillance of me and my phone calls?"

"Perhaps."

Mr. Cohen turned and faced Abbas. "The arrangement today is quite simple. We will take the hard drive with the images of the twelve tablets from you, and you will take this boy."

"Who are you?" demanded Abbas.

The Mossad agent looked at him without expression. "We are, what you might call, 'Israeli security.'"

Abbas frowned. "And why would I be interested in the boy? He is nothing to me."

Chelsea could see that Abbas was close to the end of his tether. He was clawing at his face in anguish. "If you take the hard drives, I have nothing. Everything's gone: my children, my career…" He pushed the pistol into the side of her head again. "I will shoot Dr. Thompson unless you let me go with all the hard drives." He pushed the pistol again. "That's a promise."

"Ow!" Protested Chelsea. She had a moment of panic, thinking that things were getting out of control.

Mr. Cohen held up a restraining hand and gave Mahdi a small shove.

The boy took a few tentative steps forward then stopped. He was clutching a leather shaving case to he chest. Mahdi held it out to Abbas.

Chelsea could see the light of recognition in Abbas' face.

"That's my shaving bag." Abbas said, scowling. "Was it you who stole it?"

"Yes."

Abbas, lowered his gun. "I remember you doing it. You even knew my name." He frowned. "How did you come to know it? You called me Abbas."

Mahdi shook his head. "I did not call you Abbas."

"Then what did you call me?" Abbas demanded angrily.

"I called you *Abba*."

"But *Abba* is the Jewish word for…'father.'"

Mahdi lowered his head. "Yes."

"Why?"

"I recognized you at Ebla. I knew you from a photograph my mother kept," He pointed to the shaving bag. "The photograph is in the bag."

Abbas stepped away from Chelsea, walked over to Mahdi, and

snatched the bag from him. He unzipped it, felt inside, and extracted a photograph.

For a long time, he simply stared at it. Then, his face slowly crumpled, and he started to weep. Abbas tried desperately to retain his dignity, but could not. Tears overtook him.

After a respectful few minutes, Mr. Cohen spoke up. "You have been of interest to us for some time, Mr. Shamon. We have done some research." He paused. "Let me tell you our findings."

Abbas was still trying to get himself under control.

Mr. Cohen continued to speak. "Against all protocol, you had an affair with Mahdi's mother, a Jewish girl called Sara Dayan who was at the time working as an archaeologist at Ebla. She had a son, but you didn't know, because you'd left to return to Damascus by that stage."

Chelsea could see that Abbas was now listening intently, his mouth open in disbelief.

The Mossad agent nodded. "Sara felt so compromised socially that she didn't return to Israel. She stayed at Tell Mardikh and gained employment as a teacher and a tour guide. Sara also took to using the surname, Daher because it sounded more Arabic."

Abbas held out a hand as if pleading. "She's...she's not still alive, is she?"

"Oh no. She was killed six years ago in a rocket attack—the same one that nearly killed your son." Mr. Cohen stepped forward and lifted Mahdi's arm, showing the grotesque scarring on Mahdi's left forearm.

Abbas looked at Mahdi, incredulous. "I have a son?"

"You do."

Abbas turned to Mahdi. "Why did you not think to call me *alab*? That is Arabic. What languages do you speak?"

Mahdi kept his head bowed. "I speak English, Hebrew, and Arabic. But my mother mostly spoke Hebrew."

Abbas knelt down before Mahdi, and examined the obscene scarring on the boy's left forearm. Then he took him by the shoulders and looked into his eyes.

It didn't take long before he nodded his head. "I see her. I see her...in you." Abbas started to weep again.

Mahdi stayed still and stared at the ground.

Abbas reached forward and gathered the boy into his arms.

If Mahdi was surprised, he had the presence of mind not to protest.

Abbas finally stood up, although he kept hold of Mahdi by the shoulders.

With the innocence of youth, Mahdi said, "Can I live at your place and watch TV?" He paused. "I'll clean the brass for you."

Abbas nodded.

Chelsea was welling up with emotion, but even as she watched, her mind was working furiously. There was a very real sense that she now had to rescue Abbas from an uncertain future, for Mahdi's sake. She had to ensure somehow that Abbas could return to Syria with a degree of triumph because he'd managed to get the information on the twelve tablets. She couldn't let Mr. Cohen take the hard drive from him.

She stepped over to Abbas, knelt down, and spoke softly to him. "Abbas, I want you to trust me."

He turned his head and stared at her. "You called me Abbas."

"Yes." For a moment, neither of them said anything. She broke the silence. "Regardless of what I'm about to say, know that Tony is right. You have pictures of all twelve tablets on your hard drive. Do you understand?"

Abbas frowned, but nodded.

She stood up and turned to Mr. Cohen. "May I make a deal with you?"

The Mossad agent allowed himself to smile. "What possible deal could you offer me, Dr. Thompson?"

"I'm afraid that Mr. Patterson has not quite told the truth. Mr. Shamon only has the images of six of the twelve tablets on his hard drive."

Mr. Cohen scowled and turned to Tony. "Is that true?"

"Of course it's true," interrupted Chelsea. "I put the images on it." She paused. "They are the same images I gave to you."

She was conscious of Tony looking at her with a puzzled frown. Silently she begged him, *Trust me with this, Tony.*

Mr. Cohen frowned. "What is the deal are you offering, Dr. Thompson?"

"I will give you photos of all twelve tablets, if you let Mr. Shamon go with the hard drives he has been given." She paused. "Surely you can agree to that. After all, he has been given nothing that I haven't already given you."

Mr. Cohen turned to Tony. "I presume you don't physically have the twelve tables in your car."

Tony shook his head. "No, I don't."

"But you won't mind if I check the trunk of your car all the same."

"Not at all." Tony took the car keys from his pocket and lobbed them to one of the agents standing next to Mr. Cohen.

The man caught them and went to Tony's car. After opening the trunk, he gave a small shake of the head to Mr. Cohen.

The Mossad agent smiled. "You have played a dangerous game Mr. Patterson."

Chelsea was desperate to move things on. "Do we have a deal?" she repeated.

Mr. Cohen turned to her and appeared to ponder the proposition. After a few seconds, he nodded. "I believe you will honor your word, Dr. Thompson." He waved a dismissive hand at Abbas.

"Mr. Shamon. You are free to go. Take your son and go home."

Chapter 29

C helsea couldn't quite believe it. She was sitting next to Tony, driving back to Jerusalem…and they were safe. It was hard to believe after the fear, angst, and terror of the last two days. Could it really be true?

She shook her head. Tomorrow morning the two of them would be flying back to the UK. She'd missed the last two days of the conference, but in the scheme of things, that was inconsequential. Mahdi had found a father. Abbas had found a son and probably rescued his career. One thing was certain, the Syrian academics who'd been sitting on their hands for so many years regarding deciphering the Ebla tablets now needed to get a move on. If they wanted to have a voice in the world, they now needed to compete with the best academics in the UK and Israel. Every nation now had two others to keep them honest. The events of the day had yielded an extraordinary outcome.

Just one thing played on her heart. How would Mahdi fare with Abbas? The boy had chosen to stay with him in Syria. Part of her felt a sense of betrayal. How could he choose Abbas over her? She'd seen the cruel side of Abbas, but she had to admit, she'd also seen his humanity—expressed particularly in his love for his family. The closing drama at Mt. Nebo had left her in no doubt about Abbas' commitment to Mahdi. A man who thought he'd lost all his family, had found a son. It probably wasn't a bad outcome.

She put her head back and closed her eyes.

Her action was not lost on Tony. He frowned with concern. "How's your arm?"

"Sore, but okay. Brother Makarios did a good job." She paused. "Did you know that he put myrrh on it? Extraordinary, isn't it— history coming alive."

"I'm taking you to hospital so you can get it stitched when we get to Jerusalem." He was silent for a while, and then he added, "That aside, how are you feeling in yourself?"

Chelsea wasn't sure how to answer. "It's too early to say. The pieces are still in the air, floating down."

Tony nodded. "You did well back there. I'm still not sure how you engineered it."

"Neither am I. I ran on instinct most of the time." Chelsea opened her eyes. "Thanks for playing along with me, by the way."

"I did wonder where you were going." He smiled at her. "But you'd thought it through well."

"I'm not sure I had many 'jumping off' points," she laughed. "It was my last throw of the dice."

"You were able to improvise whilst under considerable stress." He shook his head. "I'd have you in my unit any time."

As a compliment to a woman, it probably left a bit to be desired, but she accepted it all the same.

Chelsea shifted in her seat so she could lean against him and hug his arm as he drove. She needed to feel his nearness to prove to herself that he was really there. She could feel his warmth. It was a good feeling.

Twilight was falling as they pushed through the center of Jericho and on into the Judean wilderness on the Wadi Qelt road. It was a clear night, and the moon was nearly full. Moon-glow kissed the pale barren hills making them appear ghostly and mysterious. Deserts, she reflected, were full of contradictions. They were places of hellish heat and hardship, but also places of peace and elemental simplicity. No wonder the mystics of old sought out their solitude.

As they drove through the deepening twilight, a gnawing question continued to trouble her. Eventually, she gave voice to it.

"Tony."

"Yes?"

"Where are the twelve tablets from Tell Mardikh? What would have happened if Abbas had insisted on them…and Mr. Cohen hadn't turned up?"

"I had a plan B."

"A plan B."

He nodded.

"What was it?"

"The twelve tablets are currently in The British Consulate-General's safe in Jerusalem."

"How did they get there?"

"In the diplomatic bag."

"But how did anyone find them?"

Tony glanced at her. "I'm afraid you're not going to like this."

Chelsea furrowed her brow. "Why?"

Tony drew a deep breath. "The tablets have actually been kept safe in the British Museum."

She looked at him incredulously. "How did they get there?"

"I stole them from you and took them there."

She looked at him in disbelief. "But how did you manage…" her voice trailed off. "And why?" She pushed herself away from him. "Have you any idea of the angst you've caused me?"

"I have every idea of the angst I've caused you." Tony paused. "It's been a painful thing to live with."

"But why?" she asked.

"To stop people threatening you in your own home when they tried to get hold of them." Tony glanced at her. "I wanted to protect you."

"Protect me? You put me through hell," she protested.

"Yes. To protect you." He paused. "Not least because I'd fallen in love with you."

"Oh," said Chelsea. After digesting his words, she leaned back against him again.

After a few minutes, she pushed herself away again, and punched him in the arm. Then she resumed her position.

Tony nodded. "I guess I deserved that."

Chelsea settled back in her seat. "You certainly did."

They were silent for the next five minutes. Chelsea allowed the mesmerizing drone of the car and the physical presence of Tony to take her to a place of profound peace. Overarching the peace she was feeling, was the joy and exhilaration of being loved. It was an intoxicating feeling.

She was half asleep when Tony interrupted her.

"Do you mind if we make a small detour? We're going right past it, so it needn't take long."

She lifted her head. "A detour to where?"

"To St. George's Monastery." He smiled. "I need to show you off to Brother Markarios so he can see that you are safe and well."

"Sure. Great idea." Chelsea stretched extravagantly and yawned. "But won't they be closed at this time of night?"

"Not to us. Brother Petros told me that he lives in the gatehouse. I'm pretty sure he'll open up for us if I bang on the door hard enough."

It wasn't long before they pulled into the car park on the cliff top above the monastery. Chelsea had expected to feel some misgivings about being in the place where she had been recaptured, but the car park felt completely different. Perhaps it was because it was night, or maybe because Tony was with her.

She got out of the car and walked with him to the beginning of the path that wound its way down the ravine. Its pale flagstones were clearly visible in the moonlight. Chelsea glanced above her at the velvety firmament that spanned the night sky. The stars shone like diamonds, muted only mildly by the glow of the moon.

Tony took her hand and gave it a squeeze.

Together, they looked across the ravine to the monastery hanging under the rock face on the far side. It looked even more dramatic in the moon glow with the shadows of the rock face falling across it. Here and there, a faint yellow glow came from a window, indicating that the monks had not yet retired to bed.

Tony pointed out the tiny ring of lights that appeared from the windows underneath a domed cupola. "Do you see those lights there under that dome?"

She nodded.

"Under that dome, a man is praying for us."

Chelsea allowed the thought of it to wash through her.

They stood together in silence.

Then Chelsea stepped round until she was facing Tony.

He took both of her hands in his and gave her a lopsided grin. "Ours has been…" he paused, "an unusual romance."

She laughed. "You can say that again."

Tony continued. "Are the pieces…beginning to land?"

She nodded and stared up at him, drinking in the features of his face highlighted by the moonlight.

Tony let go of her hands and wrapped his arms around her waist. He drew her toward him. She could feel the warmth of his body and felt the pit of her stomach tighten with desire.

Tony bent his head down so that it hovered just inches from her own. Then, he brought his lips down on hers.

The release of tension in the warmth of the kiss left her giddy, thrilled, and bewildered. Part of her couldn't quite believe she was loved…and safe.

Then he kissed her again. And she believed.

Chapter 30

England

Tony was standing by the window of Megan Caplan's office looking out on Bloomsbury Street. Car lights reflected from the puddles left by the rain as the last of the morning commuters headed through the gloom to work. He could see that some of the shops already had their Christmas decorations up.

Christmas. *What would this Christmas be like?* he wondered. Probably very different. He smiled. Chelsea and her sister Ann would insist on it. His days of simply going to the pub with a few mates were over. He was glad. It was always a time when he'd felt his aloneness most acutely.

Sir Anthony Spiers was sitting in Megan's office chair. He had turned it away from the desk and was also facing the window. The two of them had been talking together.

Tony looked up as the door to the office was thrust open, and Megan Caplan strode into the office. She was wearing a white shirt, a brilliant multi-colored scarf with gold threads running through it, and a short black business skirt that some might have mistaken for a mini skirt. Her tanned legs were on show.

Megan saw Tony and frowned.

"What on earth are you doing in my office?" she demanded.

At that point, Sir Anthony turned his chair around and faced her.

When she saw him, her mouth dropped open. "Sir Anthony," she stammered.

The Director of the British Museum gestured to Tony. "Dr. Caplan; May I introduce you to the Chief Security Advisor to the British Museum, Tony Patterson."

Megan's brow puckered as she glanced at Tony. She was eventually able to speak. "So you're not just…"

"…a security guard?" finished Tony.

She nodded.

"No. I'm not."

Sir Anthony did not invite Megan to sit down. "Mr. Patterson has something to say to you, Megan."

Megan turned to Tony with just a hint of exasperation. "What?"

Tony drew in a deep breath. "We have discovered that you work for Mossad, Dr. Caplan."

For a moment, there was silence.

"Rubbish," said Megan. "How did you conclude that?"

"Firstly: You were abnormally keen to get the Ebla tablets scanned—but not, I suggest, purely for the benefit of the British Museum. In fact, you did not tell the Board of your actions, but acted under your own initiative. Secondly: You didn't want me to go to Israel with Chelsea. You wanted Chelsea to be exposed to Mossad's pressure without me being present. I've learned that you didn't even put Chelsea's request that I accompany her to the Board."

Sir Anthony spoke up. "I'm bound to say, I'm deeply disappointed, Megan. People who work here must have the British Museum's interests as their first priority." He stabbed the desk with his finger. "We must preserve our impartiality if we are to maintain our claim to be custodians of the world's heritage."

Megan looked at him with defiance, but Tony could see that some of the wind had been taken out of her sails.

She lifted her chin. "I can't tell you anything…"

Tony lifted up a hand. "I understand."

For a while, only the hum of traffic could be heard.

Sir Anthony Spiers leaned back in his chair. "While we might understand…you will understand when I say that your position here is now untenable."

Megan nodded.

Tony was fairly sure that a nod was as much of a concession as anyone would ever get out of Megan.

Sir Anthony continued. "And I greatly regret having to say that, because you have been one of our finest department heads."

After another moment of silence, Tony took up the conversation.

"It may interest you to know that the Israelis have been given a lot of new information on the clay tablets recently found at Ebla." He paused and said carefully, "And information has been traded."

Megan looked at him with an expression that hovered somewhere between defiance and curiosity.

"I suppose that was Chelsea's doing," she said.

"Yes."

Megan nodded. "That doesn't entirely surprise me. She has spunk, that girl." Megan turned back to Sir Anthony. "Where are the twelve tablets from Tell Mardikh now?"

"We have them here. They are available for anyone from any nation to study."

"Anyone?"

"Anyone. As I've repeatedly said: The British Museum is a 'world country.'" Sir Anthony paused. "What you don't know, is that Syria has been given the same information." He leaned back in his chair. "This means that Israel will need someone very talented and committed to head their research team. I suggest you put your name forward. You are eminently qualified."

"So I am being dismissed?"

"Yes." He pointed to a bag that had been place beside the door. "You'll find your personal effects from this office in there."

Megan lifted her chin. "Is that all?"

Sir Anthony held up a restraining hand. "Perhaps I should tell you the...er, official story." He put his elbows on the table. "As you may already know, we have given the Israelis highly detailed laser scans of the twelve tablets from Tell Mardikh."

She frowned and waited for him to continue.

"In appreciation for our generosity, they have given us detailed laser scans of the 465 clay tablets recently unearthed at Ebla. They obtained them by subterfuge, evidently." He paused. "It's quite remarkable, isn't it, that they also scanned tablets from Ebla with a scanner?"

"Remarkable," agreed Megan.

Sir Anthony leaned back and folded his hands over his stomach. He looked at Megan levelly. "Don't do it again. Understood?"

She favored him with the smallest of nods.

Tony opened the door for Megan. "I'll escort you from the building."

Megan hoisted the strap of the computer case she was carrying over her shoulder and picked up the bag. As she turned, she paused in the doorway and took one of Tony's lapels between a finger and thumb. Megan massaged it gently. "We could have been lovers, you and I."

Tony nodded. "Perhaps."

"If it weren't for another woman." She looked up at him. "Chelsea?"

He nodded.

"Lucky girl."

"Are you ready?"

Ann looked up at Tony from her wheelchair. "Yep."

Tony lifted her up and held her in his arms. She was surprisingly light. Ann's long blond hair blew in the wind, curling around so that it brushed against his back. He walked to the bottom step of the fire escape and began to mount the metal stairs.

Ann looked at him coyly as she was being carried. "You realize of course that the hero should be rescuing the maiden from the tower, not taking her into it."

He smiled. It was not difficult to imagine anyone rescuing Chelsea's sister. Ann was extraordinarily beautiful. "I'm giving you a chance to grow your hair a little longer so that a hero might climb up it and rescue you."

For a moment, her face became serious. "Do you think it will happen?"

Tony glanced at her. "I don't know. All I know is that it deserves to happen." He didn't trust himself to say anything more.

They reached the top landing. Chelsea had opened the fire door of the gatehouse and was waiting for them.

Tony carried Ann inside and deposited her gently in the recliner. As he did, Ann's head was twisting this way and that, taking in the details of Chelsea's apartment.

"Wow!" she said. "Chelsea, you have done an amazing renovation job. It's wonderful. It reeks of history, but it's spacious and comfortable."

Tony went back down the fire escape to fetch Ann's wheelchair.

A few minutes later, Ann was sitting in it wheeling herself around the apartment, exploring its features. For a long while she sat herself in front of the window and looked out at the cathedral and the ancient buildings that were huddled around it, as if seeking its protection.

Then she spun her chair around and looked at Tony and Chelsea. They were standing together, half leaning on the kitchen bench. She smiled. "You two look good together."

Chelsea grinned and sought out Tony's hand. "It feels good," she said.

Ann nodded. "From what you've told me, you've had one heck of an adventure." She cocked her head. "And both of you have come back changed."

"How's that?" inquired Tony.

"You're both deeper." She smiled. "I think you've let truth catch up with you and change you. I'm pleased to see it."

Tony wasn't quite sure what she was talking about, but comprehended enough to nod. He knew he had changed. Truth and meaning had knocked on his door. He'd been surprised by their visit, but nonetheless had chosen to welcome them in…and now he was different.

The kettle began to whistle. Chelsea broke away and began to busy herself getting afternoon tea ready—drop scones with jam and cream…and hot tea. It was ridiculously English.

Tony turned round to help her.

It was good to be home.

Evening had fallen. Ann had gone home, and Chelsea was now alone with Tony. They'd just finished their evening meal. Tony volunteered to do the washing up while Chelsea did some paperwork.

She leaned back in her chair. "Did I tell you that I've submitted the plans to extend this place to the council?"

"Good for you." He had his back to her and continued to wash the dishes. "Although I'm bound to say: The extension will be great for the short term—but this place is probably not suitable for children."

It took a moment before the full import of what Tony was saying struck home.

Chelsea furrowed her brow. "Are you saying…" she couldn't trust herself to say the words.

Tony turned round and looked at her.

She could see his love in his eyes.

Still holding the washing up brush, Tony got down on one knee. "Dr. Chelsea Thompson, I didn't quite plan to do things this way, but I'll continue, having got this far." He paused. "Will you marry me? Will you teach me how to be…a human being?" For a moment he appeared to be lost for words. "Will you teach me what to do with all this love I feel…for you?"

Chelsea put a hand to her mouth. She was in shock. Had she really heard him rightly?

Then she started to laugh. She got up from her seat, knelt down in front of Tony, and held his head between her hands. "Mr. Tony Patterson, I will." Then she kissed him.

An hour later they were both seated on the bench seat under the window. They had their legs pulled up and were facing each other. Chelsea turned and looked out at the floodlit spire of the cathedral. The last few months had been extraordinary, and she was keenly aware of the weight of history pressing down on her shoulders. Events had conspired to give her the resources she needed to make some very significant historical breakthroughs.

She started from her reverie and glanced up at Tony...her fiancee. Could it really be true? She cleared her throat. "You know that there will now be a three-way race to publish papers on the significance of the Ebla tablets. The Syrians, the Israelis, and the British Museum will all be beavering away."

Tony nodded.

"I've got a proposition for you."

He raised his eyebrows.

Chelsea continued. "Do you want to give up being a security advisor?"

Tony answered cautiously. "It's not my dream job, if that's what you mean."

She smiled. "Then why don't you resign and join forces with me in unraveling the greatest archaeological find of the decade?" She held up a cautionary finger. "I should warn you that fame will probably come your way...but probably not fortune."

Historical Notes

Ebla

The kingdom of Ebla was an early Bronze Age civilization that was the equal of the kingdoms of Egypt and Mesopotamia. It can justifiably lay claim to being the first recorded world power. The kingdom grew from being a small settlement in 3500 BCE to become a significant kingdom in 2500 BCE. It flourished as a trade center until its final destruction by the Hittites in 1600 BCE.

Ebla clay tablets

The discovery of a library of clay tablets at Ebla by the Italian archaeologist Paolo Matthiae is true. These tablets were written both in Eblaite and Sumerian cuneiform, and they are considered to be one of the earliest forms of human writing. Matthiae asked Giovanni Pettinato, an Italian epigrapher, to assist him in decoding the previously unknown written language of Eblaite. Pettinato's early assertions that some Eblaite words referred to Jewish places and patriarchs mentioned in Genesis have since been challenged. It is fair to say that a fierce debate over the translation of the tablets has gone on over the decades with Muslim scholars insisting that the Eblaite names refer to Islamic towns, not Jewish towns. At the heart of the issue is, of course, who can rightfully lay claim to being the original occupants of Palestine/Israel.

International scholars have reported being frustrated both by political interference and the Syrian civil war. Both have made it difficult, if not impossible, for them to access the clay tablets contained in museums in Idlib, Aleppo, and Damascus. It is significant that by 2019, only 48 of the 2,000 tablets had been translated. The civil war has also allowed the archaeological site at Ebla to be looted and damaged by locals hoping to find treasure.

Reference to a second find of 465 tablets in 2019 is entirely fictional, as is the discovery of the twelve 'grammar tablets' of Tell Mardikh.

Huawei

U.S. authorities allege that the Chinese communications firm, Huawei, have been circumventing US sanctions on Syria through operations conducted through Skycom Tech Co Ltd and the shell company Canicula Holdings Ltd. Canicula had an office in Damascus. Reuters reported on the alleged activities of Huawei in Syria. (See: Reuters, 19th Jan, 2019 'Technology News.')

Hydrofoil

The information in the novel about the hydrofoil built by the Russian 'Valga Craft' company is essentially accurate.

Jerusalem

The history of Jerusalem, as mentioned in the novel, is true. Similarly, the places in Jerusalem that have been mentioned also exist.

Monastery of St. George, near Jericho

The Monastery of St. George in the narrow gorge of Wadi Qelt exists in reality very much as described in the novel. The cliff-hanging complex is one of the great spectacles of the Middle East.

Mt. Nebo

Mt. Nebo exists in reality as described in the novel. It was the place where Moses first surveyed the Promised Land of Canaan. However, he was destined never to enter Canaan. The Old Testament records that he died at Mt. Nebo.

Prior's Gate

Prior's Gate in Rochester exists in reality, as described in the novel. It has always been a fantasy of the author to live in it.

Professor Eleazer Sukenick

Professor Sukenick played a key role in establishing the Department of Archaeology at the Hebrew University in Jerusalem, and was one of the first academics to recognize the importance of the Dead Sea Scrolls.

He and his assistant Nahman Avigad really did excavate the tombs of the Kidron Valley in 1941 and discovered one that had eleven stone ossuary boxes inside. Inscribed on the ossuary box 'number 9' were the words, 'Simon Alexander,' and below that, the words, 'son of Simon.' The lid of the same box was inscribed 'of Alexander' in Greek...and below it, in small Hebrew letters, 'Alexander'...and a misspelling of the word 'Cyrenian.'

Archaeologists have concluded that it is highly probable these bones were those of the son of the man forced to carry the crossbeam of Jesus' cross (see: Mark 15:21).

St. George's College, Jerusalem

St. George's College in Jerusalem exists, as described in the novel.

World Archaeological Congress

The World Archaeological Congress (WAC) exists in reality. It was established in 1986 as a non-governmental, not-for-profit organization that promotes world archaeology. WAC holds an international Congress every four years to exchange results from archaeological research.

Note from the author

Thank you for reading *The Syrian Stone*. I hope you enjoyed it. If you did, please consider leaving a review on Amazon to encourage other readers.

Inspiration for this book came from the time I lived in Kent in the UK, and from the brief period I lived in Cyprus just after the Turkish invasion in 1974.

the "Stone Collection" has grown to include:

The Celtic Stone
The Pharaoh's Stone
The Peacock Stone
The Fire Stone
The Dragon Stone
The Martyr's Stone
The Atlantis Stone
The Viking Stone
The Scorpion Stone

To be kept up to date on new releases, sign up to my mailing list at www.author-nick.com. New subscribers will receive a free novelette, *The Mystic Stone*.

About the Author

Nick Hawkes has lived in several countries of the world, and collected many an adventure. Along the way, he has earned degrees in both science and theology—and has written books on both. Since then, he has turned his hand to novels, writing romantic thrillers that feed the heart, mind, and soul.

His seven novels are known as, 'The Stone Collection.'

His first novel, *The Celtic Stone*, won the Australian Caleb Award in 2014.

Also by Nick Hawkes

The Atlantis Stone

Benjamin is part Aborigine, but nightmares from the past cause him to disown his heritage. Unfortunately, he feels no more at home in the Western world and so struggles to know his identity. Benjamin seeks to hide from both worlds in his workshop where he ekes out a living as a wood-turner. However, an attempt on his life propels him into a mysterious affair surrounding the fabled "mahogany ship" sighted by early white settlers near Warrnambool in Australia.

Felicity, a historian, is seeking to rebuild her life in the nearby town of Port Fairy after a messy divorce. The discovery of the "Atlantis stone" whilst scuba diving results in her joining Benjamin in an adventure that takes them overseas to the ancient city of Cagliari in Sardinia.

An anthropologist dying of cancer and an ex-SAS soldier with post-traumatic stress, join Benjamin and Felicity in an adventure that centres on a medieval treaty, a hunger for gold… and, of course, the Atlantis stone.

More details at www.author-nick.com

(See next page for more)

Also by Nick Hawkes

The Celtic Stone

Chris Norman's dreams of being a commercial pilot are shattered when he crashes his light plane in central Australia and is badly wounded. His life hangs in the balance—a balance that is swayed by the intervention of an Aboriginal bushman bent on his own murderous mission. The bushman leaves Chris with a mysterious and incongruous legacy, a Celtic cross made of stone.

Partly blinded and in deep grief at no longer being able to fly, Chris finds his way to the inhospitable Hebridean islands off the west coast of Scotland where he seeks to unravel the secrets of the Celtic stone.

A blind Hebridean woman, shunned by many in her local community, becomes Chris's reluctant ally, along with a seven-year-old boy who is as wild as the storm-tossed seas surrounding the islands.

It becomes apparent that the violence of the island's history has carried on into the present. Chris needs to recover from his grief, discover his identity… and avoid being murdered.

More details at www.author-nick.com

(See next page for more)

Made in United States
Troutdale, OR
09/22/2023

13099809R10171